Granite & Sugar

R. N. Arcadia

ISBN: 979-8-9999849-1-3 (Paperback)

First Edition.

Published by Obsidian Odyssey

Cover Design: WallFlower Designs.

Editing and formatting: Colby Bettley at 3Crows Author Services

Beta Readers: Lily, Chloe, Kristen, Anuschka, Kayla, Amy

Printed in the United States of America.

To all my unhinged bitches (and everyone else) who enjoy the darker side. 🤍

Content Warning

Content inside: masked serial killer; sleep token vibes; morally grey/black; kidnapping; voyeurism/exhibitionism; stalking; arson; familial issues; he changes/falls first; kinks: bondage; public play/sex; sex club; cream pies; worship; great music tastes; a neurodivergent female character with past trauma; rape is mentioned but not described in detail--revenge is had though; descriptions of sensory overload/meltdowns; anxiety/panic attacks; depression; suicidal ideation; dark banter; millennial-isms

XOXO
LOVE

Chapter One

Nikki

Life fucking sucks.

There's no way to say it *nicely*.

I'm as pessimistic as the next guy.

Oh, to wake up, be an adult, be made to feel inferior by someone else, take care of yourself, and figure out the world. *The fucking dream.*

If life throws you lemons, don't make fucking lemonade. Throw it at them. *They probably deserved it.*

Seeing the good in people has only gotten me fucked over. So no, I have nothing nice to say.

That's a *lie*, I'm a walking contradiction.

A moody bitch, rather.

Chaos consumes me. My mind especially.

I like order, but only in certain situations. Too much, and not enough, is surely to create a spiral.

Routines are great, but then I get fucking bored, feeling like I'm not a *real* person. Yet if I don't have some semblance of a schedule, I'll lose my fucking mind. Organized chaos.

Every time I open my mouth and look inwardly at my thoughts; I'm reminded of a simple truth.

My brain is wired differently.

A combination of trauma, neurodivergency—yes, I made the word up—and a bit of *what the fuck*.

A lot has happened in the past thirty years of being alive —*one way to put it, I suppose*.

I'm a millennial through and through. The weird in-between phase in the 1990s. The great outdoors, trauma from the last generation *or before*, technology, and AOL messages asking for my ASL. No, it's not sign language.

The unfiltered web was just as traumatizing as my own family. Can't forget the random commercials that pop in my brain radio randomly or songs my mother played during my youth.

Seeing people die live, weird death websites *with pictures*, chatrooms, lying about my age on Myspace, and complaining to strangers about my life. What a fucking world, but also an easier time because we as people didn't know any better.

The problem I have, *amongst many,* is how I have two brothers who are neurodivergent, and it's like we live in different times entirely. I'm the oldest and most trauma-tized, as if I'm in a fucked-up contest I didn't sign up for, which is probably a weird way to think about it. But *whatever*.

I'm like the show *The Powerpuff Girls*—mental illness, neurospice, and everything nice. Or some shit like that. Making a joke is how I get through my fucking day.

It's no surprise, but I'm not the greatest at speaking words or thinking. Emotional regulation is a bitch, but I *try*.

Don't even get me started on the sensory issues.

There are weird buzzing sounds from electrical appli-ances. Don't even think about talking to me while my socks are wet from spilling something clumsily, and the washer on the fast cycle, rattling my fucking brain and the whole apartment.

Overstimulation much?

I guess the good part about all of this is that I have the gift of masking or dissociating. Sensory input can be so overwhelming in a world that is always loud, moving, and in a rush.

Society says one thing, your family says another, and then you're left feeling confused. So, while figuring it all out and trying to blend in and trying to be left alone from the bullies for being *different,* it's hard to find balance. Hence, all the *imbalances.* Life has felt like searching for balance and trying to figure out what the hell balance actually is.

Get your ass beat by the world or succumb; an awkward place to be, in my opinion. As unhinged as I come across, I did in fact go to *therapy* in my mid-twenties.

Rewiring my brain and responses only make quirks more *noticeable.* Oh, and masking now? *Forget it.* My body told me to go fuck myself after growing up. Stress in the body affects so many things. I'm not good, even presently at this day and age, at managing it. Humor is my coping mechanism; I can't help it. Depending on the day, there's no telling what will come out of my mouth.

Trauma dumping when I meet strangers I feel like I vibe with? *Check.*

Totally putting my foot in my mouth? *Check, please.*

I could go on and on, but I'll shut up and get to the point of the present. It does take me some time to get to the point after twenty side quests and intermixing stories that strangely relate.

Today, at my ripe age of thirty, I try to keep myself motivated to have a better decade. My history—*thumbs down.*

But at least I'm the funny one in the family with a bomb-ass taste in music, which is a mix of everything, to complete the icing on my proverbial cake. My style isn't much different, a combination of all my phases growing up that I *did not* grow out of—*sorry, Mom.*

People in society never know what to make of me. I've always adjusted myself to other people to blend in better because it was the only way to survive. However, stress hits now, and I'm unwell.

I'm a part of the *diagnosed-later-in-life* crowd. Finding out you're autistic at thirty—interesting. There's such a weird connotation that comes with *accepting* that label.

I've always hated labels, for one. Why put yourself in a box that you don't belong in? *Or why belong in just one?* The only reason why it came about was from issues at work. How I react to things being said to me and about *me,* like my blank facial expression when I'm thinking, or my processing time when five questions are asked at once. Yet, *that* got me in trouble? Who fucking knew.

"Your face gives off this look that comes across as rude. And your attitude still needs work."

Internally, I'm screaming, "Oh, for fucks sake! I'm fucking thinking! Wow, this bitch really said my FACE. It's the audacity for me."

Of course, anxiety hits and twenty more thoughts follow. A girl can't win.

So, after some accommodations, they finally left me the fuck alone. *You trained me five years ago to do the same boring ass work, nothing has changed, there's no need to treat me like I'm five.* Just because I look lost, it doesn't mean I'm always lost. Sometimes I am, sometimes I'm not—let them sweat about it.

Good thing I transferred to another boss and department six months ago—she's much nicer. My mental health has improved a lot since.

Everyone takes life too seriously.

I'm tired of fitting into these molds. I have never fit into other spaces and always find myself searching for a place solely meant for me.

So, I make my own space to exist.

It's taken so many years to learn this lesson.

Unfortunately for me, the hard way is the only way I seem to learn.

I throw myself into art to stay sane in a *high-functioning* world.

Ha, that word is *laughable*.

I wish it felt like I was high-functioning.

Whatever doctor, you're the expert here.

On a particular rainy Friday afternoon in the city, I'm idly walking around. Work was lame, but somehow the rain is grounding my senses. A sensory thing, of course.

I'm wearing waterproof shoes with no umbrella. The logic of it makes sense to me. Wet socks are a no-no; rain on my face or arms, *ideal*.

I don't make the rules, I just exist.

Passing by my favorite taco place, I grab dinner and continue on my way back to my apartment.

As my old college professor said, "I'm fat, dumb, and happy."

He wasn't fat or dumb, but he was certainly happy, and he was talking about his *cats*.

My stomach is full, and all is right in the world. I'm proud of overcoming my battles with food, forcing myself to try new things instead of the same damn foods I fixated on in my younger years. *What am I, my grandma?*

You see, in my days. In the 1900s...

So cringy.

Cringe is my middle name, or it should be. Nicole *Cringe*. Sounds like a corny porn name, if I'm being honest.

I digress.

Focus bitch, remember the rain on your skin.

I do tend to live in my own world. Delusional but realistic, delulu in relulu, if you will; a strange toss to deal with.

The rain continues to fall while I make my way back to my apartment that I somehow manage to keep clean. With my recent raise after five years working my office job, pushing papers and staring at a computer screen all day, I'm able to afford to live a little bit better.

Living is hard, and I don't mean that in a suicidal way. *Not like it was when I was young.*

Exhaling, I look up and close my eyes. The sky's darkening, showing I dilly-dallied long enough.

I still have another twenty minutes of walking, knowing I'll be soaked by the time I get home, but somehow it doesn't bother me as it does anyone else I've encountered.

My doctor told me I need to walk more, so I sold my car and now I walk everywhere. It helps with my weight loss, so I suppose that's good. Twenty pounds down, and I'm hot stuff now. I finally hit my goal of being under two hundred pounds. Go me!

Proud of my hard work, I walk under the city lights, not paying attention as I like to do. People are thinning out in the direction I'm heading. Before I'm aware of anything, I'm suddenly being knocked down as sharp pain to the back of

my head shocks my system. I can't even process it as everything goes dark.

I'm sure my face is blank while it's happening.

For fuck's sake.

XOXO
LOVE

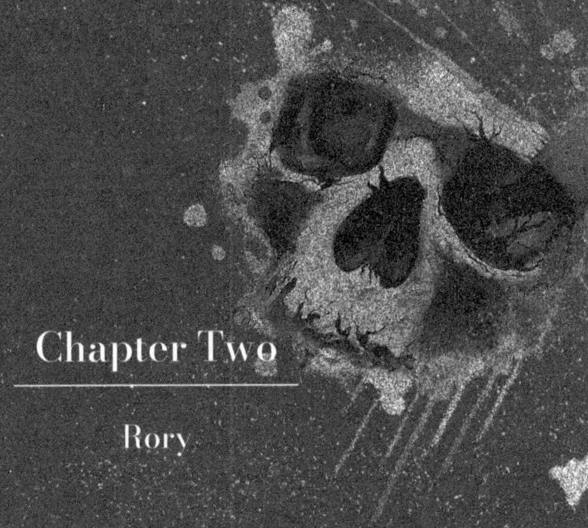

Chapter Two

Rory

Killing is like a task list, a *kill list*, if you will. Typically, I like to get the job done, but killing is similar to a full-time job; you hate it most of the time, but occasionally, there are some thrills.

1. Find a suitable person that doesn't look the same as the last.
2. Location, location.
3. Get the stuff I'll use to *take care of business*.
4. Rid any trace of me from the evidence and dispose.
5. Go home, shower, and fucking sleep.

A few kills ago...

I washed my hands as a brunette woman screamed from the other room where she was tied to a pole. This lady was giving me shit the whole time. She was heavier set and fought tooth and nail, stating that she just wanted to graduate college.

School's a fucking waste of time, or so I told her anyway. She didn't like that and started sobbing.

That's when I put the gag on her mouth and went down the hallway in the abandoned office building I found outside the city.

I was already fucking annoyed by how long this shit was taking. I should've been done an hour ago. I was missing one of my favorite movies that was playing. Whether I had seen it already was beside the point.

I wiped my hands on my pants, sighing heavily while I glanced at myself in the broken mirror with just enough light from the broken window to see my blue-green eyes reflect back at me.

Get it done, Rory, before you miss your fucking movie.

I rolled my shoulders back, along with my neck. Before marching back into the room where her muffled cries were coming from, I grabbed my knife and waltzed into the room, twirling it.

The woman shook her head, trying to plead, but it only led to muffled sounds. My obsession with completing the kill was running through my mind as I didn't half-ass these things.

"Just think of it as going to sleep. A little pain, maybe some pleasure, who knows? You're not missing anything from the college experience. All universities are money hungry, all they do is reward you with stress and debt with a piece of paper that says 'good job'."

I shrugged visibly as she squeezed her eyes shut, and I decided to slice through her stomach first then stab through her kidneys. If she didn't see me coming, she couldn't worry too much over it.

"It's not personal. I swear, I'll stop after I get to lucky number eight... Maybe ten, I'm not sure yet."

Her head slumped forward and I kicked the chair so that it tipped over, crashing as I watched her head bounce off the concrete of the floor.

I grabbed my kill bag and wiped my knife on her clothes before patting her head with my gloved hand and leaving the place.

Someone that wanted to finish college—gross. Nothing else to live for other than that; kinda sad, if you ask me.

I strolled out of the building, through the side alleyways and moved towards civilization. I took off my mask and put it away before ditching the clothes in a trash compactor outside someone's private property. I hopped the fence and stripped before pulling on clean clothes.

The compactor did its thing as I breathed a sigh of relief.

Hopping back over the fence, I made my way to one of the bus stations and got a ride back into downtown.

I dropped my kill kit off at my car and walked to the nearby movie theater for the thriller movie that I'd seen once already, but I wanted to see it again. Movies were more thrilling than my life, killing aside.

But it would have to do.

A Friday night is most people's favorite day on a Monday through Friday, nine-to-five work week—*the kill* is my Friday night. The need in me rises after some time passes. It feels like relief when it's over, like a weird release I didn't know I needed.

Without using the same methods as every other killer, I don't have *a tell*. At least to my knowledge. I switch it up to fuck with the city cops. Seven down and haven't been caught. Nor do I plan to be; I'd rather die than rot in jail and lose my goddamn mind.

The woman I set my sights on is slightly curvier than some of the others, but it's not a bad thing. From my information, the blonde woman lives alone and walks an hour through the city to get to her office job. I've never seen her drive once which was odd, but to each their own.

I work during the week in one of the stocking warehouses and sometimes overnights and weekends bi-weekly. It'll adjust so that I can keep some of those weekdays open to finding new victims. Lifting shit all day and moving things, it gives me the muscles to lift *bodies* and dispose of them. Naturally, if anyone asks or comments, I tell them I go to the gym. Who would know the difference?

I *try* not to find the same type of women, and I use different ages. The women aren't always pretty, one hair color, or occupation. The one thing I look for is differences from the last one. Different locations, looks, sizes, and the like. But the common theme is that no one will miss them when they're gone, which is why I take a few weeks tailing them to learn their habits when they think no one is looking.

I've been following *her* for weeks. My next victim.

Different from the last, but an easy target, which is something that's in common with the last seven before her. A type of person that no one will miss, who's isolated, or lives alone.

This woman seems to have her head in the clouds. Easily distracted, not paying attention to her surroundings —*check.*

I had spent two weeks finding a decent spot to take her to.

During those two weeks, I set up the basement of an unleased shop that's been abandoned for months. With the noises of the city, no one will hear her screams. The prime location is checked off my list.

How will I end her? Quick or should I take my time? Make her beg?

I like the power killing gives me; that's all I care about. To obsess over the small details and complete it from start to finish.

I wonder if I can get to my lucky number ten without getting caught? It's a life goal of mine.

Wouldn't that be something?

The rush fills me up like a kid in a candy store as I pick a Friday night to enact my plan. The plan is relatively simple: knock her out, grab her, and take her. Of course, I'd wait until she walks past the property to make things easier when I drag her down the alleyway and then the set of stairs at the back.

It makes me hard just thinking about how helpless she'll be. What should I do to celebrate lucky number eight?

I dress appropriately as the sky grows darker. A simple attire of a black hoodie with jeans and shoes that match along with my nondescript, all-matte black mask. Something simple to conceal my identity.

Keeping it tucked under my hoodie, I make my way to where I expect to find my victim.

She's getting fucking tacos. What the fuck.

Rolling my eyes, I'm on standby, watching from across the street.

She's oddly happy, not like the past two weeks with the blank face she always wore. Like there's no thoughts behind those eyes. From my observations, no one ever visited or called her. No relationships or people over. It makes me suspect that no one will miss her.

Perfect target—check.

The woman is making me feel antsy. She takes her sweet ass time before finally leaving the taco place.

Impatience floods me as I carefully cross the street and trail behind her.

The woman nears toward my mental x-marks-the-spot. I ready my brass knuckles I bought solely for my new victim's purpose.

The closer I get to enacting my plan, the more the adrenaline surges. The normal stuff right before I begin *my true Friday night fun.* I nearly shit myself when she pauses and looks up.

My heartbeat is in my ears, pounding loud as fuck. For a brief moment, my stomach drops down to my ass, too.

It takes me a second to see her sniff the air and open her palm.

This chick is fucking weird. Is she really enjoying the steady rain?

Odd, but okay.

My heart still hammers inside my cage of a body as I repeat in my head like a mantra, *"Don't. Turn. Around."*

Clenching my fist, the brass knuckles grow tighter. The pain reminds me to remain calm. Luck is *thankfully* on my side when she doesn't turn around.

I unclench my ass, relaxing as relief fills my entire body. I steal a page from her book as I sniff the petrichor scent in the air. Perhaps the woman is onto something; it is most certainly a lovely evening. A good night for an easy blonde target.

It's all working in my favor tonight.

Sleep well, princess.

I come upon her, striking her so hard I knock her down.

She doesn't realize what, or *who,* hit her until she goes limp.

I'm quick, scooping her up effortlessly, and soon I'm disappearing down the alleyway to the awaited destination.

XOXO
LOVE

Chapter Three

Nikki

My head is pounding so hard that I can't even process life, let alone *think*. As my head lulls to the side, causing the bright blurry room to shift and spin, I feel like I've been on a weekend bender.

The nausea rolls in heavy, and soon it increases tenfold, making me throw up.

I hate vomiting.

It's disappointing that I basically wasted those tacos; those were fucking good ass tacos.

Sniffling, after emptying out everything within my stomach, I try to wipe my eyes, realizing I can't. My hands are tied behind me to a chair.

My breathing steadies, waiting for my brain to catch up.

There's a noise off in the corner, and it takes me a moment to barely register one simple fact.

I've been kidnapped off the street.

I can't help but laugh over the situation.

I'm not entirely surprised it happened to me. My head is always in the clouds.

"You're laughing after throwing up?"

The deep voice startles me, and I stop all operations.

R.I.P. to those tacos. How rude.

I realized the person semi-asked a question.

"Yes?"

I try to open my eyes and groan instead, squeezing them shut. I can't even be as anxious as I should be because of the pain in my head.

"Did you have to hit me so hard?" I complain.

Whoever it is says nothing at first.

The severity of the situation begins to hit me, just like whatever the fuck I was hit against the head with. The head pain, the ties, the weird, disembodied voice echoing in the room... *Can't believe I've really been kidnapped.*

It takes me a moment to realize I said the last sentence aloud.

Why? *Not a clue.*

"Wow, nothing gets past you," I hear from a dark corner.

Curiosity brims. It's no surprise that my stupid, daydreaming ass is ill-equipped to handle such a situation, so I shut down and succumb. A rush of anxiety and depression and acceptance all-in-one.

A long-ago monster reels its familiar head again.

Good ole' *ideation.*

Not that I'm doing anything special with my life so, of course, this guy would pick me. I'm no one special. Just an idiot who doesn't fucking pay attention.

My life isn't worth anything anyway, so let's see what happens. It's whatever at this point.

Bravery fills me to say what's on my mind. *Because why the fuck not?* "You're doing us both a favor, you know."

My eyes flutter open before quickly shutting again, realizing there is a singular bright light above me.

It makes it hard to see, but with my pounding head, I

open my eyes slowly. I vaguely make out the figure in the shadows by an old, long wooden table that's barely functioning and looks like it could break at any moment.

I think I see a head tilt, but I don't know for certain. It takes a minute to realize the guy is wearing a dark mask.

When he doesn't say anything, I decide to keep talking. *I'm such a wise dumbass.*

"I'm tired, being an adult is exhausting, and I don't have enough time to do the things I enjoy like reading or creating things. Bills consume me. I'm a slave to capitalism... Dying sounds like a vacation at this point. So, yeah. Doing us a favor."

I hear a sigh, and the dude speaks. "Are you being serious right now?"

Nodding in his general direction, I reply, "Dead serious." Realizing the awful joke and situation, I can't help but giggle.

The masked guy shakes his head, and I catch him looking up at the moldy tiled ceiling as if the answers are up there.

"You must be one of *those* millennials...*great.*"

Okay, but what's wrong with being a millennial?

I frown, wondering what he's got against us nineteen-hundreders. "Yeah, because seeing a live terrorism attack as a child isn't traumatizing, or getting bullied for being different, amongst other things. Or wars. Recessions. Then there's my own personal traumas and grievances... Can't forget that."

Masked guy sighs heavily. "Of course you'd say that."

"That's rude," I say on the defensive.

Millennials didn't ask for it. I didn't ask for it.

He steps into the light more, and I make out his all-black clothing with a matte black mask.

I tuck my lips between my teeth, holding back a laugh.

My mouth runs away from me again, and I realize there's no saving me, so why not refer to all things dark and funny to me? "Could you be any more of a cliché in your dollar store ghost face mask? Who doesn't gag their victims? Sheesh."

A low growl echoes in the room and strangely makes its way down to my lady bits.

Why are you the way that you are?

"I kidnapped you to kill you, lady."

Someone seems to be *upset*.

Relaxing into the chair I'm in, I close my eyes and roll my neck so that I'm facing the light.

"Not my fault you're a terrible killer," I mumble, before raising my voice slightly higher. "Look, I'm flattered you chose me, *I guess*, but I do have a name. Lady sounds old school. Are you old? What do you have against millennials anyway?"

Masked guy slithers back into the shadows in the corner, rubbing his head.

"You have some balls, *lady*, I'll give you that."

I right my head and close one eye to squint in his general direction due to that bright ass light. If I had free use of my hands, I'd offer to show him how it's done by killing *him*. What an asshole.

"They're called ovaries, and they sit higher. What about it?"

The guy laughs this time, seeming to lean against the barely-together table, shaking his head.

"What is wrong with you?"

Of course, typical response. He's not used to someone encouraging his work.

"Well, since you asked... I have already told you part of

my problems. Tack on the mental health issues and uh, delayed diagnosis. The list goes on honestly."

"You are something else."

Okay?

"Thanks? Are you still going to kill me? Or do you need help? I can help you if you need it..."

"What-"

"Seriously though, I-"

"Stop. Talking."

Furrowing my brows, I grumble low in protest.

"I need to think."

"Or therapy," I mumble under my breath.

Masked guy takes off his mask and leans on the table with arms spread and braced. His back is to me.

I feel like the last thing he should've done is take off his mask. *Not doing it right, bud.*

"What diagnosis?" he asks quietly, and I take in his dark hair that doesn't reach his shoulders.

"Aspergers. Anxiety. Depression."

"Ass-perg-ers?"

Well, they changed the terminology, but the word is still funny to me, and I can't say it right anyway.

I stifle a giggle. "Yeah, cause this shit is ass-burgers."

He turns around abruptly. "Are you fucking with me?"

I shake my head slightly, so I don't throw up again from the movement. "I'm serious, minus the burgers. Although I could go for one. I kinda threw up my tacos. They were good, you know."

I pout about it while he sighs heavily for the umpteenth time. *So huffy and puffy.*

"It's the 'tism. You know, ASD? I'm a spectrum. Higher functioning apparently, but I disagree with that statement. It's a personal opinion."

He doesn't say anything for a long moment.

I keep it rolling. "You know people have their misconceptions, but we're misunderstood, and we're not a puzzle piece that needs solving, just built differently... I don't know, honestly, a doctor knows more than me."

"That explains the talking."

"Again. *Rude.* You removed the gag for some reason. What did you expect?"

It hangs around my neck, I'm realizing.

"A decision I'm regretting." He frowns, adding on, "And I certainly was not expecting *this*."

"The first step is admitting the problem. The second-"

"Shut. Up."

It's my turn to sigh. "Just get on with it; you're terrible at your job... Did you have to tie these so tight?"

I struggle against the binds, deciding to keep running my fucking mouth. "Why are you, uh, in this profession anyway? We talked about ME, but what about your psychological issues?"

A low growl reaches my eardrums.

"I'm wondering which one of us is the psychopath here."

My mouth falls open, offended. "Autism does not equal *that* because we're different or have sensory issues. Forget the weird brain radio and logical morals tidbit; also, I overtalk and overshare when I'm nervous, okay? The anxiety takes over. I was expecting another mindless week and relaxing weekend held up in my place. You interrupted my routine. Don't get mad at me, buddy."

He scoffs. "Just...*hush* for a minute. I'm not done thinking."

"Whatever you say, boss."

I lean my head back, sighing more, and wondering if our huffy personalities are merging. I go through the endless music soundtracks in my mind and try to figure out what song fits my situation.

Eighties? Nineties? An EDM song? All I hear is the remix sound on the old-school DJ board. *Wracka, vracka.*

Un-masked guy turns around after rubbing his face and being silent for a couple of minutes. He walks over to me with a purpose, kneeling in front of me.

Something shiny catches my eye and I take note of the knife in his hand.

I gulp. "Just make it quick, I've suffered enough in my life. Don't prolong—"

He puts two fingers to my lips to silence me.

I stop to my surprise, swallowing hard in disbelief. I'm transfixing on the male before me.

Why is he kinda hot?

Blue-green eyes meet mine, holding my gaze. I can't help my shiver.

"I'm not going to hurt you. You are not as weak as I originally thought, much to my misfortune anyway."

Raising my brow in question, I find myself distracted by those eyes. It takes a long moment to register his words.

Not...hurt me?

"Why the change of heart?"

"It's not." He brings his knife to my feet. Looking down before meeting my gaze again.

Please, stop looking at me.

"I'm not letting you leave, but you get to live, for now."

I blink. Once, twice—who knows.

"Okay. Weird turn of events, but okay. If you say so."

He raises his brow in question.

"Can you put the gag back on now?"

He laughs, clearly amused by me. "You want it on *now*?"

I shrug. "I don't mind it. I've been wiggling my fingers

behind me for stimming purposes, plus anxiety. My head hurts, and I'm tired of talking now. I got overstimulated and anxious. Interruptions and unplanned surprises are triggering. I've had enough."

He shakes his head and applies the gag rather loosely. No effort went into it.

I breathe a sigh of relief anyway.

"I'm not sure what to do with you now, but I can't let you go after you've seen me."

You took your mask off...

Idiot.

I merely stare at him as he stands after cutting my legs free of the binds.

"I'm sorry for interrupting your *mundane* day. You're right, I'm sloppy. Perhaps I can use you when the urge arises again. You seem...strangely useful."

I shrug again while he tucks one knee under him and rests his arm on the other, holding the knife. I brace myself in the event he changes his mind. The guy is clearly off his game.

"You're strange in general, but it's not necessarily a bad thing. You certainly put out whatever fire there was to kill you." He sighs in defeat, clearly disappointed and confused over the situation just as I am. "I'm not sure what that means, but you have my attention, whether you like it or not."

How kinky. I've already been kidnapped, life being turned upside-down.

I wonder what's next?

Stay tuned for next week's episode.

"Weak and alone. That's what I go for. I make sure they're not the same. I haven't chosen blonde in a while. You have pretty eyes, too. You're the prettiest I've scouted and stalked lately."

Feeling flattered yet insulted, I ponder over it. What a strange turn of events.

My mind is scrambled eggs. I need a nap or a Xanax. Both would work too, ideally.

"I feel weird without you talking now, but you asked for the gag... If you promise not to run away, I won't hurt you. I'll figure out the next steps, but you're with me now."

Unsure what exactly it means, I incline my head toward him.

My head is pounding still, and I'm crashing quicker than I'd like. *I probably have a damn concussion.*

He cuts and unties the rest of me.

I exhale through my nose at the relief.

"How's that?"

Nodding once, he takes my bound wrists and pulls me to my feet.

"Until we trust each other, I'll keep your wrist bound while I bring you to my place." I stiffen in response, and he notices. "No, that's not where I'll kill you. Relax."

This guy is delulu in relulu.

He leads me out of the basement and up a set of stairs, and I feel as if I'm not even in my body. I realize I'm dissociating to get through whatever comes next.

Do or die.

I don't even want to process what happens next, so I follow and get tugged along. The gag falls off, and I still don't want to speak.

What even is my life anymore?

XOXO
LOVE

Chapter Four

Rory

What the fuck did I get myself into?

As soon as she woke up and opened her goddamn mouth, I've been thrown off. No one has *ever* talked to me like that in my entire life.

Why didn't I gag her again?

Rubbing my temples, I groan, realizing how much I *fucked up*. My realization turns into an exasperated laugh, as I make note that this woman makes *me* look sane. Which is saying something because of *my* so-called problems.

Now, I'm at a standstill until I figure out whatever I'm to do with her.

I bring her to my home which is the top floor of one of the old-ass buildings outside of the central downtown area of the city. I wanted this particular location that allows roof access for binocular spying. It's not a fancy place, but the ceilings are high, and it has a Gotham City appeal from the comics. High ceilings with lots of tall windows that are practically floor-to-ceiling. I'm proud of my comic collection, if I do say so myself.

The woman doesn't say anything once we arrive. My

veins are prickling, noting to myself that she's the first person I've ever brought home. It's so dark outside, no one even noticed how her wrists were tied.

She's fucking weird, I'll admit it, but I wasn't lying when I told her before that she's useful.

Maybe I am a cliché. But I can improve my craft, right?

"Do you need to use the bathroom?" I ask as if we're normal people having normal conversations after the events of the evening.

She shakes her head, clearly still not wanting to talk. Yet earlier, she wouldn't shut up. What even gives with this woman?

The girl disrupted my killing plans and urges, stumping me completely. I seriously wonder if she's the crazy one.

Somehow, I even feel defeat over the fact she stopped talking and *requested to be gagged. The fuck?* I didn't think I'd ever regret keeping her quiet like I have in the past five minutes. She was so honest before, and now I'm not sure what to do with myself without it.

Has anyone ever been honest in their entire lives? *Have I?*

I shake myself of my thoughts, running a hand through my dark hair over the shitshow I've gotten myself into by not killing her.

Looking around my place with my *new guest*, it's mostly open concept. The kitchen is off to the left, the living room near the entryway with a TV stand and TV. I have a desk on the right of the TV, racks for clothes on the opposite side of the room by the bed, and a small wardrobe. The bed is tucked in the far corner of the place. The bathroom is on the opposite wall of the bed. Overall, the huge building looks like a converted warehouse space, but it works for me. Let's me live out my *comic vibes* fantasy that I grew up reading.

The woman still says nothing as I ask if she needs food or water like she's some kind of pet.

What else am I supposed to ask knowing she's stuck with me now?

Knowing I need to think about shit, I mutter to her about letting her rest before taking off the ties on her wrists since she's not going anywhere except *through me* to get away now.

She rubs them afterwards, looking around and avoiding my gaze.

Confusion isn't the right word to feel. Is she really crazy? Or are we both off?

Before I leave her for the bathroom, I tell her, "I'm only going to tell you this once. You are stuck with me, and I'm not letting you go. We'll figure out the rest as we go. For now, you'll be staying here. If you try to leave, I will know, and you won't like what I do to you."

"*Kinky.*"

Her voice is so quiet, I almost think I misheard, but it makes my eye twitch. That smartass mouth will take some getting used to, but the more I think about it, I'm not sure I mind. *I'll debate that later.*

Whipping around, I grab her chin, making her look at me. "Don't provoke me. I could still change my mind on killing you. We'll have plenty of time getting acquainted. I'm going to shower, help yourself to anything here. That's as nice and accommodating as I will be. If you're as useful as I think you'll be, then we can adjust more as we go."

She stares at me. I think it's a glare, but one cannot assume. I can't tell with her expressions as they look semi-blank. Hell, maybe she's thinking about murdering me now, and the tables have turned. It wouldn't be the worst true crime I've witnessed or watched.

To ensure she understands clearly, I say, *"Do we understand each other?"*

"Escape and die. Message received."

With how bland she says it without emotion and almost a hint of sassiness, I laugh, walking away and shaking my head.

Curious on what she'll do without my supervision, I give her the benefit of the doubt.

I shut the door behind me and strip, leaving it unlocked because I doubt she'll follow me in when she's acting weird already. I need the shower steam to clear my mind to figure out my thoughts from my dumbass decisions.

Once the water is hot enough, I step inside the shower with a heavy sigh.

Was it shock over her millennialism, or that the one time I didn't gag an intended kill that instead of screaming, she lectures and insults me? The whole situation is hilarious in a this-is-a-good-way-to-get-caught-dumbass sort of manner.

I squirt the citrus-scented shampoo into my palm and lather it up into my hair.

Maybe I should try dating her? Is that weird? Would I have to eventually kill her?

As the suds run down my body, I freeze. *Why do I feel strange?*

Strange as in the sense of not feeling relieved like I do around Friday-Night-Kills, *almost-kills,* but more of unfinished business.

I need to kill again just to be sure I'm not losing my killing touch.

Maybe this lady will help me out since she clearly has so many opinions.

Nodding to myself in agreement, I quickly finish the

rest of my shower with the rest of my citrus-scented-every-thing that I own.

I can't help but think to myself about how I can make this situation work in both of our favors. We'd have to get to know each other better, too. While she sleeps, I'll use my computer to research more about autism and the other things she named just so I have a better understanding of what the hell I'm dealing with.

If any of this is to work, we'll have to learn trust some-how. She definitely won't trust me after my *just-kidding-not-killing-you, but I-still-might-if-you-don't-behave* tone versus my already untrusting ways. I'm a loner. I don't have family I speak to, or true friends. Not anymore anyway.

However, the more I think about it as I step out of the shower, if I can accommodate my new house guest, I'll try. Despite what I told her earlier.

It wouldn't hurt to ask her questions on how to be *better* either. She did have some rather blunt opinions of me.

My thoughts wander on the woman inside my place. No one but me has been here, *ever*. I've lived here long enough that I should've brought a woman home for play or hooking up, but that was never the case. I didn't care for fucking people where I sleep. It's *my space.* I'd go to the local sex club downtown if I wanted to get laid.

My interests are rather kinky. *I wonder if she's kinky, too.*

I dry myself, wiping the mirror before running my fingers through my hair. There are tattoos that cover most of my body. Most of them are black and white, since that's my tastes for myself, and I enjoy the feel of needles. It reminds me that I'm alive, and helps rewire my brain between killing urges, otherwise I'd be up to, like, 100 in my count by now.

Keeping the towel draped around my hips, I open the

door and head to the fridge for something to munch on. I peer around briefly, not seeing her. The TV is on, so I wonder if she's on the couch while I move silently over to the back of it.

I find her wrapped in my blanket, seemingly asleep. Somehow, she looks peaceful in this state. Quiet and less mouthy. No smartass things to say while she sleeps. I stare at her probably longer than I should, and it's as if she has extrasensory perception to sense me looming over the back of the couch.

She blinks her eyes open.

We stare at one another, not saying anything for a long while. Somehow, I'm proud that she didn't leave.

"What's your name?" I should've asked her earlier, but *priorities* and my midlife crisis.

"Nicole."

Her blonde hair spills over the arm of the couch; I take note of how much more relaxed she looks.

"What's yours?" she asks, and I notice her eyes wander, taking in my tattoos. I can't tell if she's curious about me or not, but her blush doesn't go unnoticed when she sees the towel wrapped at my hips.

"Rory."

Realizing I've been staring far too long down at her, I move into the kitchen to make a sandwich.

"Want a sandwich, too?" I ask.

"What kind?" I see her sit up in my periphery. It baffles me how our interactions continue, and I find dark humor in it. A killer and a–*not victim?* Strangely, my obsessive nature with killing and completion of such feats isn't bothering me as much as it should. She's derailing me. *Am I the crazy one? Hmm...*

Smirking at her question, I read off what I have.

"Hmm, just the meat and mayo? I probably shouldn't have too much cheese. I'm one of those lactose intolerant people that don't act like it."

"You got it." She's more honest than I give her credit for. *Nicole.*

It fits her, strangely. She looks like a Nicole, not that I've met any to my knowledge. I'm interested to see what else I learn about her. Maybe it wouldn't be so hard to get to know each other. She's not the screaming type, which definitely calms me.

I make our food, making sure mine has cheese, and I grab a bag of plain chips. Bringing the stuff over, I grab water too, even though she didn't ask.

"What are you watching?" I ask, plopping down beside her.

She moves the blanket out of the way, and I watch how careful she eats over her lap to not make a mess or leave crumbs.

"It was just background noise. I didn't really search. I debated death for a second before sitting down here."

Intrigued over her words, I take the remote as she continues to eat.

"What do you like to watch?" I find myself genuinely interested in her response, and I ignore the afterthought of suddenly being interested in what someone else likes—*unless it's at the kink club and they're down to fuck.*

"It depends on the mood. Choose whatever you want. Thanks for the food."

I chuckle. "So, she has manners. I thought you said you didn't want anything." I raise my brow, giving her a look.

"You're a stranger...*a killer,* mind you. I didn't want to be a bother. You know, *bothering* might involve getting me killed."

A full laugh leaves me. She has a valid point as I steal a glimpse of her side profile.

"Just because I'm not killing you, doesn't mean kill yourself. That defeats the purpose."

She shrugs and finishes eating while I find something random to watch. Strangely enough, her company doesn't bother me. We sit in comfortable silence as *War of the Worlds* plays on TV.

The bag of chips is between us. I reach in at the same time as she does. She pulls away, letting me go first.

I wonder if she'd make a good submissive.

To distract myself on the sudden thoughts and fast-changing dynamics, I ask, "Why do you walk an hour one-way to work?"

"To lose weight."

What?

"Seriously?" *She's got to be kidding.*

"Yes. It helped me. Especially when work is boring as fuck." Honesty is the best policy, I suppose.

"Fair enough... You shouldn't worry about your weight though."

She meets my gaze. "Why?"

"You look fine the way you are..."

I didn't want to make her more uncomfortable than she probably already was. She's *hot*. Gorgeous even, without trying. I haven't seen her wear makeup but once since I've been following her.

"Thanks."

I relax back into the couch, deciding not to ask any more questions. Tonight was already fucking weird enough for us both, and I don't want to make her think I'm crazier than she already does.

"After this ends, would you like to use the bed?"

"I'm fine on the couch, it's comfy enough."

I frown, not liking her answer for some reason.

"Wrong answer."

She sighs. "I need to think, too. You can boss me around tomorrow. I'll sleep here. Seriously, it's okay. The noise from the TV turned down low will help me sleep better anyway. Just, like, don't get angry and kill me or something."

I put up my hands in defeat. Nicole is surprising me at every turn.

"Fine, alright. No killing either. Relax."

She moves the empty plate, getting situated under the blanket. The couch is long enough for the two of us, but she's short enough that her feet barely reach me with her straightened out fully. I look her over and gather she has her own processing to do. Just like I need to do. Because I certainly changed the tides this evening.

I say nothing more, and it isn't long before she falls asleep. The movie finishes, and I turn the volume down lower so that it's barely audible.

Getting up, I move a few feet away and boot up my computer. Settling in, I begin my research.

Chapter Five

Nikki

The sun blinds me as I roll over begrudgingly, forgetting where the hell I am.

My brain catches up slowly.

Oh right. A kidnapping and not dying—*yet?*

Stretching, I blink my eyes open. Taking in my surroundings, I'm on a comfortable dark blue couch, wrapped in a blanket.

For a killer, his place isn't too bad. I guess we're together now? Whatever that means.

Of course, it's me that gets in a relationship in unconventional ways. *I should probably ask instead of assuming.*

Wondering where the man himself is, I look around. I recall that I've never met anyone with his name before.

Sitting up, I sigh, turning off the TV that is still on.

Wishing I had some coffee, my bladder catches up, letting me know that I'm long overdue for a potty break.

I get up, realizing Rory is still asleep as I walk towards the bathroom near his bed, which is tucked in the corner with windows on the headboard side and the far side of the bed.

How can he sleep with the sun in his face?

His torso is exposed with tattoos and a body to drool over. *I shouldn't be thinking of a guy who tried to kill me as hot.* Maybe he's right, there's something wrong with me.

Turning away, *not ogling at how hot he is,* I shut the bathroom door behind me and do my business.

I sigh, flush, and look at myself in the mirror. Even though I was somehow able to sleep, I still look stressed and like I haven't slept. My permanent tired look.

Washing my hands, I splash my face after and use the hand towel.

What the hell am I supposed to do with my life now?

I hear a creak as I open the door and see him sitting at the edge of his bed, facing toward me. *Completely naked.*

I turn to the side startled.

"I didn't realize you slept nude..."

Not meeting his gaze, I can somehow feel his eyes on me with my senses zeroed in on the recent sensory input.

"I don't have anyone over, so I didn't think about it. Does it bother you?"

Yes—no.

"I'm fine."

It's his place, who am I to say?

I'm not against nudity; I just have to be comfortable around the person. Rationalizing my decisions is a black and white process.

The events of the past twenty-four hours have me feeling exhausted. My brain is foggy without my medication. My anti-anxiety and antidepressant combo helps level me out. Then I have meds for my underactive thyroid that I must take for the rest of my life.

Not mentioning it for fear that he wouldn't get the meds

for me or let me leave, I walk to the kitchen and ask if he has coffee. *It's a normal thing to do.*

"Yes. The cabinet by the fridge."

I go in search of the magic energy beans, while I vaguely hear him get up and use the bathroom.

Doing my best not to think about his naked body, I find the fancy machine, putting a pod in from the cabinet as instructed, along with a plain black mug.

He needs more entertaining mugs like my collection.

I sniff the caramel aroma as it brews.

"Do you use creamer or sugar?"

He startles me.

"I drink it black," I say, taking a deep breath as he moves closer to me.

At least he put on sweatpants. I hate how spacey I get and forget my surroundings because of how in my head I find myself.

The brew finishes and I take the black mug, catching his unsettled look.

"What kind of psychopath are *you*?"

I bring the hot liquid to my lips, sipping it. Huffing a laugh, I walk away. "That's rich coming from *you*."

"Like calls to like."

I can't tell if he's teasing me or not, but I roll my eyes.

"I'm perfectly *sane*. Oddities or quirks doesn't mean shit, thank you very much."

"Whatever you say, sweetheart."

Now he's giving me nicknames?

I smile into the mug. I love ridiculous nicknames, even the cute ones. Not that I'll tell him that.

I settle myself on the wood floor, next to the coffee table by the TV. Yes, there's a perfectly good couch, but I need to wake up, not be comfortable.

I hear him make his coffee and happen to look to see him adding sugar and creamer. The real psychopath likes his coffee sweet, *interesting*.

Life is fucking funny.

Sipping my coffee, the distinct caramel flavor is bold and bitterness rushes to my taste buds. It's pure happiness for me.

"So," he sits on the couch, tilting his head at where I'm sitting before shaking his head. "You said I was cliché..."

Was his feelings hurt?

Before I could ask, he went on, "How can I not be one?"

Finding a black coaster on the table, I put the mug down.

"All black clothes, the mask. I guess for your *secret occupation*, the black clothes are smarter at night... You could do with a different mask. It's basic."

He considers me, and I look him over, noticing how in shape he is. I wonder if he has any *colorful* tattoos. It's all grayscale and shading, even though he looks like a morbid work of art.

Should not be complimenting a killer—I'm mental.

"What's wrong with my mask, besides the color?"

"You need more character, a statement piece. Spice things up."

He stares at me over the rim of his all *white* mug.

He *must* be a black and white person. I'm seeing a theme, which somehow goes back to how I view the world. It's either this or that. Who am I to insult his lack of style and basic colors? Not that I mind the color black; it's one of my favorites, but I also like colors too.

"I should kill you for that."

I raise my brow. "If you haven't killed me already, you're not going to. Makes me question your judgment, but whatever. We're stuck with each other now, even if the means are entirely unconventional... Do you normally find relationships this way?"

Inquiring minds need to know.

In my neurospicy brain, if he says I can't leave and he won't kill me as a result, then that's that.

"No. Never. I don't do relationships. I just fuck."

I clear my throat, reaching for the mug to distract myself.

Nope, not going to let my mind wander on that—hold for later information.

"Then what is this supposed to be?" I ask, avoiding his eyes.

"I...don't know yet."

I give him a simple *blank* look.

"Let me know when you figure that out. Am I supposed to wear your clothes too, or use your toothbrush? Underwear?"

He sighs, leaning back fully.

"We'll work on it."

"Sounds like a relationship to me, bud."

I give him a sarcastic, smug look of *I'm right,* and he's unsettled over the revelation.

Finishing the rest of the coffee, I get up and make myself another.

"What do you do when you're not plotting and scheming? Don't you have legal hobbies you partake in?"

"You ask so many questions."

And?

"I'm inquisitive, sue me. Actually, don't. I'm not that rich."

I take a drink of coffee, enjoying the rich caramel smell,

which differs from the taste, but I enjoy that about coffee. Sweeter smells verses tastes.

"I work a warehouse job, Monday through Friday. Sometimes I work the weekend; on those weeks I get some weekdays off."

What else?

I turn around once the brew finishes, making my way back to my previous spot on the floor.

"I'll find new people to stalk, and not the same people each time to switch things up. That takes time, energy, and money to prepare for."

This guy must have a kill-kit stashed somewhere. If I check, I bet it's in his car.

"Okay... Two questions. How long have you been doing this, and it still doesn't answer my question—how do you unwind?"

"That *is* how I unwind."

"Try again. Outside of that."

He sighs, getting up for a refill too.

"I've only been doing this for a few years. I'll change locations and cover my trail."

I can't believe I'm having this conversation.

Saying nothing, I wait for him to return to his spot on the couch. I give him an expectant look, waiting.

"I like to take drives, I guess."

"Okay... That's something, I suppose. Do you only target women?"

It's a valid question.

He inclines his head *yes,* drinking down his coffee.

"Psychological issues...*with* trauma of some sort," I mutter to myself.

"What—"

Ignoring him, the caffeine begins to kick in, along with my brain power.

"I wonder if there was bullying or someone cheated on you. Maybe abuse?"

I look him over, wondering about his past and what led him to this point.

"I'm right here." He doesn't look amused.

"Be honest, have you thought about therapy or getting help? You know you can get caught and end up in prison for life, or get the death penalty, right? Not that I'm gonna rat you out; I'm not a snitch, even if I should be."

He looks up at the tall industrial ceiling. Why he searches for answers up there, I can't say. My first cup of coffee is kicking in, clearly.

"Are you being serious, right now?"

"I have a degree in psychology. I can't help but wonder. Excuse me for being curious. You need new hobbies. I'm not trying to go to prison here."

He grumbles, muttering something I can't make out despite my great selective hearing.

"I *will* go to prison if I go to therapy. They have to report shit like that." He stares at me, leaning forward to rest his arms on his knees.

I guess he's got me on that one.

"Since you have that degree, you can be my therapist for free. We're stuck together now. Tell me what I need, *doctor.*"

Still unsure if he's being a sarcastic ass, I puff my cheeks. "That's not what I meant."

His eyebrow goes up, and his face almost looks sassy—again, can't assume.

"I can't always tell when people are being sarcastic or

serious until I get to know them better. Nor do I pick up on the cues for meanness or intent. It's a 'tism thing."

He rubs his fingers on his forehead, and I can't help but appreciate his proportions. Nice forehead, eyes, face, lips, *and all the rest of him.*

"I forgot, sorry."

"Did you just apologize to me?" I'm seriously confused on the dynamic, and it makes my head hurt, or it could be lack of chemicals or not having breakfast.

I tilt my head and his blue-green eyes meet my green ones.

"While you slept, I wanted to research more about the conditions you mentioned yesterday... It was a lot of information, but I couldn't help my curiosity. I'm sorry for calling you a psychopath. I don't mean it."

His words break my brain. I'm *shook* to my core. While I wasn't expecting him to say *any of that,* I'm flattered.

"It's okay... I'm used to the names for things people don't understand. Not your fault. Thank you."

I gaze into my now-emptied cup. I'm uncomfortable, so I just sit with it.

A killer just apologized to me. And he looked up my diagnoses.

I haven't been stumped like this by someone in a long time. *Do not romanticize him.*

I ignore my inner voice, which is most definitely *right.* He's still staring at me, and I start to feel like a zoo animal exhibit.

"Could you not stare at me like that? I don't need figuring out. I experience the world differently than what society considers as normal. It's nothing." I shrug it off.

"I find you fascinating, nonetheless. Perhaps you are my new obsession."

I get up, ignoring him. Feelings and emotions are weird for me and cause discomfort. Way too soon to say things like that to me.

I clean my cup, saying nothing else, reminding myself not to fidget.

"So, you're weird with emotions too, then."

I glare. "I'm not doing this today. We don't know each other."

"Yet. We're stuck now."

It's my turn to grumble, and somehow, he finds me amusing. He gets up, coming over to my side, and I think I catch a smug look.

"I can't wait to get to know you."

I scoff and his chuckle warms my skin. I ignore the sensations, shutting down his words.

"Are you a picky eater?"

I shake my head.

"Despite what you've read about the 'tisms, I've worked *very* hard to combat my picky eating habits. Now, I'm just happy to eat food. Living on your own does that."

"Hm. Good to know. I happened to go grocery shopping days ago, after you went to work. Eggs, toast, and bacon, okay?"

I nod, happy for some upcoming food. *I'll ignore the red flags and stalking.*

"Alright. If you don't mind citrus scents, feel free to use my stuff and shower. Go through my clothes for something to wear. There should be something in there for you."

Needing space, I take him up on his offer and shower.

I enjoy his scents, finding comfort in the sensory experience. I'm able to relax and gather my thoughts before facing him again.

I've never been told words like he said before. It's

unnerving, and while he stumps me with his weird actions and change of course, I strangely want to get to know him too. *Not because he's hot, even if that's a factor.* Stupid brain.

Regardless, I don't have a choice in the matter, but I can try to make the most of the situation, even if I do question my own sanity.

XOXO
LOVE

Chapter Six

Rory

I make breakfast as she showers. Nicole seems uncomfortable when I show interest in making the most of our situation. She doesn't like it when I stare at her, and I gather there's issues with emotional vulnerability. *Trust, too. Can't forget the past twenty-four hours, Rory.*

She's right about the world putting labels on people who are different or who don't understand because they're considered *normal*. Rules that society lives by, even if we don't function at that level. I can't help but wanting to learn all about her though. There's only so much I can learn from the stalking I've done, or the internet. My research about disorders and mental health, plus autism, led me down a rabbit hole after that first night. Despite my mind swimming with information, putting two and two together, all I know from that is how my newest obsession has my attention.

I haven't killed her, and I decide not to, but I still have plans to gain her help.

Breakfast is done by the time she comes out wrapped in a towel. I can't help but look as she pays me no mind.

Her lighter hair is wrapped in a towel on her head as

another is around her body. She is tinier than I imagined previously. I can see the hourglass form and several tattoos I can't quite make out on her back.

I don't want to make her more uncomfortable, so I just observe from afar. Even if I want to see what's hidden underneath. I shouldn't be so eager when it wasn't *that* long ago when I was hunting her for sport.

Killing aside, I don't believe in raping my victims, and I haven't ever touched anyone sexually without their permission. I wouldn't start now. Not that I'm morally sound. The deeper I dive into this situation with Nicole is proof of that.

The woman herself digs through my wardrobe, grabbing black and white striped pajama bottoms, and a black t-shirt.

Pretending I'm not looking at her, I go to gather plates and turn my back when I hear the bathroom door click. Distractions, *distractions*.

Once everything is out on the island, I load my plate. I eat while standing. Maybe I should invest in a table and two chairs; I muse over the thought. It'll probably be something else Nicole judges me for in my bachelor pad.

She comes back out, and I'm impressed by how fucking good she looks in *my* clothes. I clear my throat to distract myself.

"Feel better?" *Logical question.*

"Yes, thanks."

I decide to tease her as she grabs the other plate and loads up, too.

"Did you find some of my underwear too?"

She stares at me as my lips lift in amusement.

"No. I'm not *that* weird. I don't mind going commando."

Fucking hell.

She's got me there. I can't help the desire that rushes through me at the thought. Wondering if she saw it on my face, I find her eyes focusing on her plate of food before digging in.

My thoughts roam on what she mentioned earlier about a *relationship*.

Unfortunately for me, she's right, despite her sarcastic, yet honest, remarks.

I'm not doing a good job at any of this. Not that I've *ever* done this, whatever *this* is.

Maybe I'll have her help me in my occupation? She clearly doesn't want to do the killing, but she doesn't have to. She can be the getaway driver, an accomplice. A blackmail technique in case she ever *does* think about telling anyone. It's a way to let her roam freely, knowing she'll come back. It's also a way for her to keep her routines, which I know is something relating to autism; a way for us to weirdly coexist in this mess I created.

"Will you help me find a better mask?" I ask her randomly.

Nicole swallows, reaching for the orange juice before choking. She has a coughing fit, and I move closer as she gulps some down from the glass.

"Breathe, Nicole."

Christ, was it something I said?

She shakes her head before putting her arms up to try and breathe. I attempt to pat her back, and she heaves a breath, gasping.

"For fuck's sake, woman! I said I wouldn't kill you, so don't choke and die on me."

She leans over the sink, and I wrap my hands around her abdomen to proceed with the abdominal thrusts.

"If you don't get whatever it is out, I will put my lips on you." *Maybe a threat will help?* Her dying would be counterproductive to this whole fiasco.

She jerks suddenly and spits out something, air rushing into her in a giant heaving breath.

My heart is racing as I lean my head against her back. I find myself enjoying how she feels in my arms, even if she was choking.

"I'm fine now, thank you. Fucking *toast* got me."

"Death by toast." I sigh heavily, waiting a moment to release her. "Are you sure you don't want me to put my lips on you? Do you need mouth-to-mouth?"

She shakes her head, takes another drink and steadies her arms on the counter.

I chuckle and pull away, but not before running my fingers through her hair.

"Are you sure you're okay? I'm being serious."

I hand her a paper towel to clean her mouth.

"I am now. Thank you. No kissing. *No lips are necessary.*"

"So, you don't want to kiss me?" *A valid question.*

I lean closer after she wipes her face. She turns her face so that she's mere inches away. Almost thinking I distracted her, she says nothing even though her eyes move from mine to my lips.

"Maybe when I'm clearer on this dynamic we have here."

At least it wasn't a no.

Smiling, I pull away. "Fair enough. I only kiss the willing anyway, but I'm finding how fun you are to tease."

She grumbles, deciding not to eat anything else.

I end up finishing and cleaning up while she dries the dishes. We do it in silence, but I don't mind. Somehow, it's not awkward with her.

"Will you help me find another mask?" I ask again, deciding it's safe to ask her when she's not eating.

"Sure. I don't have to kill anyone, right?"

I shake my head, walking over to the computer to begin searching.

"Okay, I suppose I can live with that."

As I search, I decide to ask her if she's truly okay with this and why it seems like she's willingly helping me. I turn my head and catch her rubbing her temples in my periphery.

"I can't explain the chaos that is my brain, Rory. We're in this situation because of *you*. As I adjust, it's easy to accept things as they are even if the processing part is severely lacking. My brain doesn't think in right or wrong."

It takes me a moment to take in the information, but somehow, I'm happy with her answer even if I can't make complete sense of how her unique brain works. She's by far the most interesting person I've met.

I give her a nod of acknowledgment once her gaze meets mine. Another minute passes before I focus back on the task at hand to find a few mask options that aren't *basic* before asking her opinion.

"Do you not like any other colors?" she protests, and I give her a knowing look.

"Black is the easiest, Nicole."

She put her hands up in defeat.

"Fine, this one. It's hot." She points to the black mask that has a skull shape with the nose and teeth. There's a hole for the eyes too.

"Did you just say *hot?*" It takes a moment for my brain to catch up after she points to one on the screen.

Pressing her lips in a thin line, she shrugs, and I gape after her as she moves back to the couch.

"Do you have a mask kink I should know about?"

A small grin slides up to the corner of her mouth. "I

don't think we're at that stage yet. Don't you think we should at least trauma bond first before we share our kinks?"

Laughter fills me as I order the mask with some paint. I want her to customize it. *I want to stand out but not too much.*

"I'm onto you."

She seems amused as I flip on the TV.

"If you help me tomorrow, I'll let you return to work on Monday." A bargain to help convince her.

She tilts her head. "I'm not killing anyone," she says adamantly.

I raise my brow in knowing. "I just need you to drive."

"To kidnap someone?"

I shake my head, realizing that the less she knows specifically the better. To ease her mind. "Dropping me off and picking me up."

She leans forward, steadying her arms on her knees with her head in her hands.

"I don't have to see anything, right?"

"No," I say with a sigh, realizing that I'm right. "Just drive. I'll give you the time and place, along with the vehicle."

I think I hear her mumble, *"Fuck, fuck."*

Letting her figure it out with her process, I wait patiently.

"Okay... Can I make a playlist?"

Confusion takes hold of me as she turns her head and straightens her arms over her knees.

"Weird request, but sure." Who am I to question where her mind is at? Maybe she needs music to process shit?

"Music is life. I need a getaway driver playlist."

Well, that answers my question.

"Fine, the music is on my computer—have at it."

Nicole's entire demeanor changes.

Grinning, she jumps up and skips over to the computer.

"You're weird, I hope you know."

I see her wave me off without turning to look at me as she scrolls through my music. I'm suddenly curious about what she listens to or if she'll comment on my music tastes.

"You like hard rock and metal. I'm not surprised," she says as if I'm not sitting from feet away.

What's wrong with that genre?

"Are you judging me?" I ask with a raised brow, and she looks at me and shakes her head.

"Oh, no! It's an observation. I like your music. I'm very eclectic in my tastes."

"I'm not surprised."

She turns to look at me again. "What's that supposed to mean?"

I return her comment smugly, "It's an observation."

The wheels are turning behind those green eyes, and I let them.

"Clever." She shakes her head, dismissing me.

Letting her have at it, the rest of the day goes by with me watching TV and her making The Getaway Playlist —*with that title.*

Tomorrow will be interesting.

I pull out my phone and make arrangements. She wasn't my lucky number eight, but someone else at random would be for nine and ten.

Chapter Seven

Nikki

I make kickass playlists if I do say so myself. Music is one thing that brings all the pieces of me together—no matter what is happening in life. I can process and do anything really, as long as I have a music playlist of some sort. Most of my playlists are mood and occasion based. I wouldn't be alive without it.

Feeling proud of myself, I talk Rory into letting me sleep on the couch again. He makes sandwiches for dinner, and I don't mind. At least he's feeding me and *not* killing me.

The next morning, I hear someone coming inside the place, and I jump up.

I quickly realize it's Rory with a couple of bags.

"I'm glad you're still here."

Not understanding what he means when I was asleep, I don't answer him.

"What is it?" I ask him sleepily.

"I brought you some things to help decorate the mask."

Wrapping the blanket around me, he saunters closer, opening the bags.

I see the mask with white, silver, and gray paint supplies.

"You want me to decorate it?"

Why would he want me to do it?

"Yes."

Thinking to myself about what to do with it, I put some of the paints in the bag.

"What if I draw a dick on it? *With balls.*"

I meet his unamusing gaze and grin to myself.

"Make me some coffee then?" I compromise.

He hands the bags over and takes off his black hoodie.

"You've got it, Sugar."

My eyebrow quirks up over his mannerisms before shaking my head and walking to the desk with the supplies.

Making room and getting set up, he brings me coffee.

"While I work on this, is it okay to listen to music so I can focus on getting this done and dry for tonight?"

He nods, giving me a panty-dropping smile. *Oh, no.*

Ignoring how his smile affects me, I turn the music on and keep it at a volume suitable for me. Not too low, but not too loud.

I get started, highlighting the different facial features in silver. I love how it blends in nicely with the mask.

I drink the cup, and he refills it without me asking— which no one ever does, at least for me. *Don't ignore his red flags.*

After he walks away, I can't help my smile as I listen to his music. *I'm saving my playlist for later, for humor purposes.*

I use white and gray paint to make a crack over one of the eyes after I finish with the silver where I want it.

Hours pass, and I let it dry, proud of my good work.

I look around, and the sun is still up, so it's not quite dusk, which means I did great with my timing.

Rory appears behind me, looking at it.

"I love it," is all he says before walking away to put on a black shirt and black pants.

The guy has no shame as he strips in his bedroom, and I watch even though he's quick about it.

"Want me to wear all black too?" I ask after he pulls his pants up, throwing things I can't quite see in a bag.

"Yes. Come here, and I'll find you something."

I sigh, getting up and moving over to the other side of the room.

He's dressed by the time I make it over, and he's already putting on his shoes.

Rory pulls a black hoodie over his head again with black sweatpants and a shirt with another black hoodie.

"How many sets of these do you have?"

"Fourteen."

I make a face as he rushes off back toward the living room. I know I'm some distance away, so I just change right there. I replace the pajamas, put them in the hamper, and replace them with what he put on the bed for me.

I've slept in my bra, so thankfully it's still on, even though I hate it. I can't have my tits all willy-nilly around a stranger I'm not comfortable with yet.

After I pull the hoodie over my head, he's standing in front of me. I catch his green-blue eyes in his mask.

"How do I look?"

Well, fuck.

My mask kink aside, I'd fuck him. Not that I'd tell him that.

"Better. I would recommend some black eyeshadow around your eyes to blend it all together better."

He takes it off, grabbing my face and kissing my cheek.
"You're so smart, thank you."

Staring in shock after him, he rushes into the bathroom and comes back out.

I can't reason within myself how hot he is, or rationalize, but my pussy sure makes note.

This is not good. I can't be attracted to a killer that I'm about to be an accomplice too.

One thing is for sure: I'm absolutely *fucked*.

XOXO
LOVE

Chapter Eight

Nikki

It's pitch dark, and I'm hidden in the driver's seat of a van in an alley. *Not suspicious at all, Rory.*

I'm listening to The Getaway Playlist on the lowest volume, feeling thankful for the shadows between the buildings.

I originally dropped him off at a location I hadn't been to before, and then he told me where to be waiting and the time.

Breaking the Law comes on through the speakers right next to my ear and I smile big, pulling the hood over my head. *I feel like a cliché, too.*

I'm laying down in the seat though, so it doesn't look *too* obvious.

Eh, I'm realizing that Rory just isn't perfect at his side hobby. My only hope is that this isn't a setup.

I can't help the nagging feeling over that thought. I'd rather die by bread.

It's ten o'clock by the time I see his masked face at my door and I yelp. I unlock the door and hear something in the back clang around.

Closing my eyes, I try to talk myself into calming down even though anxiety floods me. Without my medication, I'm more dysregulated.

I begin to feel sick, wondering what the hell he's doing, and knowing I'm a part of it.

Does this mean whatever blood was spilled tonight is also on me?

Don't spiral, hold it in.

I put my figurative mask on as he jumps in the front seat. It's too dark and I don't dare to look in the back.

"Drive, Sugar."

Let's Kill Tonight comes on as I quickly buckle in and pull away.

I'm afraid to say anything as I repeat shit to myself endlessly in my head. *Mask up, you dumb bitch. Mask up. Mask, mask. You are fine, you are alive.*

Fear and adrenaline vibrate my nerve endings, so I drive with purpose.

He doesn't say anything except when and where to turn.

In the rearview, I see an explosion in the distance.

Was it the same place? I couldn't tell.

"Just tell me if there's a body in the back," is all I say, my hand shaking.

"Nope, but that explosion was me. I'm at my ten count which is what I wanted, so we're in the clear. Well, *almost.* Turn left at the next intersection."

I do as I'm told, feeling relieved. I could barely function even *thinking* someone was in the back.

Whew.

I take some more turns that lead us to some deserted place outside the main inner city. *It looks sketchy and desolate.*

"Okay, take off your clothes and change into these. We need to burn the evidence; keep the gloves on though."

I nod without even thinking about being shy and bashful, not with the adrenaline running through me.

He hoists the bag from the back, doing the same.

The hoodie and mask come off, as I follow his movements once he hands me clothes.

I strip hurriedly, replacing what I'm wearing with blue pants and a matching t-shirt. He puts on a white shirt with blue pants.

He hands me slip-on shoes that are surprisingly comfortable. We get out once we're done.

"Leave everything but the gloves inside. I'm burning this before I put out the flames."

I follow the instructions given, moving far enough away as he takes apart something under the hood, and I see the gas tank. He tosses some fire extinguishers nearby, away from the van.

I didn't realize you could do that, or that it was in the front hood of this old van.

The old white van erupts in flames soon after as he comes beside me to watch it burn.

Strangely, I enjoy the fire. I've always liked fire, even if I got burned. Not caring that he's standing close to me, we watch it burn and burn.

"We'll be here for a while. Stay here while I wash my face off nearby."

Rory disappears, and I don't realize he's back until I happen to look beside me to see him gazing at me a short distance away.

"Call out of work tomorrow, and we'll go to your place to get things."

All I do is stare. The flames are raging beside us, and I

see the sexy look in his eyes. A dark part of me wants to kiss him. My mind is blank as he takes long strides toward me as if I am summoning him closer.

I can't believe I did all I did with him.

We're tied together now whether we like it or not.

"You look so fucking perfect right now," he says once he's upon me.

His face inches closer, claiming my lips in a heated moment. One of our own making.

The kiss is deep and consuming. This stranger, this *killer,* is claiming me in a different manner than he originally intended.

His hand cups my nape, pulling me flush to him. Closing my eyes, I don't push or pull away. As fucked up as it sounds, his lips on mine feel so right. I've never had someone kiss me next to a burning van before.

There's a first time for everything.

His tongue slides in and merges with mine. Although not unwelcome, he tastes like the mint from the toothpaste in his bathroom. His citrus scent engulfs me, and I melt into him further, my hands grabbing his sides.

After this moment, I don't think anything will ever be the same.

Our lips are molded together and soon thereafter, we watch the fire burning. I come down from my adrenaline high and lean into him instead.

It feels like we're there until there's nothing but the van frame left.

We put out the flames when I see the horizon begin to

grow closer to dawn. Then, we begin walking back. *All the way back.*

"How am I supposed to call out sick when I don't have my phone?" I ask once we make it back to his place around 9 am.

"I have the bag you carried; I just hid it."

I say nothing as he locks up behind us.

I'm wiped.

He walks to a cabinet in the kitchen above the fridge and grabs my small black backpack purse.

"What was that about the color black again?" he says, handing it to me.

I stick my tongue out as I grab my phone and send a text to my supervisor and put in the sick time in an app before putting my phone away.

To no one's surprise, I have no notifications.

"I'll let you shower first," he says as I set my bag down on the counter.

"Okay. Do you mind setting some clothes by the door for me?"

He nods, and I take off the hoodie and lay it on the edge of the couch, walking towards the bathroom.

The shower is the best shower I've ever had. We walked for *hours,* and my whole body was on fire. Aches and pains from walking, but my lips were well-kissed.

I think about it as I step out of the shower.

Exhaustion is hitting me, and I'm ceasing all functions.

I open the door a crack and grab the small pile by the door.

Smiling to myself, I dress in black pajama pants with a matching t-shirt.

I didn't have it in me to wear a bra for another moment. *Fuck that boulder holder.*

I walk out of the bathroom, seeing Rory walking in my direction.

"Will you please rest in bed?"

I'm too tired to argue so I agree and move toward it as he goes to shower himself.

Once I hear the door shut behind me, I can't help but sniff the covers. *It smells like him.* I'm finding that although he's a classified psychopath, I should *not* be getting comfortable in his bed, yet my dumbass does anyway. I scoot under the black covers until I'm at the window.

It doesn't take me but five minutes to get comfortable and pass the fuck out.

Of course, Rory's lips fill my dreams.

XOXO
LOVE

Chapter Nine

Rory

I scout for my next random victims, and I find them leaving a restaurant. They're arguing and saying terrible things to each other. It reminds me in a way of my first kill.

As I watch the man and woman from how they are inside and outside the restaurant, my mind lingers back to the first moment I took a life.

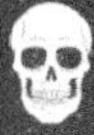

I was inside The Corner Store while my childhood friend died in front of my eyes. He was shot by his ex's boy-toy while said ex was standing next to him. I'm unsure if they saw me, but I certainly saw them.

Foreign emotions infused into my veins. There was the initial shock and anger, but then it had turned into a strange fascination. My friend was killed in front of me due to revenge or passion or whatever the fuck you want to call it. His blood splattered on the pavement while the ex and new boy-toy sped off. As I walked outside, all I could do was stare at the pooling blood beneath my feet as I crouched down over where he lay with vacant, lifeless eyes.

My reaction wasn't a normal reaction, but I'm not a normal dude. Initially, I was pissed off, because it seemed out of nowhere, but was it really?

I became intrigued by the drive and desire by how people kill people. Was it always revenge or something else? It was in that moment of standing there, dumbfounded, that I became curious to know what it was like. Maybe that's where my morals died. I didn't call for help, and someone else called the police. I wasn't sure if his ex would come back, so I walked away, mumbling, "Sorry, buddy. I'll take care of this."

So, I did that just for fun, I decide to find his ex-girlfriend and make her my first kill.

While I was curious on how killing feels, it was partially because of my last said words to my friend when I left him there dead.

Perhaps that's the truth of what started me down my pathway to hell. My hellish, curious soul. A curiosity that soon turned into an obsessive way of thinking.

It took me months to put together where his ex worked and how she hired someone and rode with her boy-toy to commit the crime.

I already had a few choice words to use when I figured out how to get her alone. It ended up being easy enough as she partied out in the city practically every weekend. It was too easy to get to her as she walked back to her car.

I came up from behind and placed my hand tight around her mouth.

"Shh, it's just me," I told her through my black mask I bought online.

"Rory? What the hell?" She turned around in her short

white dress with her hair pulled up; those heels of hers were so high they looked like they'd hurt.

"Why are you wearing that ridiculous mask?" She laughed, and I could smell the reeking alcohol on her breath.

"Come with me, I need to show you something." I held out my hand for her, feeling the weight of the gun on my hip.

"Uh, okay. Sure. Where have you been anyway? I haven't seen you since..." She grabbed my hand, and I led her further into the dark.

"Didn't you say we were still friends?" I said coolly, trying to hide my inner excitement and nervousness over what I was about to do. The first rush, I'll never forget it. My obsessive thoughts and powerful feelings rushed and molded into one force.

My heart raced with adrenaline once I pulled her around another corner, pushing her against the wall.

"Why did you kill him, and why didn't you have the balls to do it yourself?" I demanded–needed to know.

She swallowed hard. "Rory–"

"First rule: when you kill someone, make sure your face is covered, deary. I was standing nearby. I fucking saw everything."

"He deserved it, that bastard. He fucked that slut," she slurred, her eyes watering in quiet anger. Ah, revenge for passion.

"Well, I'm glad we can agree to disagree, because you also deserve this," I pulled out the gun and pointed it at her chest, finding her excuses to be bullshit.

She cried quietly. "You won't get away with this."

I smiled beneath the mask, feeling like a sick, little fuck seeking a thrill, but I supposed I would be after she was dead and gone.

"Maybe, maybe not. Who's to say? Any last words?"

"Fuck–"

Bang!

The sound of the gun made my ears ring as her insides became outsides. I'm covered in the mess as I stepped back and let what's left of her fall.

I did the sanest thing next. Relief and satisfaction, a sense of total completion. Of course, that thrill and obsessive drive would fuel me to continue down the path I created for myself. Who knew that killing would give me a sense of purpose?

Sane and content, I released a low chuckle, walking away into the night until I went into the woods, and realized that I should've brought clothes to change into. I needed to dispose of the clothes and evidence. Good thing I thought about wearing leather gloves when I grabbed her hand.

I learned a few lessons that night though.

1. *Guns were loud and messy.*
2. *Doing it out in the open was just asking to get caught.*
3. *Bring a change of clothes.*
4. *Fire?*
5. *Location, location.*
6. *Take a fucking shower.*
7. *Decide how often was too often for killing and seeking out a new target.*

What a fucking rush.

The couple walks further down the block. This time, I change it up and decide to kill two birds with one stone —literally.

Following behind them, I wait until they walk to my intended spot before I knock them both out.

Dragging them away is another challenge entirely.

Thankfully, it works out in my favor without being seen since I'm bathed in black. *Thanks, Nicole.*

I carry them, one-by-one, to an abandoned place with an entrance in the back.

It's a bitch to get them up the stairs, but I tie them up just in time for them to wake up. I feel like I've run a marathon and almost won Olympic gold for my kill-sport.

My mask carries a different weight, knowing that Nikki helped. My heart is warm as I think about her, ignoring their cries from muffled gags. I doused the room in gasoline, even though I doused various spots already that morning, along with a carefully made trail to cause an explosion which involved some math and science to complete. Timing is everything for this one.

I wave to the couple like we're good friends before I leave the place. There's a weight on my chest that I'm noticing. Why am I not feeling the same as I normally do with a kill?

I'm almost *angry* about it. The rush and power I normally get from killing.... This didn't feel the same.

What fucking changed?

I toss the match behind me as it lights up slowly.

The walk to the van is short and swift as I appear at the window, making Nicole yelp. I can't deny that I worried about her.

This is her fault.

I tell her to drive after I throw shit in the back to set the van on fire, along with my phone too.

Once we arrive at the planned destination, we change and watch it burn. Then, I wash my face off before making my way back. Nicole is still standing there watching the flames, mesmerized by it. *She might be a little pyro.*

Interesting that she's not fighting me and is going along with my twisted and fucked up shenanigans.

I pause, staring at her. A goddess disguised in my clothes. I take her in, realizing that nothing will ever be the same from this moment on. The whole situation is unconventional and psychotic, but I'm finding out how much I enjoy having her around.

There's a quietness in my mind. I'm not thinking about my next kill, *only her.*

It's fucking weird and amazing all wrapped into one.

I tell her to call out of work the following day, and we simply stare. We won't be getting back anytime soon. Moving her way hastily, green eyes soon reflect the fire meeting mine.

My freedom is standing in front of me, even if she doesn't know it yet. Her lips part as if she's thinking what I'm thinking.

There are only flames of her and I.

I tell her how fucking perfect she looks before I finally claim that smart, intelligent mouth of hers.

Losing and finding myself in her taste, I pull her closer. Her sweet citrus scent meets my own, and I succumb to my newest obsession.

No matter what becomes of us, we'll always be tied to this moment together. Never feeling like this before, her tongue tangles with mine in slow, teasing strokes. A strange dance I didn't realize I was missing out on.

There's a mold of granite in my chest. It holds black and white patterns, a hardened substance. I don't remember a time when it wasn't.

Emotions were a weakness I couldn't afford. I had found something more powerful, *playing God*.

But by doing so, fate has intervened with the woman on my tongue. The state of my mind is shifting, tides turning. Not that I think she can save me or change my ways. My granite heart is cracking. Just like the mask she painted.

I am cracking.

I don't believe in salvation, but I didn't get satisfaction from my crime tonight. It's never happened before, so once I sleep or lie awake in bed, I'll work through it.

I'd consult with my new therapist too.

We walk for hours and shower separately. I was too distracted changing earlier to even take her in. *Damn*.

I come out of the bathroom with a towel wrapped around me and find her asleep in my bed. I marvel at the sight.

She looks fucking good in my bed. I can't help but think that she belongs there.

Deciding to be a gentleman, I hang up the towel and put on checkered pajama bottoms rather than sleeping nude.

I crawl in next to her. She's on her side facing me, curled up with the covers.

Watching her is all I can think of doing. The object of my desire. Newfound and fascinating. The one person who ended up on my not-to-kill list.

Sleep escapes me. My body is tired, but my mind is working and sorting it all out.

I roll on my back and put my hand behind my head.

Before I know it, Nicole scoots closer, and wraps her arm around me, tucking nicely into my side.

"That's better," she murmurs.

Unsure if she's asleep, I wait to see if she realizes. When she doesn't, I make sure not to move.

I wonder what she's dreaming of?

My thoughts drift, recognizing we're both unhinged. Different ways, different lives, but we're undone. Even though I *illegally* obtained her, I'm not mad about where I ended up.

I found a passion before, and now it seems I'm finding another.

Not saying what I'm doing or have done is right, but maybe I can do something else that's legal—or as she says anyway. *I'll never behave to others expectations.*

Life is funny.

I'm made of granite, and she's made of sugar.

XOXO
LOVE

Chapter Ten

Nikki

I wake up to tattoos in my face. I blink, realizing what I'm doing.

Oh, no. You stupid idiot.

Tensing up, a hand rubs my back.

"Sleep well, Sugar?"

I did, but I'm *not* telling him that.

"You scooted to my side of the bed," he says as I roll away with a sigh.

"I probably thought you were a pillow; I don't know."

He sits up and looks over me.

"You were whispering in your sleep."

Turning around, I feel frantic. "What the hell did I say this time?"

A cheeky smile crosses him. "Lots of things. For me to hold in my arsenal," he taps his head and moves away as I sit up with a grumble.

"Let's go get stuff from your home," he tells me before using the bathroom.

Getting up, the sun is high in the sky, it's probably the afternoon is my guess.

He comes out, and we're soon out the door. He drives, *you guessed it,* a black fucking car, a semi-beefed up one. I look at the word *Challenger* on the car and spit out the stereotype in my brain. Sometimes, I just don't know when to shut up.

"A black challenger, *really?* Of course *that's* what you fucking drive."

He tilts his head, confused. "What does that even mean? Is it the color, or something else you'd like to share about my baby?" He pets the front hood of the car in a protective and fond manner.

Rolling my eyes, I point at the car, "Look up fuckboy and a picture of this car and your face will be next to it."

Rory stares at me seriously before rolling his eyes to the back of his skull. Then, he has the audacity to pet the front hood of his *baby.* "*Shh, don't listen to her, you're a great car.*"

I can't help but laugh at how ridiculous Rory is. Not that I should talk too loudly with my big mouth.

"Get in the car, Nicole."

I keep my comments to myself even though it physically hurts not to open my mouth. I'm sure with the look I gave him before entering his car that he already knows I always have more to talk shit about.

We arrive to my place later, making it up to my floor, and I let him in.

"After all this time stalking me, I'm surprised you didn't try to come inside."

I flip the light on and turn to find him smug with himself.

"*Yet.*"

Rolling my eyes and refusing to think about the innu-endo in my brain, I go into my bedroom and throw an assortment of clothes into a weekend bag I haven't used before.

"Give me your key tomorrow, and I'll help make it easier."

I turn around to find him leaning against the doorway frame. I ignore the thoughts of how sexy he looks just leaning there. The internal battle is *real.*

I want to fuck him and hit him.

"Am I to be living with you full time now? What about this place?"

"Yes."

Simply staring at one another, he continues, "I can think of a few things to get you out of this lease. One of them involves fire."

My brows furrow. I like fire, but not this way—*legally, thanks.*

"You can't do that for every situation you know. Are you *trying* to go to prison?"

He sighs in defeat, "I'm smarter than I look. *For a psychopath."*

I huff, dismissing him while getting my shit together. A mantra I hope to accomplish one day.

"I mean it, I'll help you bring your stuff."

Remembering that he mentioned a job, I dare to ask, "Don't you work a job, too?"

"I go back Wednesday. I work this weekend, so I already had these days off."

Gathering the rest of my shit, I grab my meds and refills in the kitchen.

"You take medication? Why didn't you say anything?"

I put them in my purse and shrug, irritated over the dumb question.

"I didn't think I could. You kidnapped me, err—*are still*

kidnapping me, and *wanted* to kill me. You stalked me for weeks; I didn't think we were on best friend terms here. Come on, Rory."

He gives me an unpleasant look, clearly not liking what I said or the tone I used. *Whatever.*

"You don't have to use that tone with me, *Nicole.* I said I wasn't going to kill you. Now that you've helped me, you can't get away even if you try, or you will go down with me."

I pause, tossing a glare his way.

"You are terrible at this relationship thing."

"It is not—"

"I'm moving in with you! *That's a relationship.* We clearly aren't just friends after the kiss we shared."

Come on, captain obvious.

I grab my bags and meet him face-to-face as I round the corner.

"Thinking about my lips, are you?" *Damn, he looks good when he's sassy.*

"Yes—*no!*"

"Which is it?"

I can feel the heat on my cheeks. I'm so irritated with him already, and his attempts at flirting are the worst.

"None of your business. Now move, psycho."

He spreads his arms out, not letting me pass.

Narrowing my eyes, he leans closer, and I think about biting him. The urge is so strong.

"You are so cute when you're fired up and angry."

This guy is so delusional.

"I bite." *Because that's the proper response to say when you are in fact angry.* It's a warning, too.

"Good to know you aren't a victim. Now, while what you say is true, I think we're working past our initial meeting, right?"

"I helped get rid of evidence for you through no choice of my own. I still think you need therapy *or a straitjacket.*"

He laughs, and the sound travels down my spine. *Fuck you, traitorous body.*

"Probably, but only if you're there with me."

All I can do is stare at this crazy killer man.

"You're going to drive me to a padded cell."

"Don't you have meds for that?"

I growl, and he finds it *enlightening.*

"Kinky. We'll save that for later, *little angry one.*"

The fucker has the *audacity* to pat my fucking head.

So, I bite him—hard.

He curses when I let go, before holding his hand and chuckling. His arm is bleeding.

"A feral woman, I love it. I've never been bitten like this before!"

I'm over him and his mouth as I walk away and grab my shit before leaving him in the doorway.

I wait by his car, and he joins me moments later.

"You got me good."

Ignoring him, he gets inside, and we drive off.

"I turned off the lights and locked the bottom door lock since you left."

The city lights pass all around us through the window reflection. I know if I answer him, I'll melt down. I can feel it coming. Like boiling water in a pot left unsupervised.

I can feel his eyes on the side of my head, and I grumble.

"What does it matter if it's unlocked?"

"Someone could steal your stuff?"

I give him a look that he catches once we're at a stoplight.

Shaking my head, all I can do is laugh.

The laughing turns into tears, then I can't stop.

For fuck's sake.

Irritated with myself, I hear him say, *"Shit."*

We get to his place, and I can tell he doesn't know what to do with me. When I don't process or regulate myself, I end up doing *this*.

I rush out of the car, not caring about my stuff. Only about getting away from him.

You live together now, dumbass.

Leaning against the building, he goes inside, leaving me the fuck alone for five minutes. I calm my hyperventilating, feeling stupid for letting him see what I don't want anyone to ever see. *Only my family, past relationships, and a few of my grade school bullies have seen it, after I pushed their books, flipped a table or two before calling them names to see how they liked it.*

In my defense, the past few days were fucking traumatizing.

As if I didn't go through enough in my goddamn life. The imbalance of everything is getting to me. Medication management or not, it's not a fucking cure.

Like I tend to do sometimes, I end up hurting myself by punching the rough brick exterior of the building.

Pain registers in my synapses, and my tears ease. I can't explain my fucked-up mind, nor do I want to. Not that I do this often.

My hands are throbbing and bleeding as I pull away and look down at them.

Larger hands grasp my shoulders.

"Let's get you inside."

I follow blindly, numb and shutting down.

He brings me to his kitchen, and I stare down, avoiding his eyes. There's no more energy left in me to figure out what he's thinking.

"I'll drive you to work tomorrow, since there will be rainy weather and storms. I want to talk to you when you get back."

He uses something to disinfect my hands before wrapping them. I don't have any more words to say as I sniffle.

"Do your hands hurt?"

I shake my head *no.*

Tomorrow they will.

When he's done, he just stares at me, and I move away and go to my place on the couch. He doesn't deserve words from me anymore.

Throwing the covers over my head, I let the quiet tears resume.

HOLY
XOXO
LOVE

Chapter Eleven

Rory

I underestimated her. *A failure on my part.*

I've never felt so shitty before.

When victims cry, it doesn't typically bother me. In fact, it irritates me more than anything.

Yet when *she* does it, my brain stops fucking working, apparently.

It's an unknown emotion that I didn't know I was capable of. *Emotions.* Nikki sure is making me go through them all.

Now, I *really* need to get to know her better. I don't know what her triggers are or how to deal with the meltdown. *At least, I think it was a meltdown.* I'm no fucking doctor.

Either way, it's my fault, and it's rubbing me the wrong way. *Guilt.*

My newest realization is that I can feel that emotion. *Who knew?*

Nicole is full of surprises. She's shown me various aspects of her personality since I marked her as *next*. Since then, I've done nothing but fuck it all up while navigating these new waters.

How can I salvage the shipwreck I've caused and get her to trust me?

First step, *apologize.*

Second, *not have her as an accomplice, or stop killing period—and mean it.*

I did make it to lucky number ten. Perhaps I can settle for that. The cops still didn't figure out who caused the explosion, and I haven't had any new killing urges. Part of me wonders if there's a therapy for that. Recovering Killers Anonymous.

RKA idea aside, Nicole already knows what I previously threatened... I should stop with any future threats.

I'll work on that.

Now, how do I get her to like me? *Guess I'll need to internet search that too.*

Search: How can a previous killer get a girl to like him without fear?

Seeing Nicole flee from me, leaning against the building, is unsettling to me. I did give her some time and brought her stuff in. On my way out, I hear *something* I can't quite make out and find her seemingly calmer. Or maybe it was a shutdown thing from what I read online. *Hell if I know.*

There's blood on her hands which startles me, but I bring her inside to clean those hands up. *I really fucked up.*

My heart twists, realizing that my own bleeding from her biting me subsided.

She fucking marked me, and I loved it. Yet, I pushed her too far. *I'm such a dick.*

Psychopath is right, according to my new therapist. *Psycho-sociopath is more like it.*

It doesn't take me long to realize she's refusing to talk to me. *It's a shutdown–thanks, Internet.*

Making small talk, I let her know about taking her to work and stuff because of the weather. I mention talking to her when she gets home.

Silence.

There's a sniffle and I dare to ask if her hands hurt. At least she shakes her head in response.

I finish with her hands, and she pulls away from me, heading to the couch. Covers fly, and I peek near the couch to see her under them.

It doesn't slip my notice of what I think is a sort of tremble and more sniffling sounds. *She's crying.*

Turning the lights off, I sigh quietly to myself while making my way to the bathroom to undress and get ready for bed.

Once I crawl into bed in total defeat, I lay on my back, staring up at the tall ceiling above me. I can't settle myself or the unfamiliar sensations in my chest. Guilt and need.

It bothers me how she's crying on my couch, and I want to comfort her, yet I don't know *how*.

Guess I'll have to learn if I'm to make this work.

This relationship.

What the hell was I thinking?

Her earlier words of *psycho* echo through my head.

How—*where* would I even begin to change? Aside from killing and threatening her.

I continue to get lost in thought while staring at the ceiling, and the city lights reflect through the windows. I get restless as time fades away.

Giving up trying to sleep, I pad silently into the living room to check on her, even if she wants nothing to do with me right now.

I can't tell if she's crying or not, so I go around to the other side and kneel beside her.

Her back is toward me, and her head is peeking out, but her eyes are closed. I lay my head next to her back and sigh.

"I'm sorry," I whisper, hoping I don't wake her.

When she doesn't stir or do anything but softly breathe, I remain that way for a while. I eventually sit back on my knees and almost reach to touch her.

My hand hesitates mid-air before dropping.

I haven't earned any right to her. I've only forced her into living with me and blackmailed her into it. She's tied to me now.

While it's the beginning, it's up to me to change the tides.

So, I jump on my computer and begin my research again.

The drive the following morning is quiet, and I notice her eyes are swollen. I almost ask her to punch me in the face so we're even.

Once I drop her off, I ask for her key to her apartment, and she tosses it in the seat without saying anything. I can't help but exhale deeply. I deserve silence and so much more.

I activate another burner phone at a cheap store before heading to her place and making some calls once business concludes.

Letting myself inside her place once I arrive, I take a good look and explore.

The kitchen is plain looking, minus a couple of dish towels hanging with funny sayings. It's clean, at least, which influences me. I'm also clean and organized, which will help in the future while we're living together. Nicole's living room is bathed in neutral tones with pops of emerald, green. Impressed with her decorating skills, I go to her bathroom and it's all bright, bold colors. Confused by the changing themes in the rooms, I enter the bedroom.

I was too distracted by her last night to really take it all in. The bedding is dark, and she has a big ass black bat pillow.

Not being able to gauge her aesthetics, I poke around her room. Her walk-in closet is even more confusing. One side is black clothes, and the other side holds all sorts of colors. Making mental notes to myself, I don't realize the time until I hear knocks at the door. *And here she complained about my black clothing.*

Rolling my eyes into another dimension, I let the movers in. I instruct them on what is trash and what isn't. If it looks like a keepsake, I had them put it in a box.

Afterwards, I make another call to deal with her lease. To my surprise, her lease ends the following month. *Perfect.*

I give the movers her new address and head to the furniture store. Once I order what I need, I check my phone and send Nicole a text.

ME:

I'm heading over.

NICOLE:

ME:

See you soon.

I get in my car, and head to her workplace, arriving on time as she's standing by the curb.

She gets in, and I can see she changed the bandages on her hands.

"Want to grab takeout tonight?" I ask before pulling away.

She shrugs.

"Chinese, Japanese, or other options?" I continue, trying to pull verbal words from her.

There's one more shoulder shrug and I huff.

"I'm not leaving this curb until you speak to me."

I see her frown. "I don't care about food. You're my kidnapper, you decide."

"*This* again?"

The sassy anger is directed at me then. "Well? What exactly is *this* then? You don't do relationships, and I live with you. You let me live, and say, 'I won't kill you,' but you blackmail me. So, please, fucking enlighten me on the goddamn *plan*. I don't care about dinner, breakfast, or anything else. Excuse me for being a fucking moody bitch."

Feeling put in my place, I take an even deeper breath.

"We'll work on *this*. *Whatever this is*. I know the fault is mine. I'll work on making it better."

"Whatever, dude."

I take the car out of park and put it into drive, speechless for a moment before mumbling under my breath, "Chinese food it is."

Nicole says nothing, simply looking out of the window as I head to my favorite takeout spot that isn't too far from my place. I'm feeling stumped. *I don't think a woman has ever scolded me like this before. It's new.* Not sure if I like it, but then again when has Nicole *ever* refrained from speaking her mind to me?

I park on the side street next to the restaurant by several other shops. "Come inside and pick out what you want."

Getting out, I'm shocked that she follows but say nothing on it.

Once inside, I debate on what I want, and she orders.

Three orders of crab rangoon, two orders of sweet and sour chicken, two orders of pork dumplings, and ten egg rolls.

I give her a look, and she smiles mockingly.

Eating my words, aren't I?

I order my short stack of ribs with two orders of white rice with lo mein. After cringing over the total, I pay before we go sit at one of the tables.

"At least I know what your favorites are, I guess," is all I can manage to say.

She shrugs, sitting across from me.

"I'm sorry, for everything," I whisper loud enough for her to hear me.

It takes me a few moments to wonder if she heard me as she's staring off into space, avoiding my gaze. Then, she speaks.

"Not the place, bud. Say it at home."

All I do is stare at her in disbelief. Her bluntness is astounding.

"You're making this difficult," I say during an exhaled breath.

Her head snaps to the side, and she tosses me a *look to kill.*

"*You* need to work on your compliments. I've done *nothing* but meet your demands," she glowers, narrowing those eyes.

I can't help but warm from within. Her inner fire radiates across the table.

Going to open my mouth, she puts her hand up to silence me.

"I've thought about what to say to you all day. The main things begin and end with 'fuck' and 'you.'"

Fair point.

She continues. "You don't know how to deal with *someone* like me. You are toxic and impulsive. I'm not even sure years of therapy *from a real professional* will help you. Instead, you get *my* ass. I'm not happy with the situation, and I'm working through processing it. I didn't expect to live past the weekend. *Don't rush me.* Too many things at once, I implode. It's unfortunate that you had to see that yesterday. A couple of days without my meds, and I have trouble regulating. I'd be as unhinged as *you* are without them. I get overstimulated, and major life changes fuck me up, and yeah, I'm feeling the feelings. I feel like I'm in the stages of grief. I've hit the anger stage—surprise! But I'm *your* fucking problem now."

I blink, unsure how to respond to how fast she spoke and enjoy how blunt she continues to be.

When I try to speak again, she holds up her hand once more. "Save it. I don't want to hear it right now. Let's get our food, and my lunch for the next few days, and go home. After I eat, *and only after,* will I hear what you have to say. Alright?"

"Yes, ma'am."

She leans back in her seat and soon my name is being called. Nicole grabs the bags, not letting me help her.

Defeated once more, I open the door, and we make our way to the car and back home in silence.

Never in my life have I been put in my place and told off. Not that I didn't deserve it, because I certainly do.

I'll respect her conditions and figure out my head from my ass in the meantime.

Chapter Twelve

Nikki

Sometimes I just don't know when to shut up.

I feel as unhinged as his previous kidnapping-kill actions were.

We walk inside his place as I guard the food with my life—*priorities when it's some of my favorites.*

I freeze, standing in the kitchen, looking around as I put the food down on the counter.

There are random boxes neatly tucked along the far wall stretching from the living room to the foot of his bed. There's a bigger desk installed, with my laptop on the right, and his on the left. How did he know I liked being seated in corners? Maybe it was unintentional.

I can't help how my chest constricts. Making my way further in, I see labels on the boxes—bathroom, bedroom, kitchen, and living room.

My head turns, and near his clothes on the far back wall that connects his bed to the doorway to the bathroom, there's a large black armoire that wasn't there before. I can't help but get emotional. It's all *real* now.

Not only was he serious, but he's deranged *and* thoughtful. I can't tell my left from my right at this point. How could one person be so contradictory?

Oh, wait...

Turning around, he's standing five feet away.

"You did all of this in one day?" I sound like a frog when I say because of how choked up I am.

He nods. "Not alone, I hired people."

That must cost a lot, but one cannot assume.

"*I* was expecting to move all of my stuff." I sniffle and wipe my eyes.

Gathering myself, I take a deep breath, and he's immediately in front of me.

"I don't understand. Are you happy or sad?"

I wish I knew too.

"I don't know. I'm figuring that out. Processing time delay, remember?"

I catch his eyes as he nods.

"I'm working on understanding you better, that's all. Is it okay if I hug you?"

Now he's asking me?

I stare at him, no longer as angry, but still very much confused and torn. Yet, I can't help but wonder what it's like to be hugged by him. I could also use one, and he asked for permission.

What is going on with me?

Somehow, he's patient enough to let me figure out how to answer.

Eventually, I agree. "You may."

Rory inches even closer, almost hesitant or afraid.

His arms open, pulling me in.

It takes me a moment for my hands to go around his waist. My head is tucked nicely under his chin. His warmth and citrus scent overpower my senses. His touch is gentle yet firm, giving me a slight squeeze. When he doesn't let go, I melt a little more into him.

I bury my head deeper and can feel the strength underneath me. With the power to kill or not, he keeps me around because I'm *different*. All I am is honest—*myself*.

None of this was okay, yet I have to figure out how to deal with it.

Guess I'm dating a killer.

Not sure how to feel about it, but here I am, hugging the guy despite the red flags.

I'm still not surprised I attracted the red flag himself.

I remember how he felt on my lips, and perhaps there's more to this killer that neither of us knows.

Life's a fucking journey either way.

I ease my hold after I relax my shoulders. *He's not a bad hugger either.* I wonder what else he's good at besides killing?

He releases me at the same time, and there's a lingering look that I can't decipher.

"Shall we eat?"

I nod, leading the way to my forgotten prize.

"I'm thinking about getting a proper table, what do you think?"

Separating the food and only keeping the crab rangoon and order of sweet and sour chicken, I put the rest away.

"I'm not picky. It's up to you."

I find him watching me.

"I want to eat properly with my room—*girlfriend*."

I still as chills crawl down my spine at the term.

"How are those things anyway?" He indicates the appetizer, distracting my brain from hyper-focusing on him declaring me *his girlfriend*.

Dating apps have nothing on this guy.

"Try one, but *only one*."

He raises his brow, opening the small bag.

"They're my favorite, okay? Don't judge. Get another bag if you want more than one."

We stare at one another as he tries it.

I grab one for myself and sigh in great relief.

Ah, much better.

When I eat my favorite foods, I tend to make happy moaning noises.

I open my eyes to find his on me as I lick my lips.

"Well?" I ask.

"I see why you like them," is all he utters before snatching the bag, and eating another one.

"Are you serious!" *Not a question.*

My Crab Kidnapper.

I reach over the couch as he sits down.

"You can kidnap me, but you *cannot* kidnap and eat my crabbies!"

He bursts into laughter before eating a third one.

"I only have two left now, dickhead!"

I leap over the couch, landing beside him. He holds it out of my reach.

"If you're trying to get into my good graces, this isn't it, pal."

He gives me a side look, smiling and winking.

Is he for real?

"Are you...flirting with me?"

He takes another one, eating it one bite with his big mouth.

I pout before shoving him and jumping up to grab the other *full* bag out of the fridge.

Grateful for it not being too cool, I toss one of those fuckers in my mouth.

"Good thing we got three, didn't we?"

He's grinning. *Ass.*

"So playful over food... *Weirdo.* Find something on TV to watch while we eat."

To my surprise he listens and grabs his food while I grab mine.

He puts on some crime show, and I roll my eyes.

"Getting ideas or something?"

He shrugs, and I eat in peace, enjoying all six of the crab rangoons.

I'm halfway through my sweet and sour before I sigh heavily, indicating I'm full. Putting the lid on it, I place it on the table.

He does the same, clearing his throat before he begins.

"I know nothing I can say will make what I've done alright..." He lowers the volume on the TV, and thank goodness, because there's no way I can listen to both properly. "But I want to try to make up for it somehow. I want to learn about you, and how to be better. You've been so honest with me, and I've been an asshole."

That's one way to put it.

I lace my fingers in my lap, and look down, unsure of where to look period. No way am I looking at him right now.

"Your bluntness saved your life, and I'm glad for it."

I glance up, holding his gaze briefly.

"You're terrible at complimenting and apologizing. Maybe leave the '*saved your life*' bit out, hmm?"

He sighs. "You're right... I'm saying that there's something about you that's worth more than death to me."

How strangely romantic.

"I haven't done a good job at making you like me, and as I've said, I've been an asshole. I threatened you and blackmailed you; of course you want nothing to do with me. I deserve it. I deserve your bluntness and being told I'm cliché."

I can't help but smile in amusement, sneaking a glance at the TV screen of a crime scene.

"I don't know how to be a boyfriend to someone, so you'll have to help me too. And please don't shut down on me again. I want you to be *real* all the time, no matter what it looks like. Somehow, someway, I'll work on getting you to trust me—the right way this time, despite how I started all of this."

I lean back, and let my head fall to the side, taking him in.

He's sitting sideways while he *apologizes*. By how he's sitting and his facial expression, I can tell he's being genuine. His tone reads right, and I haven't heard a lie yet. Maybe it's time for me to work with him too and accept my kidnapper's plea of forgiveness.

I'm delulu now, too.

Whatever, it is what it is.

"I'll work on being verbal about where my emotions are too. It can be hard, but if you're putting in effort to understand me, I suppose it's only fair. *Boyfriend.*"

We lock eyes, and I add on. "I accept your apology, just please don't make me an accomplice again. It's uncomfortable, and while I can tolerate a lot before I have a meltdown and implode, I wish you'd find more hobbies. *Less gory.*"

He scoots closer to me.

"Nicole—"

I shake my head. "Call me, Nikki. It's weird when that full name comes out. If we're living together, that won't do. Reminds me of my mother waking me up for school or reprimanding me about something."

His lips curl, and I can't help but watch.

"Very well, *Nikki*."

My name on his lips does something to me.

The toss is up in the air about fucking and hitting him. Leaning more towards the former at this time.

"Pinky promise on it."

He snorts a laugh, and it surprises me, but I'm dead serious, even if his reaction is hilarious.

I hold my pinky out. He shakes his head and takes it.

"Now, stamp the seal," I instruct, hooking my thumb up towards his.

He does it. "And who's weird again?"

I shrug, releasing my grip before he grabs my hand.

"Oh, I never said I wasn't. I'm in full realization of my own perception and my fucked-up mind plus the quirks. I've accepted it over the years."

His thumb rubs the top of my hand, and I find myself not wanting to pull away. It's the small gestures that touch me the deepest.

"You aren't on my level of fucked-up, Nikki. You haven't taken any lives."

I sigh. "It's not a contest, and I'm not God, nor will I play one. That's too stressful for me."

"Fair enough."

He studies me, and I shift, slightly uncomfortable.

"Can we come up with a safe word for you?"

I swallow and simply stare at him dumbly. "Trying to jump my bones already and fuck me silly?"

He raises his eyebrow, almost like he's intrigued by the thought.

"Not yet, not that I haven't thought about you. I just mean as a warning to me if you're in a mood or I'm pushing you too far; it can be anything, not necessarily sexual."

I blink three times, making sure I heard correctly.

Why would he think of me like that?

"Okay, that makes sense, I guess. I'll think of two words, but for now it'll be yellow and red. Easy enough, right?"

"Mine will be the same then."

Realizing his hand is still on mine, I dare to be brave with my next question.

"What about that last part...how you've thought about me?"

My throat suddenly feels dry as those green and blue smoldering gems meet mine.

"Yes."

He leans closer, and I tell him to continue.

"Don't forget the green color," he whispers, hovering his lips over mine.

I swear I can feel the blood flow to and from my heart, *and my pussy.*

"*Green,*" I murmur before his lips gently claim mine.

When he pulls away after just the one kiss, he murmurs, "Have you seen *you?* You're hot, Nikki."

Now I'm feeling shy as I pull my hand from his.

"Ah, so you're not good at receiving compliments. Interesting. At least I know I'm getting somewhat better with mine."

I puff my cheeks before exhaling. "Don't let it get to your head."

He leans closer and kisses my cheek. "On a serious note, Nikki, I really am sorry for dragging you into my life like I did last week. Plus hurting you and traumatizing you."

Looking off to the side, I can't help myself, "It's me and my mouth. I can't help myself, but thanks for not killing me... Also, that's more than what my family has said for traumatizing me. They haven't killed anyone to my knowledge, but it didn't stop them from ruining my life in a different way."

I sigh, adding one last comment. "I'll tell you all about my woes sometime, but not tonight. I'm ready to shut my brain down now."

He takes my hand and kisses it. "Of course. Can I tempt you to bed?"

Raising my brow curiously, he answers immediately, "To sleep. If you want more, you're going to have to use your words and ask for it. There's no hurry for that stuff."

"Whatever you say, boyfriend."

He sighs, standing up and gathering our leftovers to be put away.

"I'll sleep on the couch tonight," I say, and he turns to the side briefly.

"I can sleep on the couch too, and you can always take the bed."

I shake my head, and he doesn't seem to like my answer but accepts it.

"Alright, if you change your mind, the offer is always open."

"Thank you," I tell him as I stand and head to the bathroom.

I end up grabbing his clothes to wear to bed, since most of my stuff is in boxes that he so helpfully labels for me to sort through at a later date.

I tell him goodnight as he goes to prepare for bed while I situate myself on the couch.

It's been so hot and cold lately, that I'm mentally and emotionally exhausted. Who knows what's next at this point?

XOXO
LOVE

Chapter Thirteen

Rory

When I wake, it feels as if the playing field is more level. We reached an understanding the night before, and dare I say it, I have some pep in my step.

I can't believe I have a goddamn girlfriend. Thirty-five years later. Got to start somewhere, right?

Dressing for work, she says she'll walk which doesn't sit right with me.

"The only one kidnapping your sexy ass is *me.*"

She blinks, shaking her head in disapproval over my shenanigans.

"It's too early for your dark jokes. I'll be paying atten-tion to my surroundings, thank you very much. *Or fucking let them.* What's another round?"

I frown, not finding it funny, and I mean it seriously. "It's too early for your dark jokes," I repeat back, and she huffs a bitter laugh.

I make her coffee-to-go as she dresses. To give her privacy, I keep my back turned.

"I'll drop you off and see if I can switch my schedule so

that it's the same during the week, or figure something else out," I tell her, placing the lid on top.

"You're so bossy and talkative in the mornings. That coffee better be for me, or it will be me trying to end your life next."

Laughter leaves my mouth, and I can't help but find her comment adorable. "Does this mean you're still mad at me?"

"Depends on if that coffee is mine," she says suddenly at my side with a blank face that makes me wonder where her head is at.

The grin on her face is sexy as I hand the thermos over.

"A few more of these, and we just *may* get somewhere."

"You have strange priorities, Niks," I say without thinking as I recall her earlier compliance for kills nine and ten with her music playlists. Nicole is an odd and fascinating woman, even still.

She grabs her bag. "Let's go, bossman."

As Nikki turns around, black thermos in hand, her ass bounces as she walks to the door—I resist the urge to smack it. *Not yet,* I remind myself.

Now that she's being more open and honest with where her head is at, I'm enjoying our banter again.

"I'll pick you up when you get off," I say as I pull up on the curb to drop her off at work.

"Yep," is all she says, and I watch that ass as she walks away.

"*Damn,*" I comment to myself, waiting until she gets inside the building before driving off.

Work is a fucking drag, but at least I was able to change my hours to match hers, not that it was off by much. With warehouse work though, an hour difference sometimes matters with deliveries and shipments.

When I pick up Nikki, we ride in silence until arriving

home. The more I refer to home as our place, the more it fully sinks in on the situation and acceptance for us both.

"Office work is so boring," she complains once we enter my—*our* place.

"I agree. Have you thought about changing jobs?" I ask, making basic conversation.

"It was a lot of work to get it in the first place. The money is decent enough to live on. It's just mind-numbing and boring. I suppose it helps, not having to use my brain as much, since it's mindless." She kicks off her shoes and flops on the couch.

Finding her amusing, I lean over it and offer a suggestion I recalled from some time back. "Leftovers and trauma bonding?"

She considers me. "Sure, why the fuck not?"

"I'll heat up the food. Get comfy?" I suggest, pushing away from the couch and making my way into the kitchen.

"Yes, mom," she snarks.

I wiggle my fingers to restrain myself as she stands up, giving me a questioning look over.

"Why are you doing that with your fingers?" she asks as I stop and pull the leftovers out.

"I'm resisting the urge to spank you," I grumble. "Your sass gets me going sometimes."

Placing her dumplings in the microwave first, I find her eyes locked on me with an equally satisfied smirk.

"Kinky," is all she says while walking off to steal my clothes and shower.

I can't help but picture her tied up with a pretty rope tie of mine or *stuffing something in that smart ass mouth.* A guy can fucking dream.

Forcing my mind to blank, the food is reheated and ready by the time she's done. Seeing her stroll in with my black t-shirt and pajamas makes me drool. The pajamas hug her ass quite nicely. *I wonder how her ass will feel in my palm or how red it will turn with spanking.*

I steadily control myself. *I haven't been perverted like this in a while.* Perhaps that's the surprise and excitement of it all. She's unlike anyone I've met. Her mind is curious and sensitive to the world around her. Nikki views things with color, sound, and texture. Unsure on the taste bit, but damn, do I hope to find out.

Next weekend off, I wouldn't mind a visit to kink club. I decide to ask her when the timing is right. *Maybe after trauma bonding and dinner.* Maybe that should be the proclaimed *'Flix and chill'*. Or whatever the saying is with kids these days in the hookup culture.

We situate ourselves on the couch, eating and watching the news initially.

"Explosion from days ago is linked to a gas leak," the announcer says while cameras show past footage.

I can't help but feel smug. Except, I turn to look, and Nikki is shaking her head with a weird laugh that I can't decipher.

"Well, damn."

I can't help but grin over it before I steal a dumpling, and she huffs an inpatient sigh.

"I will bite you again."

"Someone doesn't like to share, I see," I tease back. *She's like a little piranha when it comes to sharing food.* It's fucking amusing to me.

"Just my food," she retorts.

"And sharing other things?" My curiosity peaks, and I'm wondering where her mind will go with that statement.

She doesn't answer until she finishes eating, and she certainly doesn't disappoint with her honesty.

"I'm bisexual for one, kinky, and I have no problem sharing anything else of me, whether it's trauma, my opinion—all that stuff. When it comes to food, maybe it's because my brothers liked to steal my food and things that were *mine* that I liked growing up. Now, I have this weird food habit in adulthood."

She places the emptied container on the coffee table while I finish mine.

Thinking over my next response, I set my stuff on the table too. "I wasn't expecting you to say that... I'll ask more on some of those topics later." *I'm not even sure how to address sexual things in general, at least in our scenario. What do you do in these relationships? Communicate, right?*

"Are your brothers the same age?" I ask, distracting myself from asking kinky-sexual questions.

She lifts her hand and makes a so-so gesture. "I'm thirty, you know, the *baby* millennial."

Tossing her an unamused look, I dare to say mine after I gave her so much shit in the beginning.

"I'm *thirty-five...*" She fucking notices it immediately, because, of course she does.

Jerking her head to the side, she narrows her eyes. "Are you *kidding* me? You're an elder millennial! *Asshole.*"

I tuck my lips between my teeth, amused by the whole situation. Next thing I know, a pillow is flying at my face, making me blink.

"Don't start something you won't win. *Because I will win.* I know how you brats are."

Her eyes darken as if I gave her the green light indicator to fuck around and find out. Her own hand gets twitchy and fidgety. *Hmm, interesting information to put in my arsenal for later.*

"I thought you wanted to trauma bond?" she interrupts. Herself or me, I can't be too sure by her own reaction to such a temptation.

"I'm easy, there's not much," I admit, and she gives me a knowing look. I can almost hear the words in her mind. *There's no way a psychopath like you doesn't have trauma.*

Instead, Nikki adjusts herself to sit leaning against the back of the couch while facing me. Listening and waiting for my response.

"Well, there's no siblings. That I know of. My parents are divorced, both of them cheated, and weren't really around to raise me." I shrug it off as I speak, knowing that I'm not the only one with that kind of sad-sack story to share. I'm not unique.

"I know what your psychoanalyzing brain is about to say." I give her a quick side glance. "I'll spare you the theatrics. I felt detached growing up, rebelling and running with the wrong sort of crowd, doing what the fuck I wanted."

Nikki gives me a small smile, which answers my question of analyzing me with that brain of hers.

I heave a sigh, getting to the point. "I fucked at sixteen and discovered kink at seventeen. I moved far away from home to start over where no one knew me. That happened after witnessing the death of my best friend."

Pausing, I catch Nikki's frown. Before she can ask for more details about shit that don't matter in the grand scheme of things, I continue. "I suppose that event was life-altering for me. I grieved in a way that probably isn't considered normal or whatever. Of course, I had to avenge my friend who didn't deserve to die. It's not morally ethical, and I knew that, however, revenge and fascination aside, I wanted to know what it was like."

"Not surprised," I barely hear her whisper. She speaks so softly, I question myself on if I heard anything at all.

"Whether that event broke my brain or not, I experimented, hence where I am today. No relationships, just fucking with large side order of kink and plus *that* side hobby. That kind of power is—*was*—a rush."

I heave a final sigh, signaling that I'm finished speaking. Silence buzzes in my ears, and I realize for the first time in my life I was honest about myself. Nikki was rubbing off on me, in more ways than one. Some of that power exchange I've done both consensual and not—*talking about the murder part here.* I experienced some of it while being a dominant kinkster. Yet, I wanted to take something too far in the beginning when I started down this killing road. Not that kinky shit and killing are related, but it helped my fucked up mind in-between. The battle for control, *the fucking rush.*

I'm so lost in thought, I almost don't hear Nicole's comment.

"I beg to differ on what broke you," she says, making direct eye contact.

I recall from my internet research about eye contact and autism which equals avoidance of it, for the most part. Part of me is grateful while the other is unsettled, because this woman is looking through me, right through my demented, fucked up soul.

"Yes, please counsel me," I whisper without thinking, staring at her in turn, those green eyes reflecting with the TV lighting which has been muted without me realizing.

She tilts her head confused, "I can't tell if that's sarcasm or not by your tone."

"A mixture of both," I admit honestly.

She sighs, not pushing further on that thought. "Well,

divorce is hard on a kid. I'm a kid of divorce too. It's isolating especially when the parents don't really parent the best."

Nikki adjusts how she's sitting to stare at the TV absent-mindedly, almost as if she's reminiscing. Part of me wants to tread her mind and explore all the depths of her, not just her body. My *sane* part knows she's far too complex and that I'll get lost or drown trying to figure her out. Not that she needs figuring out. I have no intention of changing her. Now that I understand more about her, trauma aside, I'm learning how to adapt and adjust to her needs. What may be defined as quirks are merely idiosyncrasies that make her, *uniquely her*.

Distracted by the intelligence of the woman in front of me, she continues to speak as my brain catches up to speed. "Development for kids is crucial from around age five to prepubescent years. Then, there's the whole puberty changes in the body and mind as the brain continues to develop deeper..."

I gather she's about to go on a psychological tangent, so I redirect her because I want to learn more about *her*.

"Your turn," I interject in, "Please continue. You're probably right on the money; you don't have to give me details I won't remember."

Nikki stops from whatever she was about to say, sighing in defeat.

"I know I'm *right*. Thanks for the reminder, *Rory*. I know we don't process or react the same, and we were born in different environments..." She stops, running her fingers through her hair, making a frustrated noise. "I think I need a drink to talk about mine... I've been in therapy, so it doesn't hurt as much to talk about, and it has helped with my PTSD immensely, but it can still be a lot. It'll also take my mind off the weird fact that I'm having this conversation with you, Mr. Serial-Killer-In-Recovery."

Rolling my eyes, I simply stand up, "Coming right up."

I hunt for the tequila in the top cabinet and mix some up with some leftover mixer and salt for the rim that I had from Cinco de Mayo last year.

"I *love* these," she says in a more animated tone that tells me she's happy; she even does the little happy wiggle, taking the glass from me.

Seating myself closer to her, but not too close as to not make her uncomfortable, she takes a few satisfied sips before continuing.

"Tastes good, Rory, good job." She takes another big sip. "So, my parents divorced, and I'm the firstborn. My mother was busy trying to support us as a single parent and she had my brother ten years later." Nikki pauses to take another sip. "My dad was kinda neglectful and didn't want anything to do with me, so like, he got remarried and had a boy. No dad wants a depressed kid, I guess. I used to think it was just because I was unlovable, not that our genetics just screamed *autism-galore*."

I frown at her statement of being unlovable and her father being neglectful. *Why would no one give her the attention she deserves? The fuck?* Before I can process fully and dive further into my downward spiraling thoughts, she continues.

"My mom did her best, but she dated shitty men, and I obviously took after her—*it is what it is*." Frowning still, the way she sounds like it's nothing, I just sigh heavily, doing my best not to interrupt. "In high school, I got into one of those high school relationships to try and ease the bullying, but he ended up taking advantage of me."

I'm unsure if I should hug her or move closer. Not

wanting to make her uncomfortable–wait, did she say *taking advantage?*

"He raped you?" I ask immediately when my brain fucking catches up.

She finishes her drink with a quick nod.

"Fuck, Nikki," I say, downing the rest of mine.

Then, she has the audacity to downplay her trauma which pisses me off.

"Unfortunately, I'm not the only woman with that type of story. I guess that's why I needed a drink, because I don't want pity or anything. I went to therapy to deal with my shit. It took *years*, naturally. I withdrew into myself to deal with life back then. After I graduated high school, I went off to college for Psychology, far away from everything. Unfortunately with that newfound freedom, I experimented with drugs and drinking before going into therapy," Nikki takes a short pause, blurting out further truths and honesty. "I graduated, finished therapy, and learned all about where my kinks came from. I got a delayed diagnosis at thirty and medication to stabilize my moods which helps with emotional regulation, honestly. I started my thirties off to a great start."

I can hear her sarcasm oozing, bleeding out as she trauma dumps.

"Well, I take back what I said before. I have no problem making room for a *number eleven*. If ever given the chance."

She shakes her head as I frown at my empty drink, wishing it wasn't. I can't help my rising anger that echoes in her favor.

"This isn't *Stranger Things*; we don't need an Eleven. That bastard isn't worth it anyway. He's probably balding, continuing to be the waste of human space he is, and I got hotter. *I am not my trauma.*"

Her comment makes me scoff. Her last statement repeated in my mind. *I am not my trauma.*

Am I?

"Well, I'm glad one of us is healed," I say, not knowing what else to say at this point. *He'll be number eleven if I ever see that motherfucker.*

Nikki shrugs, "If that's what you want to call it, I guess... Make another one of these?" She gestures to the glass, picking it up and holding it in front of me.

I take it and say nothing else. It takes no time at all to whip us up another round, only that time I brought the ingredients with me, so I didn't have to get up again for a while.

"Thanks." She takes a drink, making a dramatic sound as she swallows, indicating her pleasure of taste.

"You know, I spent most of my life as the black sheep. The delayed diagnosis aided in lifelong questions of why I was different from most of the other kids."

I observe her over the salted brim of my glass. In a way, I'm a black sheep too.

"What fucking gets me going," she looks off to the side with wide eyes, "Is that my brothers get all the help and I got the fucking neglect and trauma. Sounds fucking dumb and unfair, if you ask me. I resented my parents for a long time—which I came to terms with in recent years." She huffs a breath, taking a big swig of her made-with-love-by-Rory margarita. "Then with my ex and that whole shebang... Trauma this, trauma that. Of course, I had to experiment with drugs to find out for myself. It wasn't shit. I don't know how people do it for a long time when I got bored after a year..."

Sipping and staring at her, I can't help but be amazed by the woman in front of me. I went through less, and *she* didn't kill anyone as a result. Maybe I am the socio-psychopath she says I am. We're not cut from the same cloth or even the same side of the street, but there's a connection. We relate to one another in strange, twisted ways, and I'm not sure it's a bad thing. But who am I to say?

"I will say, healing in my twenties gave me all the self-awareness I can ask for. A perspective that's uniquely my own," she halts my lingering thoughts. "Just so you know, I don't really chat with my family as it still can be triggering, so I find keeping my distance to be healthier. For me anyway."

With a slight nod, I can't help but scoot closer until I'm next to her. After our trauma dump, I found that I couldn't be far away. *We'll psychoanalyze that later.*

"It's a good thing we aren't our traumas then, isn't it?" I say, catching those pretty green eyes smiling at me.

She clinks her glass against mine in agreement.

"I'm not on your level, though," I comment, and she turns her face to the side, holding back a laugh.

"Ha, as if." She meets my eyes again. "Don't put me on a pedestal, Rory. Just because you've killed and I didn't or was an accomplice—whatever, doesn't mean I'm better than you. At least in my brain anyways... We're all fucked up in one way or another, whether we come that way or are made that way. It's up to us to rewrite those pages in our fucked-up history. We can start and stop at any time with it."

It's my turn to clink my drink against hers this time. *So wise.*

"I guess I'm at that point now..." *Because of you,* I almost voice aloud, but instead I crack a joke. "Are you sure you don't want to be my therapist?"

Smirking, she huffs her laugh, staring into her glass. "I'd make it worse, knowing my luck."

"What if you make it better?" I counter her, raising my brow.

Nikki peers deep into my soul after that–too deeply in fact.

"You're optimistic for a killer," she says randomly.

My lips twitch, and I can't help but let my laughter slide out of me. "Why, Niks, I do think that's *a compliment.*"

Ignoring my antics she laughs, and I can't help but admire the sight. Being the reason she laughs is far more preferable, so I'm finding.

"I *could* give you more, but you're already so full of yourself."

I pretend to be offended, clutching my drink to my chest as if she shot me. "Ouch."

With a cheeky smile, she asks, "Have you looked in the mirror though?"

Maybe once or twice.

"You're hot, too," she speaks, far too honestly. "I shouldn't be as attracted to you as I am. Maybe that's why I'm in the acceptance stage of things."

The stages of grief. My psychological girl.

I lean closer, smugly, *"You're attracted to me?"*

Green eyes search mine, and I'm being pulled into her depths once more. Only this time I don't have to wonder.

Her lips meet mine first.

When she pulls away, I wonder what cloud I've drifted to.

"I wouldn't have kissed you at all if I wasn't. Also, can't forget the whole, *'sorry, I'm a killer but I'm sparing you'* thing." I laugh, claiming her lips in turn as the chuckle remains in my throat.

"You have a point. But I think we're trying to move forward, right?"

"I guess." She narrows her eyes playfully, the mirth prevalent.

We keep our playfulness as we finish what's left in our glasses. By the time we get through our third round, I say something dumb, and she's laughing and leaning against me. I join her in her laughter, and suddenly it feels so easy to be around her. We're able to be ourselves, with no judgments or worries about tomorrow.

Laying my head on her shoulder once we catch our breaths from laughing, my words slur as I say, "Thank you for trauma-bonding with me."

"Interesting thing to be thanked for, but you too, Rore."

My heart skips a beat over her nickname, and I nuzzle my head into her neck. "Will you cuddle with me in bed? I don't want you to think you have to keep sleeping on the couch. The bed is big enough for two."

She sighs, giving me a languid smirk. "I didn't realize you're a cuddler. You're full of surprises. Sure. You made me margaritas, after all. I'm in the palm of your hand."

I perk up at that. "Oh, really?"

"Cuddling is all you're getting out of this bitch tonight," she counters back in a matter-of-fact tone.

I fake pout. "What do I have to do?" Moving my head so I can see her better, the room spins slightly. *Fucking tequila.*

"Hmm, I'll let you know. An activity that should be discussed first *in sobriety*. If you behave yourself, of course. I can't give you the goods all up front, you know."

"*Tease.*" I sigh in disappointment, but I'm more than ready to get to bed and snuggle. Before I can move to get up, she's moving and straddling me in my lap.

In a dizzying daze, my hands go to her hips.

"I didn't say I wouldn't kiss you though," she says in a low tone that I feel tug at my balls.

Her hands go to my shoulders as she leans down and kisses me, gently at first, before pressing closer.

I'm greedy for more of her taste and my hands slip into her blonde hair. Sensuous in my pursuit, I'm reminded of the first time I kissed her next to a burning van. The adrenaline from us both after committing a crime and the look on her face. Lips that begged to be kissed in that moment.

Now, here she is in my lap, brave with alcohol, yet I'm content all the while. She's right, as much as I'd love to go further with the indescribable beauty in my arms.

One of my hands slides down her side, to her hips, and over her round ass. I can feel those delicious curves, begging to be tasted and cherished. *Soon, I'd lick every inch of that body.*

Her tongue plays well with mine, and suddenly I'm being wrapped around her finger. That didn't take long.

I pick her up, her legs hugging me as I stand up and bring her to the bed.

"Fuck, you're so sexy, Niks."

She moans in my mouth, and I'm feverish for more the minute I lay her down on the plush mattress.

"I want to taste the divine," I murmur, tugging up the shirt with my teeth.

"I want you to remember the taste of me," she says with the purse of her lips that I want to bite.

"As if I'd forget," I lick up her stomach as she tenses, her hand goes through my hair.

"Fine. Bring those lips up here. Your hand can wander," she says, growing breathless already.

"Fucking deal." Intoxicated me *can* compromise.

My lips meet hers eagerly as my hand roams down her

chest, groping twice with the promise of more later, sliding further down.

"I wonder how wet you are, and if I can bring you to the other side with just my fingers."

Arching her hips up for me and widening her thighs, I find my answer on how wet she is. Groaning and wishing I could taste for myself, I tease her entrance with a single finger and circle her clit in tempting strokes.

Nikki's panting as I devour her mouth. I continue to tease her until she twitches and writhes under me.

Good, just where I want you.

My fingers slide into her wet cunt while my thumb continues at her clit.

One of her hands scrunches a hold of my hair while the other fists my shirt. Her reactions are giving me oxygen in my lungs. So, this is what rebirthing feels like. *Only this is just a taste.*

I stroke her, curling my fingers until she swells and comes at last.

Tasting her breathy moans has made me as hard as granite.

When I pull my lips away, she has the best bedroom eyes I've ever seen, so glassy and dreamy from what I just gave her.

Removing my fingers from inside her, I bring them to my lips.

"I'll be thinking of this taste, tequila or not," I say with unmoving promise.

She reaches for me as I pull myself to stand at the side of the bed, humming around my fingers leisurely. Her hands immediately go for my pants, and I shake my head. *Fuck, what's wrong with me?*

"Remember what you said," I remind her from her

earlier request that she communicated. "Rest, Niks. My cock isn't going anywhere. I'll join you in bed shortly."

She relaxes, seeming disappointed, which brings me more joy than I care to admit. The fact that she's consensually willing means a lot, but I won't do more tonight.

Once I'm in the shower, I jerk off to the taste and feel of her. Then, I make good on my promise of cuddling. The warmth of her lulls me to peaceful dreams which only exist because of her.

XOXO
LOVE

Chapter Fourteen

Nikki

I spend the next few days unpacking, getting most of it done while Rory works late hours during the weekend. *I do not think about how good his fingers and lips felt that night we drank margaritas.*

I unpack the bathroom stuff first, placing my favorite scents of the week in the shower. I find various storage spots for makeup and necessities. His bathroom is in need of décor, that's for sure. It's so *plain and unlively.*

I move onto my clothes next since I'm clearing out his wardrobe. The weather is getting warmer, so I keep a mixture of shirts, long sleeves, and sweaters. It's thoughtful of him to buy things he thinks I need. *When everyone else is lacking in that department of thoughtfulness.*

I didn't realize killers could be thoughtful. Or is ex-killer the proper term? Is that proper dinner table talk?

Holding the great internal debate, Rory arrives home that Sunday, full of exhaustion. Checking the time, its midnight, and I got distracted. Apparently, his job only adjusted his work hours to match mine.

"I'm surprised you're still up."

"Me too honestly," I say kneeling next to the armoire with a box.

"I'm wiped. Working until you die sounds fucking insane."

Or you can always just be kidnapped or killed, but I'm not saying anything.

"We have to pay to live, and live to pay? It's ass-backwards."

"Hmm," he considers me, coming to stand next to me, "what's not backwards, is coming home to you. It seems I look forward to it every day."

I give him an attempt at a smile. "A psychotic symptom, I'm sure."

He bends over, leaning in, "You need to work on accepting compliments, Sugar."

Unamused, "I ain't gonna change, but maybe I'll find another face to make, who knows. Is it bedtime?"

Rory chuckles and kisses my forehead.

"You're wifey material."

Disgust fills me, "Ew, stop. I'll barf."

"So dramatic."

I give up on clothes for the night, taking off my bra, and jumping into bed.

He turns off the lights and strips down, crawling in next to me.

"Can I ask you something, Nikki?"

With how he says it, I can't help but be concerned. "Yes."

"So, I don't know how to say this in a way without sounding like...weird."

"Just say it, I'll figure it out if needed," I say, suddenly getting impatient but ready to sleep.

"Okay, so, there's a kink club not too far away, and I

wanted to ask you if you wanted to go with me, but we haven't defined the boundaries of our relationship. We also haven't fucked around, so I didn't know if that would be uncomfortable for you. Or if you would interested in fucking this week beforehand, you know for practice."

I blink in the darkness, taking in the information, processing, and doing it again until he points it out.

"Got anything there for me, Niks?" He almost sounds anxious over what I might say.

"Give me a second, still processing here. One, you asked to *fuck me*. Two, you want to take me to a sex club when I didn't even know there was one. Third, and most important, *what do I wear?*"

I hear a stifled laugh behind me as I roll over on my side. I see him smirking while I stare at him, intrigued by this new development and request. *How did I not know there was one in the city?* I wrack my brain, realizing I'm a closeted kinkster.

Rory scoots closer so that part of the lighting from the window above reflects on part of his handsome face. The muted rays paint him in a sultry way, yet somehow gentle in a sense too. It's captivating.

"You never cease to amaze me, Nikki."

I blush in the shadows of soft light from the window from feet away.

"There's no rush for any answers, but I wanted to bring it up to you. Think on it and let me know?"

Of course, he gives me things to think about before I go to bed. Rude.

I nod my head, murmuring a soft *okay,* before rolling back over. Rory snakes his arm around me, pulling me close. The steady up and down of his chest against my back tells me he's already fast asleep.

I stare at the ceiling listening to the sounds of cars passing by, soon the ceiling turns black, and a dark and sultry club appears around me, people in masks flash in front of my face as the lights pulse in time to the music. Sin is thick in the air. Sin I definitely want to be a part of.

When I dress the next morning, I find myself gravitating towards a black pencil skirt with a button up blouse, the typical office job attire. As I'm sliding the stockings up my thigh, and hooking them to a garter, a devious thought crosses my mind.

I smile, sliding the next stocking up and finishing the outfit with a pair of black pumps. Making my way to the front room, I find Rory, waiting by the door. His eyes meet mine, then slowly trail down my body, locking in every inch of curve I have to offer. My ploy is working. Rory is sizing me up just like his pants. Now this, I could get used to. Rory's eyes on me, daydreaming about me while he's at work. Who knew an outfit could be great foreplay.

I sashay in front of him to the car, clearly putting on a show. After his whispered words about getting more *acquainted.*

I'm not thinking about his fingers in me at all, nor has it been all I thought about.

Even in my thoughts, the lie tastes good on my tongue.

He drops me off at work, and I make my way through endless paperwork and mailing them. I fax, make copies, and check my emails.

A daydream snatches my attention while the mundane tasks of work drag on.

As I sashayed in front of him earlier, his hand pops me on my ass, making me yelp. Energy and nerves tingle from the base of my spine. I don't hear him get in the car.

Turning around to see what's up, he's right there, tattoos exposed. I don't give myself time to wonder why he doesn't have a shirt on, I just roll with it.

I give him my best sly smile before he grabs my face and plants a good one.

I imagine his skin as rough but that there's soft tenderness, too. My fingers glide up his inked arms as I slide my tongue inside his mouth to taste the divine. A taste that devours and consumes me.

Before I know it, I'm spread out on the hood of his black car–his baby.

My stockings are ripped as I watch in fascination and lust while he rips his belt off, unbuckling his work pants.

I'm ready to go as Rory's cock springs free and my mouth salivates for a taste.

Rory says dirty things, lining himself up at my wet cunt, my underwear disappearing.

I'm a fucking goner.

The daze doesn't seem to end when the work day does. Rory appears at the curb in the car he adores.

I've been needy all day, fidgeting with rising sexual energy. Now that we're heading in that direction, my thoughts turn into a dirty trash can of tangled sighs and his hands on me—in a different way than ever before. The daydream of him fucking me lingers on the surface of my mind.

I wonder what he tastes like. I can potentially add sucking a killer's dick to my resume, right?

Maybe not, but for my mental resume, definitely.

Once I slide into the passenger seat, I find those lovely eyes on me.

"Good day, Nikki?" He asks before pulling off.

"Same shit, different day." A basic bitch answer even if it is the truth. Well, mostly.

I wasn't sure about mentioning how he was on my mind *all* day that I had to double-check the paperwork I mailed out every time.

"Same here." He turns the volume to low, and within ten minutes we're home.

I enjoy the silence, walking inside and kicking my shoes off before picking them up.

When I stand up fully, Rory is right there in front of me.

"So, shall we continue from yesterday?"

My mouth is suddenly dry.

"Green."

He lifts his hand to my chin to tilt it up before a sweet kiss consumes me and leaves me longing for more as he pulls away after one.

Walking to the couch, he sits down with a hesitant sigh.

"We need to have *the talk—sex* that is."

What is this, Sex Ed?

"Okay," I say and find myself standing at one end of couch, my shoes in hand.

"You mentioned you're kinky... Can you give me some background on that? Likes? Dislikes?"

I'm thirsty over the thought.

"Restraints. Rope in various positions are good. I like hair pulling, throat holding—aka hand necklaces, props, paddles, and the like. I'm sensory oriented as you know. So, tastes, sounds, touch, sights, and smells are always good in combination. Depends on what the day calls for."

He's taking off one shoe while his eyes look to the side seeing me standing there.

"Okay. Do you consider yourself more submissive or dominant?"

Good question.

"You didn't say both," I mention, and he raises a brow in curiosity.

"In the bedroom, I mean."

"Depends on the person, honestly. My head space is important."

"Good to know," he says, removing the other shoe.

"Do you want to dominate me, Rory?" I can't help myself or my low tone.

Something flashes in his eyes, one that resonates in my pussy.

"I can be flexible, but at this moment, *yes.*"

I open my mouth, my heart rate rising, feeling flush. He watches me carefully.

"Remember your colors. Where are you now?"

My entire nervous system tingles.

"Very fucking green."

Rory rises, and he takes me in fully once more before taking two steps right up to me.

My pumps slip from my hold, and his lips find mine eagerly.

His hands dive into the hair at my nape as the other arm pulls me flush to him.

Before his tongue slides into my mouth he whispers between kisses, "I've been thinking about undressing you all fucking day."

I'm already slick between my thighs.

"You aren't alone in that."

He licks up the column of my neck, grabbing my ass.

"It's time for me to undress my girl then."

Pulling away from me, he grabs my hand and leads me to the other side where the bed is.

Before I can register all that's happening and if it's really happening—*it's apparent that it's not a dream.*

"I've been wondering what you taste like all day," I bravely speak up.

We're standing at the side of the bed then.

"It's only fair if I taste you tonight." With how he tugs on his bottom lip in contemplation, I'm quickly sinking to my knees while looking up.

"What's your color?" I ask him.

"Very fucking green."

I grin as he cups my face and I begin to take him out of his dark jeans. The feel of his bulge is powerful and playful under my touch. Once, its free, I take an eyeful in. The girth and length of it will break me. *Fuck.*

I'm not even a tiny person, but *what am I supposed to do with the thing staring at me?*

Fuck it. I don't waste time and lick up the column of it.

His hand goes in my hair.

Enjoying it there, I continue to tease him with my licks. I grow eager with each one.

The way he tenses and relaxes because of all I'm giving him—*I'm so fucking wet.*

Once he's wet enough, I slowly take him into my mouth, careful of my teeth because of his sizing.

Rory curses, tilting his head back in what I hope is bliss. I keep my eyes on him until I try to take him further.

He sighs through his teeth, "I can't wait to make your mascara run in the future. I can see it now."

I can see it too.

Wrapping my hand at the base of him, I moan around

him while closing my eyes. I can still smell his citrus body wash even though I can't taste it. I find his taste new, one I can't name, yet delectable all the same.

"Fuck, yeah. Just like that, Sugar."

Encouraged by his words, I increase my pace as my stomach growls to let me know it's time for dinner. I'd have to dive into him more when it's not before a meal.

"Look at you," he whispers, and I find I'm more ravenous than I thought.

His words do something to me, and I'm realizing that the few words of praise stick more—they mean more.

Guess I'm a praise girly.

"Fuck, I'm about to cum down that pretty throat. Almost there, baby."

I nearly come with him as I keep my pacing. He stiffens before hot, salty cum spills down my throat.

Almost gagging at first since it's been a while, I'm proud that I don't.

His hand tightens briefly in my hair before releasing. His panting has me nearly feral. I nearly tackle him as I stand up.

My stomach interrupts to growl loudly.

He sits on the bed, opening his eyes.

"I'll make dinner," he offers, and I swear I'm pouting.

"Don't worry, that pussy is mine the minute we're done eating food."

I shiver at his declaration, watching as he stands, putting himself away.

"Tongue out," he says, and I'm confused as I do.

He licks it. "Mmm, I taste mighty fine on such a sumptuous tongue."

Merely blinking at him as he pulls away, but strangely turned on, he winks, walking away.

Following behind him, "That was okay for you?"

He stops, turns, and I nearly run into him.

"Okay? No, Sugar—that smart mouth of yours did wonderful."

I can't help my smile as he returns it before he walks away to start dinner.

XOXO
LOVE

Chapter Fifteen

Rory

I barely remember dinner or what I ended up making.

All that overtakes me are those dreamy green eyes. Ones that have haunted my dreams ever since I first gazed upon her.

The woman before me has awakened something inside of me, and while I process it, I'll taste her *more thoroughly* this time.

Once Nikki's back hits the mattress, I hover over her admiring those curves with hair splayed around her. My hand settles on her hip as I take it all in. I can't wait to undress her, but I didn't want to rush to taste her and miss out on her precious reactions.

I peck her lips quickly, and instruct her, barely touching her sweet little mouth. "Move up further on the bed, Sugar."

Nikki wiggles to do so immediately. A sly smile draws upon my face. I crawl further on the bed with her, telling her to open for me.

Green eyes lock with mine, a soft sound escaping her while her thighs part.

"First," I hook my fingers at the top of her skirt, "Tell me what you thought about today that wasn't work." Nikki lifts her hips to aid me in pulling the skirt down and off.

"I..."

I toss the skirt elsewhere, sliding my hands up her tights. "Use your words, Sugar. Don't hold back on me. This is all *for you*."

Her chest rises and falls heavily. "I thought about what you said last night. About getting acquainted this week and figuring out our dynamics before the weekend."

I massage her inner thighs. "As have I. Go on, what else?"

Swallowing her saliva, I catch her lick her lips. "I've been fantasizing about your cock in my mouth all day."

My smile grows, "Oh, really?"

"Yes," she breathes out, as if the honest words are a release of their own.

My fingers slip into the top of the stockings, "Once these stockings come off, I'm going to discover how wet you are, aren't I?"

"*Yes.*"

I savor the sexy goddess underneath me as her skin comes into contact with mine. Once they're off, I toss them too. Smooth skin greets me, along with my own eagerness to taste and touch her again and again.

"I've only tasted briefly, and while I wasn't disappointed, I'm now unable to stop myself from drinking whatever nectar you give me. My only thought has been to consume your pussy all day *with my tongue*."

I see her release her breath, biting her lip and watching me to see what my next move is.

"To make things easier for you, we don't have to do anything you don't want to. You know the color-words if you find yourself feeling overwhelmed, not just now, but the future as well. That alright with you?"

"Yes, Sir."

The words are my undoing as I trail soft kisses from her feet all the way up her thigh, then I do the other leg the same way. With skin so soft, how could I ever think of killing her?

I'm coming to terms with how early in this *relationship* she's affecting me, ever since she was tied to the chair.

I have a treasure on my lips. My hand trails up to tease her outside her damp underwear. It doesn't go unnoticed as I nibble on her inner thigh. She jolts slightly before relaxing.

Wondering if she's been wet like this most of the day, I find my cock coming to life.

"So fucking wet," I bring my nose to them and inhale deeply while gripping her thighs.

Her skin pebbles under me as I kiss her pussy once, then twice. However, it's not enough. I look up to find her on her elbows looking at me with her mouth lax. Those eyes are so fucking dreamy.

"Has anyone sniffed you and told you how fucking divine you smell?"

She shakes her head no, eyes not leaving me.

"That's a fucking shame, because now this pussy belongs *to me*. This scent is *mine*." I inhale her underwear again and find her tugging on her bottom lip. "Now, I'm going to worship and savor the scent *and* flavor until you come on my tongue."

She gives me a nod once my fingers massage her labia. Nikki's head falls back with a soft sigh.

I'm so turned on by the sight that I can't help myself

when I move her panties to the side for a slow lick up her cunt.

I can already taste her divine; she's soaked and ready. It takes everything in me not to push my cock in where it's meant to be. Instead, I allow myself to growl low in my throat.

"These are coming off," I say before sitting up and pulling her panties down and off.

My hand finds her inner thigh, rubbing the nerve endings gently. The other teases her slick folds. She writhes at my touch, and I can't describe how much joy it gives me to see her lose herself to sensation. Knowing that I'm doing it for her makes it all the better.

Nikki moves her hips, and I'm more than ready to devour as my tongue finds her clit, moving around in teasing circles. Lapping up what's already there, I groan in delight.

She tastes so fucking good.

I make sure to tell her as much before I lick her cunt to the finish.

A curse leaves her lips above me, arching her back and opening herself more, a full feast spread for me. *And I'm fucking here for it.*

Moans echo from us both as I tease her entrance, licking up and around in gentle motions that have her grabbing the black sheets below us. I hold her leg up with one hand while the other grabs her inner thigh.

Keeping my pacing, she swells under my tongue.

"Come for me, Sugar. Give me my holy drink."

I hear her panting, and I don't relent. Waiting until the right moment, I place my lips around her clit to suck, using my tongue for added assistance.

A hand flies into my hair, gripping it tight. The most beautiful sound leaves her lips as she falls into my worship.

What Nikki doesn't realize while I gaze up at her as she comes is that she's my goddess. I serve *her*. Everything I needed all my life hadn't found me until I kidnapped her and took my destiny into my own hands. *Well, mostly*.

Now, my destiny is on my tongue, and my killing days are over. All I need is *this—her*.

My name is a whimper on her lips, as I clean her up with my tongue.

"Rory."

The calling of my divinity, the altar of that I worship.

My lips meet hers, letting her taste herself.

"I'll save the fucking for another night this week," I whisper as she adjusts and gets in her spot on the bed, opening her arms.

I hold up my finger in wait as I undress, leaving my underwear on even if my dick is begging to break from it.

"How'd I do, Sugar?" I murmur into her neck as I snuggle up into her arms.

I feel her sigh in what almost sounds like relief.

"That was great. I know what to do now when you get on my nerves or piss me off again."

Laughing into her neck, I hold her against me.

"That's one way to shut me up."

And there wouldn't be one complaint either.

XOXO
LOVE

Chapter Sixteen

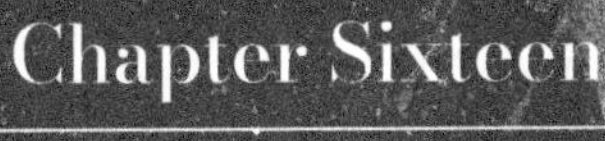

Nikki

Well, *fuck.*

Not only was I thoroughly satiated, but I passed the hell out the minute we curled up in bed. Never thought I'd be mentally complimenting a killer-man for pussy eating or for having a pretty tasty dick.

As I've thought before, *I'm fucked now.*

I'm dating a killer, and I'm not even mad.

Do I need to be committed now?

Waking up the following morning, I couldn't remember what I was uncertain about to begin with. Nothing made sense anymore, and I didn't have the energy to fight or resist. A killer accepts my ASD, but my family ignores it—what the fuck?

Life is ass-backwards.

Opening my eyes to the sun rays dancing across my skin, I realize I highly doubt Rory would fuck bad, and if he did at least he eats pussy good. I'll settle either way, choice in the matter or not. For me it's about silver linings to get through the day, or whatever the fuck I can do for my sanity.

My senses kick in: citrus, warmth, and a tattooed arm around my stomach. I don't even mind it to be honest. In fact, my brain isn't fully awake for processing much anyway.

I wiggle in his hold, trying to scoot closer. He lets me, and it's not long until I realize what's poking behind me.

Do not think about his dick. You have to get ready for work. Do not think about his dick.

I repeat the mantra hoping I believe it.

"Good morning."

With how sexy he sounds, I almost turn around and eat him alive.

"Mornin'."

He buries his face into my neck, kissing a tender spot that leaves goosebumps behind.

"I don't want to work today," he murmurs, and I have to agree with him.

"Same." *I sound like such a millennial.*

His arm tightens around me, and I'm now flush against him.

"I think we have time for breakfast."

Remembering my thyroid meds, I realize I have to wait thirty minutes until I can eat. I remind him as much.

To no one's surprise, he's not talking about real food.

Rory moves his arm and helps move me to my back, then he's hovering above my face with a salacious smirk that I can feel in my pussy. She's awake more than my brain is.

Before I can register anything, he kisses me firmly before kissing down my body until his tongue greets my-already-waiting pussy.

My hand drifts above to the edge of the pillow as I grip it for dear life. Rory wastes no time and quickly consumes me. Last night was slow but all-consuming. This morning is a fast consumption that makes my head spin.

It doesn't take long before I'm gripping his head with my thighs and my other hand. I'm not a loud porn screamer, *as I like to call it,* yet I'm still vocal enough with my soft sighs.

Rory pauses, and I'm delirious while he makes eye contact. "I can't wait to fuck you for the first time, but I'll happily eat your pussy for the rest of my life."

I groan, pushing his head back down and falling back into the sensation of his sinful tongue. Warmth fills me from his words, realizing that no one has ever said that to me before.

The rise of orgasm floods me as I encourage him not to fucking stop. The fucker has the audacity to smirk.

I shiver as endorphins flood my bloodstream and spasm through my cunt. I have to process being awake and Rory's pussy consumption.

Breathing out a sigh of release, my eyes are half-lidded once he pulls away.

"And I'm supposed to function today after you say some shit like that?" I finally say.

He sits up fully with a wicked ass smirk, using a thumb to wipe the corner of his mouth.

"Say 'ah' and see how fucking beautiful you taste."

The gesture is so fucking sexy, I swear I think I'm ready for round two as I listen and open my mouth, sticking out my tongue.

I soon taste myself, and close my lips around his thumb, sucking and teasing him with my tongue.

"Mmm, aren't you such a temptation to take again," he whispers, brushing his fingers against my cheek.

He pulls away from me, and I find myself in a gloom of disappointment as he dresses for work.

Rory grins at me, but I find myself more distracted on the ridges of his abs and how his jeans do a little pop as they glide over his ass.

"You're evil."

This fucker knows *what he's doing.*

"I'll only tolerate those words in these scenarios."

I roll my eyes, puffing my cheeks while I get out of bed not caring if he's serious or not.

I can't help but ask him on the way to my job, "So, are you going to fuck me tonight or tomorrow?"

He casts a quick glance, keeping one arm on the wheel and moving the other to settle on my thigh. All I can focus on is his large hand. On my thigh, or in my pussy. *Fucking me.*

"For me to know and *you* to find out."

I keep a raised brow until he looks at me briefly. He squeezes once before smirking to himself.

It seems to me, he gets a rise out of torturing and teasing me, and it's going to drive me crazy. I can't help my excitement, nor the anticipation. It will be another day of hyper-focusing and fantasizing.

We arrive at the curb of my workplace, and I sigh in disappointment once he removes his hand.

"Don't think about me too much today," he says *sweetly*.

I get out and roll my eyes before giving him the finger and leaving him there.

It's going to be another long day.

XOXO
LOVE

Chapter Seventeen

Rory

Teasing Nikki is becoming a new favorite thing.

Part of me wants to be *evil* and let her stew for another day, yet another part of me isn't sure if I can wait.

You waited this long, what's one more day?

Throughout my workday, I toy with various ideas on whether to fuck her or feast on her for dinner, and by the time I leave, I settle on teasing her again tonight.

My main dilemma is how eager I am for another taste. She's in my veins now.

Once I'm outside her work, I eagerly await her presence while tapping my fingers impatiently on the steering wheel. It's all but forever when she finally steps to the curb in her office attire, getting in my car.

"Hello, Sugar," I greet with a smirk as I try to read the encyclopedia of her facial expressions.

"Hi... I'm in the mood to make dinner tonight."

Letting her take the lead might be a better plan, I decide, as I give her a nod and drive us home.

"I'm interested to see what you make," I start off, and while she stares off outside the window, I ramble on. "I have the dry erase board on the fridge if you want me to order or pick anything up for you. Any necessities, really." I pull into my designated parking spot in the lot outside the building.

She says nothing as I kill the engine and follow her up to our apartment. My usual confidence is waning.

Once inside, Nikki takes off her shoes and gets to work silently. Only once I ask if she needs help, and she waves me off.

Putting my hands up in defeat, I opt for a shower and leave the door open.

Our morning was fucking glorious, and now the vibes with her are different. Her standoffishness makes me feel insecure.

I strip bare and take myself in when I look in the mirror. It's like I haven't truly looked into my reflection, if ever. Suddenly I can see who she once saw.

A killer committing crimes with questionable morals.

Who am I to her now?

As I scrub myself, I wonder if she had a bad day or something. She's typically only silent when she's in a certain state of mind that usually involves her being stressed.

The shampoo bottle is in my hands as I blink in and out of reality. I'm in a fucking daze, trying to figure out her moods or if I'm good enough for her.

I debate on asking her what's up when I finish my shower and head into the kitchen, still wet with my towel wrapped around me at my hips.

Nikki is stirring something on the stove as I sneak up behind her, wrapping my arms around her. A short, startled yip leaves her, and I kiss her neck.

"I think I died a little. Don't sneak up behind people with anxiety, for fuck's sake, dude."

"*Sorry,*" I murmur against her skin, tugging on her earlobe while trying to ease my own nerves.

She wiggles out of my hold, pointing a large spoon at me.

"Nuh-uh!"

Raising my brow in amusement, I lean back against the counter. "What are you going to do about it?"

I can't help but taunt her as those green eyes narrow on me. It seems like she's not as stressed as I thought, just focused. I'm immediately at ease, feeling silly for my earlier existential crisis in the shower.

"I'll either fuck you or bite you."

I'm so scared.

"So angry and bitey, Sugar." She's not, but I have to tease her anyway.

Nikki swats at me before turning back to the stovetop, grunting, "Get out of my kitchen and go on somewhere. I'm almost done."

I laugh, doing as she says and grabbing my newly acquired phone. Leaning against the opposite side of the island furthest from Nikki, I order a table for us online, just big enough for two, while the smell of garlic bread wafts through the air. "Whatever you're making smells fucking delicious."

I can hear a snort from Nikki before she says, "I wanted to be bad and have emotional support alfredo."

I can't help but laugh. "The lactose pills are in the cupboard."

With a thumbs up to me, she distributes the food on two laid-out plates. Then, she pulls garlic bread out of the oven.

I move out of her way and hunt for some wine to share between us.

"I ordered us a table, so we don't have to keep eating on

the couch or standing at the island counter," I tell her as I pour the red wine I end up finding.

She nods, handing me a full plate while I hand her a glass of wine.

"Thanks."

For jokes, I put on another crime show as we settle to eat. Initially, she gives me a knowing look before focusing on her food.

We eat in silence, and I take her plate, wondering why she wasn't as chatty and why she referred to pasta as emotional support. What does she need support with?

"That was tasty," I praise as she agrees with a long satisfied sigh.

Nikki follows me, writing some items on the fridge list. *So, she was listening earlier.*

"I'll clean," she goes on, standing at the sink after I take the marker from her to write *sandwich stuff.*

Perfect timing.

I time it right to come up behind her after she rinses out the pot, placing my chin on her shoulder. When she doesn't say or do anything, I place my hands on her hips, kissing her neck. Once, twice—three times.

She shivers under my hold, and it doesn't slip past me how much slower she's moving with cleaning up the dishes.

Evil teasing plan, check.

I hum in approval as I run my hands under her red, dressy top. *She's so fucking warm with skin so soft.* If she needs emotional support, I'll be happy to help.

Nikki leans into me, forgetting about the dishes.

"Has something been on your mind today, Sugar?"

She sighs softly, a breath of a whisper. "Yes."

"*Go on.*"

I lick up her neck before sucking on her earlobe. She

sucks in through her teeth, and I unclasp her bra from under her shirt. I tug it off with her top and toss it to the side as a gasp leaves her lips.

My intention is to only tease and touch, giving into one of her senses.

Hopefully, I can behave.

Cupping her ass and squeezing, my other hand casually fondles one of her tits. How I haven't played with them yet astounds me. They're full and bigger in my hand than I thought they'd be.

As if it's my first-time feeling tits, my cock grows against her ass.

"You've been such a tease, it's time for me to return the favor," she says sweetly.

As soon as I process those words, she twists out of my hold, kneeling with those lovely tits on display.

Underestimating her *again,* she smirks up at me before ripping the towel from my hips.

My hard cock springs free, and in that moment, I'm speechless when she takes me into her wet mouth. A delighted groan leaves my lungs as I stare down to watch and admire the incredible sight.

Nikki's tits are bouncing, her dusky rose nipples begging for my tongue and teeth. I see parts of me disappear and reappear, slick with her saliva while she bobs her head. Her focus and enjoyment with my cock is all I need to live.

"Fuck." The only word I can even say, but it says it all.

The *sight* of her on her knees, sucking my cock with her eyes closed—golden.

The *feel* of her tongue and suction brings me closer and closer to my peak—heaven.

The *sound* of her slobbering and all she's giving me—fucking bliss.

The *taste* of her from this morning still lingers on my tongue, and I'm aching for more.

Nikki moans on my cock, and suddenly all my senses flow into one as I tense up, releasing into her talented mouth with a stifling groan. I couldn't even give her a fair warning.

My hand scrunches into her hair as I climb down my ladder of ecstasy.

"Who's evil again?" I huff out breathlessly, releasing her as she makes a popping sound with the tip of me.

"Still you," she says, licking her lips as if I'm her dessert.

I growl as she stands, and I pin her to the counter but not before reaching around her to turn off the water that was forgotten about.

Her eyes are glued to me, and my lips then lock onto hers in a frenzy. I bask in the taste of me merging with her. My hands grip her hips, and the naughty thing has the audacity to smirk between our kissing.

It takes me no time to lift her up onto the counter next to the sink and slide my tongue inside her teasing mouth eagerly. Her thighs hugged me, and I hurriedly tug off her pants. Remembering that she didn't put on underwear, she's soon bare before me and ready for the taking. *Almost.*

Desperation peels at me by the layer; I need her more than I need to breathe.

Before I think of checking in or returning the same torture, she opens her mouth. *As she always does.*

"Fuck me. Fuck me right here on this counter. Neon green light, Rory."

My dick twitches at her chosen words. I cup the back of her head. "Are you sure?"

"Fuck yes, and don't fucking stop, whether you fit or

not," she says in a sultry, deep tone that I've never heard from her before.

Not saying no to *that*. Her desperate needs match my own.

I waste no time easing my cock into her slick heat. Taking my time, I keep her head cradled in my hand, using my tongue to lick along her pulse. She tastes like all my favorite meals eaten with her—*which is all of them.*

"I'll fit perfectly, Sugar, don't you worry your gorgeous head."

Her pussy is fucking wet and tight, and I can't help but slide deeper until I pump a few times and reach my hilt.

"Fuck, yes," she encourages, and I grunt my approval.

She stretches snug around me. Her hands don't know where to touch and stay on me, but she settles on holding me tight. Nails scratch at my back and sides while my hands go around her body and in her hair. It's as if I need to be closer until we're one.

Her noises are normally softer as I'm eating her out, but as I fuck her on the counter, I can't tell if I'm hurting her or pleasuring her. She's louder but not screaming. I happen to enjoy the sounds she's making, but just to ensure she's okay, I ask her.

"Are you enjoying this cock I'm feeding you?"

"It's all I thought about all day—God, yes."

"The only God here *is me*." I reach down to circle her clit to prove my point, slowing my pace just a bit to look at and revel in the sight of us connected.

"Look at you," I tell her, and those *fuck-me* eyes lock onto me, reading me for who I am. *Hers.*

"This pussy was made to take me, all of me. Look how well you take it, Sugar."

Her mouth falls open and she rolls her neck until she's

leaning back on her elbows. Naked glory, pert tits, and divine curves fill my vision as she moans perfectly.

Feeling encouraged and increasing my pace, I keep circling and teasing her clit. She starts to swell around me, and I know she's close. It's only been hours in the grand scheme of things, but I'm in tune to her.

"*Fuck,*" she moans, the familiar curse leaves her impeccable lips, and it only makes me want everything—all of her.

"Your life is mine," I groan, grabbing her hips tight.

Her softs sighs are all I need to hear.

"Come for me, Sugar," I beckon, not relenting to my pressure and pacing.

"Ohhh!" she cries out, jolting, her inner walls clamping around me as she comes.

The sensation is overwhelming as I groan and find myself spilling into her shortly after. I fill her full of me, making sure she takes it. Her hands grip the edge of the counter as if to keep her afloat, and I find myself pulling out of her and sinking to my knees to taste us both.

The minute my tongue tastes my cum and hers, I find there's nothing better than the taste of us together. She looks to see what I'm doing before making noises above while shaking.

I don't move until she comes for me again. Her hand is clenched tight in my hair, and I'm lost there—in her. In me. *In us.*

I've found someone that's worth my time and energy. Who belongs with me. I may have taken her, but now she's simply mine *to keep.*

So much for waiting until tomorrow.

XOXO
LOVE

Chapter Eighteen

Nikki

After licking me for all of my worth, I'm soon carried to the bed where he fucks me on all fours, smacking my ass and pulling my hair. *Just as I like.*

When I come the final time for the night, I come so fucking hard I see stars. He went harder and faster than on the counter, and I wonder where this psychopathic sex *god* has been all my life.

Damn, he certainly knows how to fuck my brains out. I'm practically putty in his palms.

For the first time, fucking someone isn't awkward and cringy. Normally, it's the weird phase of figuring out what each other likes, *not orgasming,* and taking a few times to get the hang of things with someone new.

So, I thought.

Turns out a person just needs a psychopath that's a *hot* walking red flag.

It's clear that I'm not the best person to judge, morally sound or not, even if I come on his tongue and enjoy returning the favor.

The morning after is the hardest, because adult responsibility calls me back to reality. *I hate it here.*

Sunlight reaches across my face as I blink my eyes open. There's a delightful soreness between my thighs which causes me to relax back into the tangled sheets. I stretch out slowly, making ridiculous stretching noises before humming my approval at the male curled up next to me with the sweetest smile plastered on his face.

"Good morning, Sugar."

"It's definitely a good morning, now."

He chuckles, tugging me closer for a peck on the cheek. His warm arms caress my synapses as I realize we both have to work.

Groaning, I begin my complaints. "Let's play hooky and skip work. I don't wanna go."

I feel him press a kiss to the top of my head.

"I know, me either. But we have a busy day scheduled at work, and I'll get my ass chewed out if I don't go."

I sigh in defeat, his warmth leaving me against my wishes. Reluctantly, I get out of bed and start the day, and we're both off to work before I know it.

The day drags on and all I'm thinking about is the next round after he picks me up.

A habit of mine involves getting fixated on new sexual partners when they satisfy me. Although it's not quite a fixation, I just like sexual activities—*kinky activities.* I crave the feeling of walking funny and feeling a cock, *balls deep, inside me.* A carnal craving; an awakening perhaps. That's what Rory has done to me.

When the man himself is at the curb that afternoon when I get off, I climb into his *baby* with a cheesy grin, clearly overexpressing myself with it.

"I don't think I've ever seen such a greeting from you before," he tells me as if I didn't know myself and how grumpy I normally am.

"Getting dicked down might have something to do with that. Speaking of..."

He tilts his head with a cute look that makes me melt. Rubbing my thighs in anticipation, I pull the parking brake and climb in his lap.

"We're at the curb—"

I initiate a quick make-out session, his hands cupping and squeezing my ass as my work dress slides up. The sound of his moan has me *swooning* and ready.

"Let me park us somewhere more discreet, at least?" he suggests, and I huff, falling back into my seat.

Rory pushes the parking brake back down and looks me over, his hand falling to my thigh, slowly moving up under my dress.

A smile curls upon my lips as he shifts the car into drive and I learn over, my hand sliding to the front of his jeans, working to unfasten them.

His thick cock springs free from his jeans, and I look up at Rory through my lashes. "Don't kill us," I murmur before licking up his thick vein.

I'm eager for a taste, and I can't help but bask in his sweaty man scent from working hard all day. *Fuck me.*

While focusing on sucking him off, he sucks in his teeth, cursing to himself.

"A woman on a mission, I see," he exhales, and his driving is erratic. "Fuck." His hand flies into my hair, scrunching a handful of it. "I'm almost to a spot, slow down just a little—I'll come if you don't."

Smirking, I decide to listen...*kinda.*

I give him one last lick, his tip popping out of my mouth

before leaning back into my seat. Rory grunts, whipping us into an unknown location.

Smirking over at him, Rory looks me up and down, grabbing my waist and groaning, "Come here."

I lift up my dress, sliding my panties down my thighs, then crawl over the center console and into his lap.

He cups my face. "Fuck, you're gorgeous when you're unleashed."

I claim his lips, positioning myself perfectly to take in his cock.

He eases into me as I hold onto the seat.

Rory makes it easier by pushing the seat back and laying it down. His tongue toys with mine. Here, in his car, we're matching each other in energy.

My hands grip his shoulders, and even though there's the lingering soreness between my legs, I'm greedy for more. I bask in the pleasure and pain he's giving me. It's been less than twelve hours and I'm already fucking dropping my panties for more.

Good news is that Rory isn't complaining about it either.

"That's it, Sugar, take me; use my cock."

I toss my head back, moaning over the sensations he's giving me while his hand squeezes my breast before trailing down my body. Settling that callused hand from working all day on my waist, he steals my breath away. The sensation of his warmth and that thick cock easing in and out of me, I pant heavily.

Fucking him in the car is far more worth it than my previous daydreaming of *on* the car. I don't want to stop at the car, I want to fuck him *everywhere*.

My dress lifts, and I happen to glimpse how he's watching me take in his cock. Gathering that it's his thing, he angles his hips while I lean further back to take him deeper. I decide to watch too. Granted, I find I enjoy watching Rory's reactions to me *and* him more fulfilling. His mouth is slightly opening, and he does this little thing when he slides all the way in me that I find endearing. A little biting of his lip before softly sighing, as if my pussy is where he belongs.

What a powerful feeling.

That man himself catches my ogling, and smirks, adjusting slightly before pumping at an angle that makes me cry out. It's so pleasant as I steady my hands on his thighs for emotional-sexual support.

"There you go, just like that. You take everything I'm giving. Keep it up, Sugar."

My pussy answers with a grip that makes him groan. I quiver and wish all our clothes disappeared so I can lick the salty goodness of his sweaty skin.

"Fuck, I'm gonna come soon. I'm going to pump you so full and taste our divine flavor once we're home."

Taking in his praise, he keeps hitting deep within so much that I'm panting desperately with the rush and rising of a needed orgasm.

"Fuck, yes, come all over me—make me yours."

Realizing his words, I fall apart all around him, crying out as he pulses and shudders with me.

Filled up with his hot cum, I tug on my lip and let my neck roll as I feel him empty out into me.

My eyes fly open once he pulls me toward him, kissing up my chest and neck.

"I won't be able to function if you do this every day, baby."

I use my inner muscles to squeeze him in response as he makes unholy sounds.

"Evil, evil woman."

I huff out a laugh at how the tables turned while leaning forward to wrap my arms around him and plant my lips on his.

His words ring in my skull. *"Make me yours."*

I kind of just did, didn't I?

Chapter Nineteen

Rory

This woman turns me on like no other. As she thought about me, *I thought about this.*

We stumble through the front door of our home. I lift Nikki onto the island, her legs falling open as if an answer to my earlier prayer. I crouch down, my tongue lapping at the mixture of us. The impromptu fuck in my car was—*I can't even begin to describe it or what Nikki does to me.*

I'm brought back to the present as Nikki's legs squeeze around my head, and her fingers tangle into my hair, pushing my face into her sweet pussy.

I relish the sounds of her moans which only grow louder the closer she is to coming on my tongue. Until she finally moans a soft, *"Fuck,"* before her legs go lax on the counter.

Wasting no time, I scoop her up and carry her to bed.

Crawling in next to her after I strip down, I wrap my arm around Nikki, pulling her into me. My life has done a complete one-eighty since I kidnapped this beautiful crea-ture. I no longer have thoughts of killing. Not even an urge —well, except for when we trauma-bonded, then I wanted to murder her family and her *fucking ex,* but I guess that would be wrong.

I digress.

It's strange though, how Nikki was the one thing that would turn my life on its head and send it in a healthier direction. From victim to roommate to savior.

Nikki's breathing deepens, and she falls into a deeper sleep. The sounds of her sleeping next to me lull me into a deep slumber of my own. My last thought is Nikki and my newfound energy for *life.*

Friday after dinner, I decide to ask more about her tastes in kink.

"I was thinking," I begin, plopping down next to her on the couch.

Nikki gives me a *blank stare.* "That's scary."

I can't help but laugh at her jab. "I was thinking about the kink club, and I wanted to get a feeling of what kinks you're into before we go. I want you to be more comfortable in that type of space with me."

She blinks, once, twice, three times, and my palms begin to sweat.

"I have a high pain tolerance," she begins without missing a beat, twirling her pasta on her fork. "I like bondage, being tied up or restrained. Sensory impact is also a favorite, t*o no one's surprise.*"

My mind runs a million miles a minute over her words, and suddenly I can see her strung up in my rope ties, unable to move. Various scenes flash of such dark dreams; I nearly drool, and my cock is ready to fucking go.

She's tied up and helpless, consensually, of course. Moaning and coming on my tongue too. I can see it so clearly in my mind's eye.

My fantasies continue to run away with me as she eats and continues rattling off more things that don't help my mental imagery. *I'm harder than sin, and that's a lot coming from me.*

"I don't care for anal, although licking is fine. Electro stuff or things involving scat or piss—not for me. Exhibitionism is good and voyeuristic stuff too. Toys are great, never tried nipple clamps... Hmm, what else am I missing?" She pauses and the room feels too hot as my cock throbs.

"I mentioned being open to multiple people before, *I think.* Oh! I'm definitely a bottom, but I'm open to trying to top. That's it, I think."

I can't think straight as her eyes find mine. A bead of sweat is making its way down my neck as I nod, stuffing my face quickly before I drain my glass of water. She's watching me carefully, no doubt wondering why I'm acting weird.

"What about you?" There's uncertainty in her tone when she asks; my hands grab my knees to focus on what I like. Suddenly, I can't seem to recall a single thing.

What is wrong with you, Rory?

"I like doing everything you described and I'm open-minded too."

She considers me, finishing her food. "Are you okay?"

I shake my head, stand up, and try to remember if I have anything to use. Since I've never brought anyone home, I don't have too many materials—only my kill kit that I burned in the van.

Shit-fuck.

"Rory."

The soft calling of my name brings me back to the

present. Nikki gets up and follows me to where I grab two ties that go with suits that I'm shocked I have. *When did I buy those?* I'm not a fancy guy.

Her hand rests on my back.

"I don't have much, but I wanted to test things out in a different way tonight, if you're open to it."

"I don't care about that," she says as I turn around with the ties in my hands.

"I'm not okay. My problem is," I begin, backing her into the wall near the bathroom door, "the imagery you gave me. *I'm so fucking hard right now.* I can't fucking think or breathe, Niks."

She tilts her chin up, her hands on my chest before the other travels to my cargo pants.

"Oh really?" Her voice dips, and I nudge myself flush to her, my dick practically in her hands, begging for it.

"My other problem is," I lean close to her neck, inhaling her sugary scent, "It's only been a few days and you're all I think about. I don't think about killing, *I think of my newest obsession—you.*"

Running my nose up the column of her neck, she smells sweet—like *sugar. My Sugar.*

"I've developed a taste for you, one I can't survive without."

I hear her exhaling and I lick her neck hard.

"Rory, I can't think when you say things like that."

Placing a kiss on her collarbone, I can't help but smile.

"Then, don't. Let me tie your hands to our bed and tease you until you beg for me to fill you."

"Fuck me," she says breathlessly, and I take her hands and lead her backwards to the bed.

Her words are in her eyes, glassy and lust-filled, the pre-bedroom eyes look I'm finding I adore.

I undress her, gently pushing her to the bed.

"Remember your colors and get in the middle with your arms raised."

"Yes, *Sir*."

My dick twitches as I take in her curves. Her perky, full breasts beg for my tongue and teeth. Her hips dip down towards those thick thighs that I love gripping or having them wrapped around my fucking skull. Green eyes are on me as her arms rise to the iron bar headboard.

"I'm going to tie one around your mouth, and the other for your arms. Alright?"

She nods, and I strip bare, my hard cock like a beacon while I climb in and straddle her. Nikki keeps her eyes on me while I wrap one tie around her mouth, but not tight, because I still need her to beg for it.

"Too tight? Say something."

It's slightly muffled but I still hear, "Eh goo," which translates to *it's good*.

Smirking, I tie her arms around the iron bar above her head. Making it tight but not too tight, I take my hands afterward, and rub down her body, admiring the hourglass shape of her. That warm softness beneath my fingertips. I can't tell if her skin is heated or if it's mine.

Pliant beneath my touch, I lean down, planting soft kisses to her cheek then down to her shoulder. Trailing kisses down to her hip, Nikki wiggles slightly underneath me, arching her back. A sly smile crosses my mouth, and I gently grab onto her hips, my tongue tracing circles around her navel then down to her thighs right down to the sweet spot between her legs.

"My greedy slut."

Throaty noises escape her even though they're muffled.

I spend adequate time licking her cunt and gripping her

luscious thighs that wrap around my head. Not quite wanting her to come yet, I feel her swell and try to begin to fuck my face.

Although I enjoy how she fucks my face, that's not my purpose.

I kiss her inner thigh, holding her legs apart so she can't squeeze my skull, and I hear a groan above me.

"Beg for it," I murmur against her skin, kissing down her inner thigh.

Mimicking the movements on her other leg, I move so I can flip her over on her belly.

"I'll give you this cock once you beg," I say as I pull her hips toward me and rub my dick where she's soaked.

Nikki tries to move her hips, but I swat her ass in warning.

"Use your words, Sugar."

I move my throbbing dick and lick her from entrance to rim to prove a point.

She's making grunts and noises, and when she speaks clearly, I know she's pulled the tie loose from around her mouth. Before I can react, she says, "Please, fuck me, Rory."

I lick her ass in response.

"Which hole? Fingers or cock?"

She sighs as I lick her clit.

"Put your cock in my pussy and *fuck me*."

Magic words earn what she begs for.

I pull her hips up and back, so she's flat minus her ass while her arms are tugging the tie restraint.

"That's my girl," I praise, sliding home.

Holding her glorious round ass, my head tilts back. I go slow at first, enjoying her tight walls wrapping around my cock like a little cock sleeve. The relief I finally feel is almost too much, because apparently, I'm going too slow.

"Harder, Rory—*please.*"

"*So sexy when you beg for me.*"

I build my pace and strength, hitting deeper.

Her sounds turn unholy and *fuck*, it's undoing me. I'm practically possessed.

"I'm going to come, and then you're going to come all over this cock."

She cries out in agreement as I bend and circle her clit with my thumb. The moan of my previous fantasies reaches my ears as she squeezes my cock, and I pump her full.

I squeeze her ass in appreciation, catching my breath on the comedown.

Slowing and stopping, I pull out.

"How are your wrists?" I ask and untie her quickly.

"They're fine," she says once she's free, rolling onto her back with heavy breaths. Then, she puts her hands to her temples before making an explosion noise, "But my mind is blown."

I kiss her cheek in thanks, moving to grab a towel and a wipe to clean us up. It takes no time at all. Once I finish, I crawl in bed after turning off the lights. The only light is cascading from the city beyond the window.

We roll to our sides, facing each other. I grab her hands, linking our fingers and folding our arms between us. I place a gentle kiss on her hand, and she does the same, a gesture I find to be sweet, just as she is.

XOXO
LOVE

Chapter Twenty

Rory

Once we clean up the place Saturday, Nikki glances at me from her armoire.

"What does one wear to a sex club? Nothing?" She focuses back on finding something to wear as I smirk.

"It's *kink*, but on the other hand you aren't exactly wrong," I say, pulling on black pants that are comfortable and movable. "Legally, you have to wear clothes *in*. The rest is optional. There are private rooms you can go in and observe too. Some are staged and some are free reign. A dance floor takes up the main space where you can view public scenes and play around to those who are consenting. There's a rig setup too for rope suspension scenes"

She looks back behind her, meeting my gaze briefly. "What else?"

Nikki continues rummaging through her clothes as I put on a plain black t-shirt, recalling how the club does things.

"Well, there's various bracelets depending on what you're looking for. First time guests are purple, which you'll get. There are memberships people can get if they want to be a part of the VIP club. There are also options for those who go on occasion, it's just a cover charge like everywhere else, except pricier due to the nature of the place."

"What are the other bracelet colors for?" She leans into the armoire, digging around.

"Yellow is curious, green is for submissives only, orange for switches, and blue is for dominants. Gold is for top tier VIP patrons who pay monthly fees. They kinda get free reign of the place and can take classes for free. I'm sure there's other perks, but I'm obviously not some rich asshole."

She snorts a laugh. "Fair enough." She strips out of her clothes, not caring that I'm there watching. "What do you typically do when you go?"

I rub the back of my head, sighing. "I mingle and fuck."

Nikki pulls a black dress out of the armoire, looking over her shoulder at me. "Oh, right, you did mention that... Quite the fuckboy, aren't you?"

She pulls her black dress over her head, adjusting it to her body.

I stare at her blankly, my lips pressing into a thin line.

My eyes narrow at her as she meets my gaze again. "Tell me I'm wrong," she insists, and *I will not*.

I groan, pushing my tongue into my cheek trying to calm my rising irritation that I suddenly feel.

"You know you're not wrong, Nicole, but I also don't do this whole–" I pause my hands moving in circles in front of me as I search for the words. "You know, the relationship thing."

Nikki chuckles, pulling out a pair of black pumps. "Yeah, sounds like a fuckboy to me."

I bite down on my lip watching as she pulls on the first heel then the second.

"I'm not a goddamn fuckboy," I snap while she balances

herself in the heels. "And I haven't been since I fucking met you."

Nikki smiles, coming over to wrap her arms around my neck, "But you're a little fuck toy, aren't you? *My* fuck toy." She wiggles her eyebrows at me, trying to make light of the situation.

I decide to give up on the conversation since she's not fucking getting it.

I place my hands on her hips and gently push her away from me, stepping away from her. "What happened to the boyfriend-relationship and living together? A *relationship,* as you spelled out before."

She bends over to adjust something on her heel, and her round ass is nearly on display, distracting me.

"Yeah, yeah. You can still be my fuck-toy tonight, though. Don't be so grumpy about it. I'm only teasing you. Labels are dumb anyway. Our relationship is unconventional, Rory."

I run my hands through my hair, taking a deep breath. "You drive me crazy, Niks."

"Likewise, fuck-toy," she says nonchalantly.

Marching over after she finishes with her shoes, I smack her ass one good time. The yelp she gives me satisfies me enough.

"So, it seems like you're in a *brat* mood, no surprise with your *mouth.*" I pause as she turns around, looking up slowly at me under her lashes. It does something to me as I distract myself with a question and a statement. "What do you want to do while we're there? I recommend watching and observing for your first time. It can be overwhelming."

She raises a singular brow, daring to say something smart. "I'll let you know what I'm not ready for. I am a woman who can use her words, as you like to point out with *my mouth*. Neurodivergent, sorry, *neurospicy*, doesn't mean inept—thank you very much."

"Yep, *brat mode*," I mumble under my breath.

"What are *you* in the mood for tonight?" She changes the topic to me while moving to the bathroom to apply some makeup.

Nikki fixes her hair back and grabs her makeup bag for something and begins painting her face. I don't know shit about makeup, so I'm not sure what she's using on her face to cover it.

"You don't need makeup, you know that, right?"

She gives me the side eye and shrugs.

I lean against the doorframe, watching her paint her face and adding something that makes her cheeks darken. Moving my attention from her already beautiful face, the black dress is suitable for her, hugging those curves in all the right places. Simple, but so fucking sexy. She doesn't even have to try hard to be sexy. She just has to *exist*, and I'm itching to fuck her. Not just fucking, but being around her, and dare I say it, *her smart fucking mouth*. She may not understand my irritation, but I'm trying to show her a different side of me *as I'm learning this new side too*.

The line between the past and present still seems to blur together, and it gets under my skin, as I'm finding out. How can I make positive changes when she takes these digs at me?

Snapping out of it, I come back to said present. She's applying something to her lips and another thing to make her eyelashes darker and thicker.

"I never said or thought you were inept or incapable. I'm just looking out for you, Nikki. I keep trying to show you that I'm trying to change and be better. *Not* a fuckboy or that serial killer you met in a crappy ass basement."

Green eyes meet mine briefly before fixating on the mirror to apply finishing touches to her makeup.

"Interesting choice of words, but I'll take it. I wasn't trying to upset you. I don't always know when to back off, and I know I can be a bit much. Thank you for telling me. I do appreciate you looking out, Rory."

Any earlier tension melts away with the look she gives me. Although she looks fantastic without makeup, I can't help but enjoy how she transforms with women's face paint, as I like to call it. She looks sultry and tempting all dolled up. My name on her lips is all I want to hear.

I cross my arms and wait a moment before answering her earlier question of what *I'm in the mood for.* Her. *Naked and being fucked by me.*

"My only plan tonight is to fuck you. How it happens, and the specifics, I'll leave up to you, Sugar," I say in a husky way that brings a smile to her face.

I'll take her any which way. My eyes won't be the only ones on her.

"Are other people off limits?" she asks once she sprays something over her face, a setting spray of some sort from what the bottle says on the counter.

"I'm not sure, I've never been in this situation before," I admit. "Do you want to fuck other people?"

She shrugs. "I'm not against it. If anything, I'll be flirty? But I don't expect anyone to talk to me as a newbie and with you by my side."

Uncertain of myself or her meaning, I move off the door frame, walking away before I start another argument. I don't think I can fathom anyone else touching her, because I won't fucking let them.

Instead, my mouth utters, "Live your best life." I move to grab my own shoes and wallet.

"Likewise." I catch a glimpse of her, and I can't tell if she wants me to be jealous or not, or if it was my nonchalance or reaction. I seriously can't tell anymore.

"What's the cover fee?"

"I got it," I tell her while walking toward the door with her in tow.

On the way down, I cross my arms and lean against the corner as she stands nearby. Her eyes are on me.

"I'm not going to touch anyone else or have them touch me. I was just saying earlier."

I avoid looking at her. "Okay." If I say anything past that, I'll give away my jealousy. *The fuck if I let someone touch her.*

Her hand on my shoulder causes me to finally look at her as the elevator shakes when it gets to the bottom.

"I mean it." Her expression is softer, along with her tone. "We're figuring each other out with our relationship. It wouldn't be fair to either of us to introduce more people. I just keep messing up tonight with my words." She takes a deep breath, letting her hand fall from my bicep.

I uncross my arms. "I'm navigating just as you are, Niks."

Nikki gives me a half-smile, and I pull open the doors for us to walk to my black car. I rub the hood of her in appreciation before I open Nikki's door.

"Let's have a good night, Niks, alright?" She nods, touching my hand as she gets in and I shut the door after she's seated.

We both buckle in, and I drive to the club.

A minute after being in the car, she randomly asks, "Did you like that Getaway Driver playlist I made?"

Trying to remember, she decides for me by snatching my phone and putting it on. "To *refresh your memory* on my kickass music tastes."

Shaking my head, I laugh low in my throat.

Song titles like *Bad Decisions and SICKO* are just some of the few that play before *Hunting We Will Go* goes on.

"You think you're funny, don't you?" I ask, amusement dangling from my lips.

The grin on her face says it all to me.

"Pain in my ass," I mumble to myself.

She makes a kissing sound with the face to go with it.

Chuckling to myself, we arrive in the private lot and pay the parking fee before being escorted in. Nikki takes a hair tie from her wrist and does a messy bun while we walk in the doors. After we get ID'd, she gets a purple bracelet, and I decide for blue.

First timers get a tour of the club by a staff member of their preferred gender. Nikki has no preference so a person who identifies as non-binary gives us a tour. They tell us their name is Bunny.

Bunny has a purple pixie cut and is wearing a latex onesie with—*bunny ears*.

I find it amusing as I follow them through the tour. The dance floor dungeon that's largely spaced out with play areas: a large rig with various rope and safety notes for patrons, a spinning wheel, a Saint Andrew's cross, benches and tables, and a large four-poster bed in the corner. The bar is in a separate room off in the back.

Bunny leads us down past the room with the bar to the long hallway with endless seeming doors. They show us the voyeur room, *the communal fucking room,* and make a mention of special nights throughout the month dedicated to various fetishes and classes—at an extra charge, of course.

We make it back to the dungeon room where people have already gathered to dance, watch, or begin scenes.

Bunny waves at us before walking off.

"Wanna grab a drink? I'm overstimulated and need a minute," Nikki says immediately after Bunny disappears back to their station near the front.

I take Nikki's hand without question, leading her to the quieter backroom where the bar is.

She's squeezing my hand, and sighs in relief once we make it to the bar.

"A margarita, please," she says to the younger blonde gentleman working the bar. He's wearing an orange Switch bracelet.

There aren't too many people in the bar room, and I often wonder if it's on purpose for those seeking a quieter space.

He looks at me for my order. "Bourbon on the rocks," I answer.

"You okay?" I ask quietly, wondering how the night is going to go. Sometimes, I realize how overstimulation is not always bad and can be good too—I couldn't tell which was which at this point and time though.

She nods, sitting at the bar stool.

"A lot to take in. I'm not sure where to start either."

I sit next to her, trying to be encouraging but also feeling relieved. "There's no hurry to decide. Enjoy your margarita. Let me know if you need space and want to go around and explore or watch with or without me."

"I'll let you know."

A margarita is placed in front of her and my drink too. I pay right away, leaving a tip.

Deciding not to talk so she gets a minute to process the tour, I enjoy the burn of my bourbon. Drinking it slowly, I debate on what I want to watch in the main dungeon room.

My thoughts then drift on picturing Nikki on the cross or bent over the spanking bench. Not being able to help my dirty thoughts, I feel her eyes on me as if she too can picture it.

"I'll start at the main room, observe and go from there. Do you dance at all?"

She finishes her marg, and I shrug.

"I'm indifferent to dancing honestly."

She huffs and puffs. "For a kinky bastard, you sure are *boring*."

I look at her in disbelief. *"Excuse me?"*

"Did I stutter?"

My hand gets twitchy to paddle that ass.

"Keep on with your sassy attitude, and I'll have your ass red over that spanking bench for all to see. *Don't test me.*"

She smirks, looking so smug with herself.

"Ready when you are," I grumble, pushing away my empty glass.

Leaving the bar, sultry music draws us closer and closer to the dance floor dungeon room.

The people moving their bodies on the dance floor are *mostly* clothed. The others participating in scenes are not.

Curious about her reactions to all of it, I follow her lead toward where a couple of others are watching a scene of a woman on the Saint Andrew's cross.

The submissive for the scene is strung up with a blind fold. The female domme is doing sensory play with a flogger. Nikki's eyes are locked on them, and I find it hot *how* she's watching them with this smoldering, turned on look she has. It sort of reminds me of her pretty bedroom eyes. This is different though. *That* is for *me only*.

I can tell she doesn't care much for the couple fucking on the bed for all to see. The two women in front of us in their scene have all of her focus.

While *she* has all of *mine*.

XOXO
LOVE

Chapter Twenty One

Nikki

The women in front of us has me hyper-focused. The pro domme has this transfixed look upon her face, and it almost looks romantic how she's using the sensory flogger on her sub for the scene.

The sub's eyes are closed, her mouth slack with a look of utmost bliss.

Suddenly, I can feel myself in her shoes, the sensations of flogger and the binds on the cross. Wet warmth pools between my thighs, and I'm lost in the scene. I forget about Rory for a while, at least until the pro domme kisses her sub.

He's behind me with his chin on my shoulder, his breath lingering in my ears. Despite the music, I can hear him breathing.

"Do you want that to be you, Sugar?"

Leaning slightly into him, I nod. *It's fucking hot*, obviously I want to be on that cross being worshipped.

Rory tugs on my earlobe as I watch the domme switch gears and toys. I see her whisper something in the sub's ear, and the sub nods in agreement. It's sweet how she caresses her face before bending down and taking out a vibrator.

Oh, fuck.

Other people are around us, and I don't have a care in the world. Rory and I watch while the sub shakes and cries over the pleasure from the toy.

I'm so wet, I almost can't think straight. Live scenes are better than internet porn any day.

Rory's hand finds my ass, grabbing slightly before I turn around in his hold.

We're being locked in a sensuous stare down, blue-green eyes staring into my heated soul.

"Dance with me," I say, nudging him away from the watching crowd to the dancing one.

I'm slightly overstimulated again from watching and need to get out some of the energy, yet I want to channel it instead of quieting it.

I place my hands on his shoulders and swing my hips, rolling them. Sexual energy has a hold of me, and I'm feeling incredible. Although, that sort of sexual energy permeates the entire dungeon.

It doesn't slip my notice how Rory's eyes occasionally glance down to see how I'm moving my hips, even with his hands on them.

Then, he licks his lips as if I'm something to devour, and it gives me the ego boost I need to step up my sensual dancing. I turn around and throw my ass back against him, moving it in circles before dropping down to sit on my knees briefly. When I come back up, I bend over and wiggle my hips.

His attention is *all on me* by the way his dick presses against me, and I roll my body, until I'm standing. I keep throwing my ass back until he joins me. Pressed tighter to me, his hands then wandered. We're both leaning into each other, and I let sensuality take over me.

The heat of the room, the booming beats, his whisky and musk scent mixed with sweat, and the way his hands travel and claim while we move, I'm riding a fucking high. There's someone fucking on the bed in the corner, another couple on the spinning wheel, and the sexy couple at the cross are finishing their scene.

My senses zero in on Rory's heat against mine, and we get a couple of onlookers before they go off their own way or dance with whoever they're with. It doesn't matter much to me.

I'm focused on the sexy male behind me.

Despite him appearing indifferent about dancing, he's moving like he's almost fucking me. Part of me wonders if he would.

We could really shake up this party by fucking on the dance floor. I'm horny enough to not care, so I'm curious if he'll lift up my dress and try.

My hand travels to his zipper, undoing it.

His hand flies into my hair, pulling it back at my bun so his lips are at my ear.

"You want me to fuck you, right here?"

My hand takes him out, palming him as I nod hastily. His cock is already semi-hard, but with my teasing it's a solid force to be reckoned with.

I think I hear a grunt, but I'm unsure with the music.

"Dip down and up again for me then."

My scalp prickles at his grip before loosening. I raise the back of my dress up while his finger swiftly glides through and I hear him suck his finger.

Once I repeat my move from earlier of dropping down while I dance, I bend over. Rory slides home, pumping twice and pulling me up against him. His hand slides in my hair as my messy bun unravels.

"So fucking wet for me. Goddamn, Niks, you're so fucking sexy."

I can tell by the way he says it, he's in *dominant-mode,* or so I like to think anyway.

He stretches me while we gyrate on the dance floor. I'm slightly surprised we both lasted so long without doing something of the sort, but now that he's in me, *I'm in heaven.* Forget overstimulation, who's she while I'm getting fucked?

My eyes drift close as I arch my back, still moving my body to the beats while he speaks his body's language by rolling his hips, pumping my pussy full of him.

A curse leaves me as he sucks on the side of my neck. The music aids in the mood, otherwise I'd question if I'd be able to do what we're doing period. I moan as he begins to fuck me harder. Then, he teases me by slowing down, leaning into my ear.

"We have an audience, Sugar. Slowly get on your knees with me."

Fluttering my eyes open briefly, we both go in unison down to the floor slowly. I'm spread on all fours with him inside.

His hand rubs up my spine before entwining his fingers in my hair. Cock consumes me while he slides in and out, until I bend further, and he hits deeper. *Jesus, Mary Mother, and Joseph.*

Lost in how hard he's fucking me, I feel his finger on my clit. My pussy swells excitedly, swallowing him up with every thrust. I am swimming in it as my head tilts back in his hand and I practically yell out a moan. *Part of it was for show,* but the other half of me knows it wasn't.

With the break in the music, I know it's heard by Rory

and whoever is standing near enough. My eyes remain closed though.

He pulls me up against him with his hand wrapped around my throat in a lovely hand necklace that has me coming all over his cock. He puts his face beside mine grunting before slamming home one final time, coming with me.

It's unbelievable as I dive headfirst into *space*.

"Fucking hell. *You are perfect, Sugar.*"

Taking deep breaths, I feel him pull out and fix my thong before helping me stand.

Before I can even think or speak, his lips are on mine with his hands cupping my face.

When he releases me, my eyes struggle to stay and remain open. Rory leads me off the dance floor to where some empty booths are. He pulls me into his lap, cradling me as I bury my face into his neck, inhaling his sweaty, sex-filled scent that I find I'm beginning to enjoy.

"You did so well. I'm proud of you," he praises, kissing my forehead.

I'm on a happy little cloud, proud that this killer-man is practicing good aftercare. *Boy, do I feel cared for*. Never thought I'd ever think *that*.

Barely coherent, we stay there until I sit up, running my hand up his chest.

Concern laces those green-blues as they search my face.

"Are you okay, sweetheart?"

I nod. "I am now. Thank you."

He runs a hand through my hair before leaning in to kiss my cheek. His care for me breaks my heart.

I want and need to dislike him for all he's done to get us here to this point. Except, the more he acts like this, the more I find how much I *like* him.

That part is unsettling in itself.

Do I dare let myself fall, knowing disaster probably awaits?

My mind drifts on those thoughts as we leave the club and head home. Then, we continue our aftercare by curling in close in bed with me as the little spoon.

I wonder if my heart will let me fall, or if I will even have the choice in the matter.

As if Rory would let me have a choice. The man has consumed my body and mind.

Now, he's worming his way into my dark heart.

XOXO
LOVE

Chapter Twenty Two

Nikki

Weeks pass by me in a blur. Sometimes I simply check out. I remember working and falling more *into depth* with Rory since I refuse to say "love"—*yet*.

My apartment has been squared away and taken care of. It's all so *official*. The rug has been pulled from under me, and it feels crazy to say *I love you* to a previous serial killer.

Part of me wants to go away for a while to figure it out, and the other part of me is unbalanced. The situation with Rory hits me in waves as I try to rationalize it, *again*, for the thousandth time.

I wonder if he'd let me take a weekend trip away without fear of me ratting him out. I haven't had a single moment to myself for longer than a few hours. I *need* time to myself.

How do I talk to him without him freaking out? Do I love Rory or do I just love to fuck him? *Fuck, I need space.*

I sit at our high top table, the one Rory was aware enough to invest in for me.

Poking around at the chicken and veggies on my plate, I

struggle to find the right words to tell him how I'm feeling without setting him off.

Rory beats me to it.

"What's up with you, Niks? You've been acting strange lately."

His statement baffles me. Rory is apparently more in tune to me than I realize.

I exhale, setting my fork down. "I–" A short pause, and I twist my hands in my lap. "I'm not really sure how to talk about it."

Even though I'm staring down at my plate, I can feel Rory's eyes boring into my head.

"Well, *try* anyway," he states.

I don't respond right away, still finding the right words. "Nicole?"

I take a deep breath, still refusing to meet his eyes. "I– Well, I'm used to having time to myself that lasts longer than a few hours."

After another steady breath, my hands are clammy. I try to shake them out, trying to get rid of the extra stimulation that's flooding through me.

"I'm feeling out of sorts not having it. We live together now, which is fine, but something essential in my routine has been taken away from me and I want—no, *need*—to find a way to get it back. I wasn't sure how to bring it up or ask, or how to make you feel safe trusting me away from you."

I gulp in air, not realizing how fast I was talking.

The silence between us is heavy, and my mind feels like scrambled eggs. I'm not sure how he's taking it. All of a sudden, I'm hyper-aware of everything and how afraid of his response I truly am, so much that my leg starts bouncing in anticipation of the outburst he's bound to have.

Rory sighs heavily. "Why didn't you say so sooner?"

I find a crumb to look at on the floor.

"Nikki," he says calmly, and with how he says it, I slowly meet his gaze. "I was wondering why you pulled away from me." He gets up and moves over to my side.

The chair I'm in rotates, and soon I'm face-to-face with him.

"I want us to trust each other. If you need a weekend away from me, that's *okay*. Remember, I'm used to being alone too, not that I'm bothered by your presence or need time away. In fact, I want to be glued to your side most of the time."

I catch a hint of a smile as he holds my face in his hands, rubbing my cheeks with his thumbs.

When I don't say anything, mulling over his words, he continues. "For your safety, at least keep your location on? It's for my own peace of mind too. Can we compromise on that?"

I nod in agreement while he kisses my forehead, trying to ease my shaking.

"Do you have a particular place in mind?" he asks quietly, searching my face with a look of concern.

"The beach sounds nice."

"Well, I work this weekend. Want to do it then?"

Nodding once more, he kisses me and wraps his arms around me. With the squeeze he gives me, it's as if my body recognizes the fight or flight state and decides to ease up.

I find it more comforting than I should, and I can't help but begin to cry at the agonizing relief I'm too shocked to feel. All the worries and tension I've been holding in rush out.

Rory went from *being* unsafe to *feeling safe*.

My mind can't fucking comprehend it. Too many

changes so soon. My processing time may be more delayed than most people, but *damn.*

When he notices my shoulders shaking and a sob escaping, his hold tightens. "Oh, Niks."

Releasing my emotions is sometimes uncomfortable for me, and I hate myself for crying in his arms. Men may be told about withholding emotions to remain strong, but I disagree. Women are held to a similar standard, otherwise we're deemed emotional crybabies, more or less.

"Let's go sit on the couch," he suggests, and I don't want to let go, so we awkwardly make our way to the couch with me attached to him.

"I don't want you to be afraid of me anymore, Nikki." He keeps his calm tone and demeanor once we're on the couch, and I lay my head on his lap, burying my face into his stomach.

He brushes my hair with his finger while the other hand rubs my arm.

I hiccup, feeling *so stupid.* It always happens when there's an emotional outburst like this. I expect the worst and then when it's the opposite, my brain hits a wall, so crying is how I respond.

"I'm not going to hurt you, unless you ask for me to—in kinky situations."

I sob harder, trying to calm myself, but my body decides otherwise. He continues comforting me while I release the pent-up emotions I've been holding in a tight little box. Eventually, the water works ease up, and my head is fucking pounding. A side effect that I fucking *loathe.*

Emotions are stupid, and I hate this regulation bullshit.

"I hate crying like that," I mumble more to myself than to him.

"Don't apologize. I should apologize to *you.* I'm the

asshole here, not you. I'll say it as many times as I need to. *I'm sorry, Nikki.* I love you and I'll spend the rest of my life making it up to you if I have to."

I glance up at him after wiping my face.

His hand caught another tear, rubbing his thumb over my cheek.

"Want me to book your weekend for you or do you want to do it?"

I shake my head, laying my hand on his stomach, feeling his wet shirt.

"I'll do it. Sorry about your shirt."

He moves slightly to pull it off.

"There, now it's no concern. It's all yours to use."

Rory places it in my hand before going back to running his fingers through my hair.

In that moment, the gesture is extremely comforting.

I close my eyes as my scalp tingles in wake of his gentle fingers massaging me. Taking deep breaths, I manage to calm myself down completely.

My thoughts drift back on his words, and my eyes pop open at a realization. Rory is already looking at me in a fond way that makes me squirm.

"Did you say you love me?"

"I did."

We lock gazes, and the longer I stare, the more *I see.* He's vulnerable and bare. Based on the life he lives and told me about, I don't think he loved anyone, *ever.*

While I'm flattered, I lay there exposed and vulnerable too.

How would I know if I love him out of fear or for *him?*

"There's no pressure to say or return the affection, Niks. If and when you feel the same."

All I can think to say is a low murmur of, *"Thank you."*

"Do you want to eat, lay in bed, or lay here?" His voice is quiet, and I find I'm not hungry.

"My head hurts, so some aspirin and laying in bed sounds good."

"Okay, I'll put dinner away."

He carefully moves me so he can get up.

I stare up at the ceiling, feeling weird for not returning his words. I need to figure that out for myself. Did I ever truly love anyone or just the idea of them?

Familial love is different, and even then, it's kind of forced because we're born into our families. He's given me a lot to think about, that's for sure. *Future me problem.*

My heart aches over his tenderness of bringing meds and water before snuggling in bed with me as the little spoon.

XOXO
LOVE

Chapter Twenty Three

Nikki

The ocean waves crash at my feet. The water is warm against my heated skin from laying in the sun. I made sure to use all the sunscreen for my pale ass self. It's refreshing and freeing to be there in the moment. A peace I didn't know I needed. The word *peace* is a concept I hardly ever understood. People talk about it, but it's hard for me to experience and get out of my noisy head. While medication regulates me better than without it, it's not a cure. All I know is the chaos in my mind and life. If I didn't have my therapist and meds, I'd be more lost and unregulated.

The water crashing against me reminds me that everything will be okay. The tides change all the time, and in the grand scheme of cycles, there's always ebb and flow. I'm the same way in a sense as most human bodies are made primarily of water.

I want to *forgive*. I want to be able to reciprocate other things outside of sex. *Even if the sex is worthy enough on its own.* Sex doesn't cure everything...*just most things.*

The sand between my toes is grounding me back to the

planet. I would need to be better about my coping mechanisms, so I don't fall into a dark pit of doom. As my therapist says, "Feelings need to be felt, not ignored. If they're ignored, then it comes out whether we want them to or not."

She's a pain in my ass, but the good kind. *She's right.*

Wading further into the water, I tilt my head back to the sun.

Part of me wonders if Rory would like the beach or doing various activities outside of kink and lounging at home.

I put the mental note away for later and enjoy the rest of the afternoon swimming and laying under the sun. I get slightly sunburnt considering the time outside, but I knock out hard in my hotel room. After eating a mean breakfast of protein and orange juice, I spend the Sunday doing the same thing on the beach, reading raunchy romances on my phone.

Rory says good morning and good night both days. His location says he's at work, so I resume reading a fantasy book after the raunchy one. It's nice to check out and get out of my head. *It's exhausting being in there, honestly.*

I wander into a seafood restaurant nearby, eating all the seafood I can manage before walking on the beach at sunset.

The weekend getaway was needed, however, I find my mind drifting. I hate to admit to myself, but Rory should've been here with me. Often, realizations happen like this for me—delayed, like the internet explorer browser with 124 frozen tabs.

Next getaway.

Next.

I'm already thinking about a future with him. *Fuck.*

The more I think about it, the more I realize whatever

feelings I have for Rory are not completely out of fear. When he's not getting on my nerves, I happen to enjoy his company. Our quirks somehow mesh well with each other, oddly enough.

Driving the rental car hours back into the city the following morning, I can't help but feel excited to see him. Once I drop the car off and get a ride near his place, he opens the door for me when I tell him I'm home.

He's wearing sweatpants and no shirt.

"Fuck, I'm happy to see you. I missed you."

Like a dog wagging his tail when he sees his owner.

I smile as Rory squeezes me into a tight hug.

"Come drink coffee with me and tell me about your weekend." He leaves room for me to walk inside, and I head in where I drop my bag off next to the couch.

After I kick off my shoes, he joins me with a fun, spooky Halloween mug. I smile over it, because as much as I'm changing because of him, he is too. Never thought I'd be any kind of influence over someone else before. Strangely, I don't mind it. At least he's not killing, but there's no way that I *saved* him—what a ludicrous thought.

He places his arm on the back of the couch behind me, rubbing the back of my head.

"I saw you didn't leave the beach. How do you feel?"

Leaning into his hand, I hear him sip his coffee.

"Much better."

I move my head to the side to take him in, admiring the various tattoos he has on his arms and chest.

"Do you have any interest in going with me somewhere next time?"

He holds his mug, those pretty eyes finding mine.

"You want me to go with you?"

I nod as he takes another sip.

"Then, I'm there."

"Really?" I question, surprised by his response.

"I want to be where you are... Even though I missed you and having you next to me in bed, I'm happy you got the R&R you needed."

I lean against his arm, kissing his inner elbow.

"It's as I said, sometimes I need a getaway from the same four walls. It's why I used to walk to work, minus the exercise part."

"Fair enough."

I wait a few minutes before asking him another question so he can enjoy his coffee.

"I guess I don't know what you'll enjoy doing."

"If you're around, I don't care what we do. I'm happy being around you, so I'm simple in my pleasures, kinky activities aside. If you want to go to a water park or amusement park, then I'll go. I want to experience life with you. You're *mine*."

It never fails; the minute he says *'you're mine'*, I'm a bitch in heat.

Once he finishes his cup of brew, I move so I'm straddling him. My summer beach dress rides up to my thighs.

"I'm learning how to figure that out, too."

I drape my arms over his shoulders, leaning in for a short and sweet kiss.

"I'm yours every time you look at me with those pretty eyes of yours. Every time my cock is in your mouth or when I can manage a smile out of you. Every time I don't see you looking at me with the same fears, it is a better day for me."

Relaxing as his hands settle on my hips, I breathe him in. Today he smells like coffee and whiskey. His scent changes in various stages. I enjoy it, whether he's fresh from the shower, drinking, or fucking me.

I enjoy *him*.

"I love you, Nikki. Probably have since the first time you opened your little millennial mouth to insult me." My lip twitches while I play with his hair.

His eyes are brighter today, focusing those lovely irises on me. I poke his ribs. "As much as you cringe over it, you are one, too," I comment while he sticks his tongue out.

The gesture is so cute, I can't help but giggle.

Rory sets his empty mug down, smirking to himself before his eyes find mine. "I feel like I haven't heard that laugh in so long."

I frown at him and he shakes his head. "That just won't do."

Wondering what he means, my question gets answered once I find myself quickly underneath him. He begins poking and prodding at me.

"Don't you dare," I warn, and he narrows those eyes playfully before grinning.

This man is trying to tickle me, and he succeeds. He continues to do so in random various areas until I'm turning blue from all the squealing and giggling.

"You're so fucking perfect," he says, straddling and looking down at me.

I catch my breath moments later, running my hands up his thighs.

"Alright, tickle monster," I puff out.

With how he looks, straddling me all sexy like, I'm turned on by it.

I swear, my pussy has a mind of her own.

"Someone needs to get used to compliments." He's practically reprimanding me with those words.

"I can't help it, Rore."

His pupils dilate.

"I like your nickname."

I just gave him a nickname, didn't I? One that isn't *psycho* or *killer-man*.

"I like yours too," I comment back.

"There you go, Sugar."

Swooning over him, I sigh. "You make it very difficult to resist you."

His brow quirks up with intrigue.

"You find me irresistible?"

"I came here feeling better and more relaxed, then you have to be all—"

"All *what?*"

"Irresistible and sexy. God, you make me so horny, I can't even think sometimes. You unnerve me with how attracted I am to you. I have to rationalize in my brain, and it's a battle."

And there goes my word vomit. Fuck my life. *He* didn't need to know all of that!

The corner of his lip curls up. "Battle of?"

I sigh in irritation.

"Whether I want to try to love you or hate you. *Forgiving you.* Strangle or fuck you. Most of the time I want to kiss your lips off."

I remind myself to shut the hell up. My heart is thumping hard in my chest.

Rory releases me, moving down to hug me and bury his head into my stomach.

"Minus the hate and strangling, you aren't alone, Niks. You drive me fucking insane."

He looks up as I adjust my head to gaze down upon him. I can't help but appreciate how cute and cuddly he's being.

"As fucked up as it sounds, I don't regret *you.* The

methods to get here, *yes—probably—*but never *you* coming into my life."

I still debate *that,* but I don't voice it. For once, I shut up.

He grips my sides as if he can't get close enough. For someone so obsessed, he's *sweet.*

"So, sounds like we're both in a situation," I say with defeat, not being able to help but run my hand through his dark hair, enjoying how soft it feels.

"I thought I was made of granite," he whispers. "After seeing my friend die, it changed me. I fixated on the aftermath of revenge and wanted to know what it was like to take a life. Thus began my weird obsession to continue that thrill of killing. A trail of unhealthy habits followed. I don't claim goodness or to be morally sound. But... I *want* to be good *for you.*"

I'm still not surprised that I attracted a serial killer with my weird ass personality.

"Do you think you'll want to kill again?" The question of the millennia.

"No. Everything I thought I needed wasn't what I needed, after all."

"How do you know what you need?" I focus my gaze on him, wondering if this *not-killing* isn't just a phase. *Am I enough?*

"What I need is right in front of me."

Okay, Romeo. My lips curl up.

It's all so interesting to me. The changes between us both. I couldn't even begin to fathom on how to psychoanalyze the man even still. He wants to be *better.*

"So... you're granite and I'm sugar?"

"Yes, but *we* are so much more now, Niks. Perfectly misaligned. *'I've got a river running right into you.'*"

Realizing his words are song lyrics from one of my favorite artists, I swoon.

"Someone's been listening to my playlist," I remark quietly.

"Music speaks what generic words fail to say."

"You're so smart."

His head pops up, pulling up my dress.

"So is the woman under my touch." His hands caress their way up to my breasts under my bralette.

His nose dips, inhaling my pussy.

"So, I ignite the sex drive for you, hmm?"

I open my thighs in response while he adjusts himself. His chuckle is low; so low, I feel it in my core.

"Are you ready for me to show you how much I missed you? A reminder of *who* worships this pussy?"

"Please, by all means," I whisper as he blows air outside my entrance.

"I'm glad to know I do it for you. Now, it's time for me to drown in your wet cunt."

I gasp the minute he claims me. All previous thoughts and conversations from before are out of my mind.

It's quite possible our honesty—err *mine,* was needed. Now, he knows exactly where my head's at.

I've been wet since we sat on the couch. With how he's lapping me up eagerly, one hand teasing my breast and the other on my hip, I'm finding how needy I am for that tongue and his touch I've missed.

"Fuck, I've missed that tongue of yours."

"I'm all yours, baby," he murmurs between licking my clit.

Melting further, my hand guides his hand to my other breast.

"Rore," I moan, arching my back as my orgasm rises within me.

"That's it, come for me, Sugar."

When I do, he doesn't stop. I'm shaking under him in pleasurable torture. The man never relents on his intentions toward me, not sure why he'd stop now.

XOXO
LOVE

Chapter Twenty-Four

Rory

My home doesn't feel like a home, not without her.

There's no one to banter with or tease; it's just *empty*. A crushing hole in my heart.

Fuck, I miss her laugh, her curves, and her strange but fascinating brain.

I couldn't stand to see her pulling away from me. For weeks, she wasn't herself or as chatty. We just went through the motions.

It wasn't until she broke down in tears that I realized how neglectful I'd been, how afraid of me she still was. So, I let her go.

She asked for the beach and the beach is where she's been according to her location. I'm realizing I'd give her a burning star if I could.

In her absence, I've realized three things.

One: I need to check in with her more often. I can't let her go so long stewing in her emotions or hanging out in her head.

Two: I'm a fucking dick, even if it's not intentional. I

need to learn to become more aware of my actions and reactions to her. Show her that she doesn't have to fear me.

Three: It wouldn't hurt for us to learn how to better trust one another. To learn communication and compromise. Not just sarcastic banter or half-assed conversations when we aren't aware that we have issues.

I do my best not to look at her location on my phone, but I find making sure she's safe is comforting. Her little dot location remained mostly on the beach or at the hotel restaurant.

On Sunday, I find myself constantly checking my phone. I don't think it spends more than a full two minutes in my pocket. I should probably find a way to put her location on my TV, so I can watch the little dot move closer to me.

I find myself pacing around the space, cleaning already clean counters, remaking our bed, and fluffing couch cushions to keep busy.

I can't fucking think straight.

When she finally walks through the door, it feels like sunshine after a storm. My heart is racing in my chest, and the blood is roaring in my ears as I take her in. Her floral dress and her little sandals.

I pull her into my arms, my face going to the crook of her neck so I can breathe her in. She smells like sunshine, salt, and sunscreen, a heady scent that I want to burn into my senses.

They say distance makes the heart grow fonder, but whoever said that was a fucking moron.

This was fucking miserable.

I finally get my shit together, and pull Niks over to the coffee machine, not quite ready to let her go just yet. I know she's a coffee lover, and I love her; I want her to feel like she's back at home. It's a revelation to realize how in love with her I am.

Is that what this insanity is, the way I struggle to breathe when she isn't near me? Or is it finally listening to the playlist she made just for me and my killing sprees? Whatever the case, I don't fucking care. All I know is I never want this feeling to leave me.

Handing Niks the steaming cup of coffee, I breathe her in one more time before letting my piece of sunshine go. My sexy woman walks over to the couch, curling her legs underneath her as she sits. I follow behind her like the lost, love puppy that I am, sitting beside her.

Her fingers wrap around her black skeleton mug that's giving a middle finger as she blows on the steam.

"I listened to the playlist," I admit.

Her green eyes glisten in the sunlight coming in from the windows. My breath catches in my throat as she smiles. It's also *very* possible I made my own playlist for her, but I'll keep it hidden until I'm ready.

Her lips curl up. "I do have good taste, if I do say so myself."

I nod my head, knowing that it was her playlist and the stupid fucking red dot that kept me sane all weekend.

Her perfect smile, the way her blonde hair looks in the morning light in bed, and her smooth skin against mine, warm and soft... I'm learning to be sweeter and gentler with her. Thankfully, she makes it so easy. Loving her is easier than breathing air or thinking about things I can't change. All I can do is pave a better way forward where she feels safe and loved.

That's what this insanity is—*love.*

At the realization of this over coffee, I make more and ask her all about the beach.

"It was needed," she says, handing me her mug once the coffee beeps in indication that it's ready.

"But," she pauses and continues as I refill her mug and bring it back to her, "There was someone missing from my adventure. Someone I realized I didn't need until it was nearly too late."

My heart skips a beat inside my chest cavity.

I lean closer to where she sits, eye level with her now.

"I'm not going anywhere, Sugar, take all the time you need."

Her eyes mist as she nods, and I place a gentle kiss on her forehead.

"Do you want to help me decorate this place more, so it feels more homely?" I offer, before moving away, to fix my second cup with cream and sugar into my black mug.

"Really?" she asks quietly, and I turn to lean against the stove, setting the spoon down.

"Yes. You put more colors into my world, so why not continue doing so?"

There's a faint blushing creeping over her cheeks as I smirk into my mug, taking a sip. *This woman does it for me.*

"I'd like that, Rory."

She looks behind her and frowns.

"What is it?"

Nikki gives me a once over, taking a sip before speaking. "It'll be hard to decorate the windows, but it wouldn't hurt to put up some lights. Can we find a ladder big enough to reach that high?" She indicates upward towards the high ceiling.

I reassure her with a smile, happy to know she already has ideas in her pretty little head.

"I'll find the ladder, you find the lights."

Her face lights up. "Deal."

"There's enough light from the windows, so it makes it hard to decorate the space, but the lights make it feel more ethereal in here now. A place worth coming home too."

I catch a glimpse of her smile, and dammit, I'd *kill* for that smile.

It's her that's ethereal and lovely. The lights enhance what is already there.

I won't lie and say I don't do purposely sexy things to have her eyes on me or full of lust—that part is enjoyable. *But I do things on purpose.*

"You're worth coming home to," I say, coming behind to wrap my arms around her.

She leans against me. "Do you like it?"

"I do. I like you under them more." I kiss her neck, admiring the woman in my hold and the lights all decked out above us.

"Do you always have to say sweet things to get under my skin?"

Yes, as long as you don't leave me alone for a weekend again.

"In a non-creepy way, I love getting under your skin," I say instead.

She lightly taps my hand, giggling.

"I love getting it *in* more," I add while quickly scooping her up, moving to lay her in bed.

"Rore—"

Placing my fingers to her lips, I silence whatever she's about to say.

"Just let me taste you under the lights for the first time. I need to see you come."

"Rory," she moans out the minute my lips meet her pussy.

It's enough to quiet her words, and I worship it all the more.

This. It's better than anything else.

Next time I'm off work, we make it down to the kink club.

There's a rig set up for suspension, and I see how her eyes lock onto it.

"Want to?" I offer with a grin, itching to do so.

She nods her head, looking at the contraption as a smile spreads across her face. I beam at the thought of her suspended in front of me.

"You're so precious," I say, licking her cheek.

Excitement coils my brain as I think of possible ties Nikki would be interested in. Should I leave her arms free? What angle should I have her, maybe horizontal?

While we wait, we watch a tasteful spanking scene of two men using the spank bench.

My eyes are on Nikki the entire time while her eyes are fixated on the scene. Those lovely eyes are bright with unadulterated hunger under the low sensual lighting as each blow to the bottom's ass is given firmly.

The dungeon room is big enough to incorporate different lighting for various scenes and flashing lights for the dance floor. Aside from the spanking bench scene, there's another couple making use of the bed in the corner which is always a popular display in the club. The crowd seems to be split between the three scenes.

I can't wait to see Nikki tied up in a sexy way that leaves

pretty little rope marks on her body from chest to thighs. *One not of force.*

Taking in her little black dress that hugs her curves, I wonder if she'll take it off for the rope scene.

Nikki catches me staring at her. Tilting her head to the side, she asks, "What?"

I smile, shaking my head, pulling her into my body.

Before I know it, the person tying the rope from before taps my shoulder, indicating they are finished. They ask how much rope I'll need, and I tell them.

Once they wander off, I turn to Niks. "How do you feel about a whole-body suspension?"

Tilting her head to think it over, she asks, "Like tied-up mummy, or can I have my head and hands free? I need a visual here, Rore."

I chuckle, kissing her swiftly before explaining and negotiating.

"We can do a leg tie where your legs look like bent scissors, and I can do a pretty little chest harness that cradles you. How do you feel about spinning?" I suggest, and she nods eagerly.

"Sounds perfect! Can I have my hands free and my head comfortable?" she questions, and I think it over in my mind, nodding.

"Yes, and I'll request a Sleep Token song just for you." I toss her a playful wink, and she wiggles, grinning as I grab some rope to get started, standing in front of her. "Ready, baby?" I ask sweetly.

She nods excitedly, her kissable lips stretching into a smile and pulls off her dress, revealing a strappy black bra with the matching underwear.

Practically drooling over it, I begin the various ties to prepare, doing the chest harness first before doing her thighs. I create the uplines, where they connect to the spinner ring that she'll hang from. I make note of her pressure points and nerves, ensuring to avoid any major numbing areas.

"Check-in. How are we doing, Sugar?"

She answers with a cute little smile. "Green, keep going."

I chuckle, telling her to look away from the rope as I connect one of the uplines from her chest harness as I don't want to pop her in the face with rope.

I continue to check in frequently once she's partially suspended. She says, "Green," each time, and starts relaxing into the rope. I take notice of the rope sheers nearby in case of an emergency, which every rope top should have.

"Be right back," I say to her as she stands on one leg, half-leaning back. I leave her for a few moments to request a special song before returning.

"What's your color, Sugar?" I ask, breathing into her ear gently.

"Neon green."

I grin, tugging the other line. When I'm done, one of her arms is free. Her legs are tied to where they look like bent scissors, and I have her in a suspendable harness that crosses all over her chest and back, linking to her hips.

Nikki is now completely off the floor and at my mercy. She is high enough off the ground, and since there's plenty of space, I give her a little spin. She giggles, looking upside-down at me with the prettiest smile that I'd die for again and again.

I mouth the lyrics to the song as she tells me to spin her again.

My heart is full of seeing her in my ties and having a

good time. When she slows from spinning, she mentions wanting to remain suspended for the remainder of the song.

The lights flash and turn blue, making her look like an ethereal rope bunny. Her gorgeous eyes meet mine, and I can't help but kiss her upside-down. Her free hand goes into my hair while I slide my tongue in and play with hers.

Once the instrumental finishes on the song, I sing the words. *"Oh, and my love. Did I mistake you for a sign from God?"*

Her smile grows.

"Or are you really here to cast me off?" She mouths the words after.

"Or maybe just to turn me on," I say back.

Our scene draws a small crowd. I move my body to the beats, rolling my hips as she raises her arm, trying to wiggle hers.

I'm so in love with her it hurts.

As much as I wish for her return of words, moments like this are everything to me. Moments where she feels safe and comfortable to be herself without a care. Her enjoying kink with me makes my heart grow fonder.

I love how things are changing between us so we can have this dynamic. I feel I still have a lot to make up for, but I'm trying for her.

Before I know it, the song ends, and I check in with her as it's time to get her down safely.

I release one of the lines, freeing her legs first, so she can stand while I undo the rest. After ten minutes, Nikki is completely free of rope. Seeing my work of art indented across her skin in hues of red makes my dick beg for freedom.

"You're so beautiful, Niks," I praise, pulling her into me for a needy kiss as she stands wobbly.

"You're handsome too, you know," she says tugging on my leather harness that I forgot I was wearing.

"I'm yours," I mumble against her lips before bending to pick up her dress and supporting more of her weight.

I assist with putting it back on her, knowing that some people can feel woozy after spinning and being suspended.

We leave the dungeon area, heading for the bar for some quiet. My nerves are zinging with newfound energy; a rope-tying high.

I order two fruity drinks, walking with her tucked into my side as we grab a corner booth to snuggle in.

While I'm riding a high, I wonder if she is too. No matter who's doing what, whether topping or bottoming, everyone needs aftercare.

"How are you feeling, gorgeous?" I say to her with her nestled into my side, my arm around her shoulders, rubbing her upper arm.

She sighs deeply, nuzzling her face into my neck. "I feel...invigorated. *The Summoning* was the best song to do that to, my God." I lean into her, those marks of rope I left her stuck in my mind. If only she was naked so I could lick them.

"You did so well. You make a great rope bunny," I praise again, making sure she knows how cherished she is.

"I know, I do," she states proudly as I squeeze her.

"You—*we* drew a crowd too, and fuck do you wear my ties well, Sugar," I add while downing the sugary drink, sliding over hers.

"You know, I think I'm good, I don't need a drink. I find snuggling with you to be better." She climbs into my lap, wrapping her arm around my neck and leaning her head against mine.

"Yes, ma'am," I say, downing the second drink before folding my arms around her.

"You were amazing, too," she comments quietly, and I lean to kiss her neck in thanks. I rest my head on her chest, feeling the *thump, thump* of her heartbeat as we soak up the aftercare before doing some dancing and finishing our night at home.

I could certainly get used to this.

XOXO
LOVE

Chapter Twenty Five

Nikki

Dare I say, I'm enjoying being around Rory.

So much so that I invite him to attend as my official boyfriend for a charity event for work, to which he agrees. I settle with the idea that he's actually *my boyfriend*. I toyed with the idea originally, not really processing it, but now it's fully sinking in.

My brain really irritates me, I swear to God.

Future work event aside, for the next kink club night, I decide to wear red.

Somehow, tonight, I feel unstoppable, sexy even. Maybe it's my color choice of the evening, or a newfound confidence I didn't know I had within me stewing.

When I walk out of the bathroom, Rory's gaze lifts from his untied shoes and travels up my body. His mouth hangs open slightly.

"What's your problem?" I question, trying to stifle my smile.

Rory strides over with his one shoe untied, running his hands up my body.

"That dress won't stay on long; shall we start taking it off now?"

Swatting at him, I take a step backwards. "This dress is for *me*. You'll be lucky for a taste, hot shot." I laugh, putting my hand on my jutted-out hip.

Rory groans, running his fingers through his hair. "Fuck," he accentuates, "I can't think when you look like that."

Raising a brow, I shoot him a look. "Like what?"

"Like a divine goddess. Your confidence is oozing, Sugar."

"Hurry up, Rory." I ignore the blush rising to my cheeks despite my makeup.

He huffs a breath, putting on his other shoe before adjusting his netted shirt.

"Every woman is going to want to lick you," I can't help but say to him as we ride the elevator down. He says *I'm* hot, but *him?* The man is a fucking sex god.

Rory places his hand beside my head, leaning in close. My breath catches in my throat as my brain malfunctions at his closeness. He presses his lips into mine as he runs his nose along the side of my neck, breathing me in. I shudder, my legs opening slightly to adjust to his body. Rory bites my collar bone gently before licking back up the side of my neck.

"The only one I want to lick is *you*." He sighs deeply, tugging on my bottom lip with his teeth.

"I won't make it out of this building if you don't stop."

I clench my thighs together. He leans back, licking his lip coyly. *Sly fucker*.

"You aren't the only one, lovely."

The old elevator dings then, reminding me that we

haven't even left the building yet, and I'm ready to mount him.

With a swift kiss, we maneuver to get in his car and drive off.

"What do you feel like doing tonight; voyeur room?" I suggest, a tingle of excitement traveling up my spine. In fact, *it's all I can think about.*

"Sounds good. Also, the next weekend I'm off, I want to travel somewhere with you."

I settle my hand on his thigh, rubbing in response. "I'd love that."

"When's your company party again?" he asks, and I'm grateful he gives me moments of breaks before firing off one question after another. I don't want to embarrass myself with flappy-overstimulation-hands.

"Next month."

"Formal wear, right?"

"Yes." *Please, no more questions, Rory.*

Thankfully he doesn't ask anything else as he pulls into the private parking lot for the kink club building.

"We'll go shopping for it soon," he says while we get out of the car.

I grab his hand which earns me a sweet smile. We check in and get our dominant and submissive wristbands.

"I wouldn't mind you topping me," he whispers in my ear once we find no one in any scenes yet.

Pulling me to the dance floor, I place my hands on his shoulders with a sly smile.

"And what would you have me do?"

His gaze drifts off in thought.

"I can think of *many* things. If you feel up to it, maybe you could tie me to that bed in the corner? Let everyone see just who owns me."

Fuck.

His words hit their mark. "Should we wear collars just to confuse people?"

He considers me. "I like that idea. I know generally it's for pet play or in more serious dominant/submissive dynamics, but I don't see why we both can't wear one. While we lean towards one dynamic, doesn't mean we can't switch to the other." He shrugs. "Fuck em'."

I play with the hair at his nape briefly, a coy smile placating my lips in agreement. "I never liked abiding by society's rules anyways. Who are they to put us in a box?"

Rory gives me a devilish smile before kissing my lips. "I love you, and you are so right."

The heavy beats turn to something more fast-paced. The lights pick up on the rhythm, and I can feel the electricity in the room rise with the increasing beats. We sink and swim with each other on the dance floor.

Sweat is trickling down my back, my body invigorated from the beats and energy in the room. Rory grins at me, pulling me closer. "I need a drink. What about you?" I nod, throwing my arms above my head and moving my body to the beats. Rory swats my ass as he moves past me towards the bar.

Warm hands glide over my hips, and I smile as I turn around. To my surprise, it's not Rory but another man. He towers over me, his dark hair wafts beautifully in front of his mask. His jade green eyes glisten like the harness strapped to his torso, a dragon tattoo wrapping down his arm.

"Well, aren't you a fiery little devil in red."

Unsure on what to do, I ease up my dancing to pause and take a step away from the masked stranger. I look over my shoulder for Rory, but I can't see over the crowd of people. When I turn back, the masked man has taken another step towards me.

"As cute as that mask is, not interested, bud. My man is at the bar getting drinks," I shout over the music.

Thank fuck the guy is decent enough to put up his hands in defeat and wanders off respectfully with a nod. My thoughts travel back in time to where I made fun of a certain man's mask. *Then, the bastard felt bad and had me help him.* Again, life is fucking weird.

I giggle over the thought before I turn around to a dark-haired goddess staring at me. She indicates her head for me to follow her.

Confused, but dumb enough, I decided to go along with it.

The lady takes me to a dark corner near the front where conversations can be had without shouting over the music.

"So, you're with Rory? Another new toy?"

I purse my lips, wondering how petty I want to be. I don't like the lady's tone.

"Why does that concern you?" I begin and wonder what this lady's motive is. *Besides jealousy, of course.*

I'm autistic, not delusional. *Well, not today anyway.*

"He's been *mine.*"

Oh, that explains it. *Here we go.*

"When's the last time you heard from him?" I ask, ignoring her statement. I fiddle with the side of my dress casually to keep my hands busy.

"Well, it's been a few months, but he works a lot."

Gosh, this lady is on the delulu track.

"Interesting. So, why should it bother me that he hasn't seen or spoken to you?"

She gets in my face. "I'm telling you to back off, bitch."

My temper flares at her deciding to get in my bubble. I

resist the urge to bite her. I realize the tendency is a weird habit that I try to control.

"How about you get your stinky breath out of *my* face?" I step back, waving my hand in front of my face, and she stares at me, surprised by my gesture. "Secondly, I'm his girlfriend. So, why don't you get a fucking clue and stop being a skeeze? He's not interested, so *you* back the fuck off."

I push her out of my way so I can leave. She shouts words after me that go in one ear and out the other, and I flip her off for good measure.

Walking out the back door for some air because I'm fucking irritated and need a damn minute, I lean against the building.

The masked guy from before is smoking a cigarette.

"You good?"

"I'm fucking peachy," I retort.

"Do you smoke?"

I shake my head, wondering why I don't, but then I remember being eighteen and choking on that nasty shit.

"I did it once and choked. Not the kind of kink I'm into."

He leans his head back, laughing.

"You're funny, I dig it. Sorry about before; I didn't mean any offense."

"You're good. Thanks for respecting consent and boundaries... Anyway, I'm just irritated because my boyfriend was a playboy before me, and I happened to run into one of his conquests."

"Ah, I see. Sounds like quite the predicament."

"I told her off, so maybe she'll take a hint. Maybe not. Hell if I know."

He takes a drag, and I watch the smoke drift from his

lips up into the night air. I imagine myself as smoke wafting through the air instead of the irritating emotions I'm having trouble regulating.

I take some deep breaths and tell him to enjoy his cigarette, heading back into the main room.

On the way, I peek into the bar room, not seeing Rory. Wondering if he's looking for me, I make it back to the dungeon room. Trying to find him feels difficult, so I stand near a wall to get a better picture of people. I do my best to ignore the creeping anxiety that curls like a snake at the base of my spine.

Then, I find him, leaning far too close to that dark-haired lady from before. She puts her hands on him, and they seem to be in some sort of heated discussion. *Wonder what it's about?*

Rory has her back against the wall, kinda similarly like in the elevator earlier, and from my vantage point, I can't tell on the intent. It makes me fidgety regardless.

Annoyed all over again, I head to the bar for a drink to try and calm my nerves that's spiked into full blown anxiety. Not the night I wanted to have.

Had the lady been nicer, maybe I wouldn't feel some sort of way. *She* got territorial over someone who isn't hers. He isn't, right? Rory spoke previously of never bringing anyone home, and how he didn't do relationships. Maybe he was just telling me that since I talk too much. Who knows, though.

I rub my temple and ask for two shots of tequila once I'm at the bar.

The masked guy from earlier comes beside me.

"That bad, huh?" he asks, leaning on the counter. I can't help but take in his black dragon tattoo that starts from his pectoral muscle and swirls down the entirety of his arm. The shading and line work is quite lovely, I must say.

"Yep." I down the two shots without making a face.

"Well, what are you going to do?" He looks at me, impressed at how I downed the shots.

"I take back my statement from earlier. Let's go make someone jealous. Want to dance suggestively enough to make a point?"

I see his grin. "I'll be on my best behavior, little fire sprite."

Offering my hand, I drag him to the dance floor. I'm still pissed off, but dancing should help me.

Once I find a good dancing spot, I pull the guy to me. "Show me your moves then," I tease.

"I'll play innocent until we see him, alright?"

I nod as we keep things friendly.

He does some silly move that makes me crack up, and I can see he's trying to cheer me up. It ends up working, and the song changes right when I see Rory in my periphery. I give the masked guy the go-ahead with an indication of my head, and he drops down in front of me. When he comes up his hands *appear* to roam over the surface of my body but he's barely touching me.

Apparently, it's enough to hit the mark, because soon Rory's upon us.

"Nikki, what the hell?"

I have to admit, Rory looks *sinful* when he's upset, and I mean truly upset. It's quite the look for him.

The woman from before comes up behind him, making me forget how hot Rory looks angry. "See! What did I tell you? She's not good enough for you!"

He snaps his head to the side. "Enough, Rachel!"

"We're just dancing, Rory," I say over the music, and he frowns.

"Doesn't fucking look like it."

I begin to feel overwhelmed and push away from everyone. Escaping Rory's grasp, I rush out of the room.

The first door I see down the hallway, I dart into quickly.

Of course, it's the voyeur room.

People look at me for being noisy, and I hold up my hands whispering sorry.

I find a place in the back, catching my breath and calming myself.

We were supposed to be in this room together.

XOXO
LOVE

Chapter Twenty Six

Rory

My eyes are on Nikki, in her red dress. *God, I could fuck her.* Over the couch, counter, elevator—doesn't matter to me.

At the kink club, she teases me with how she rubs her body against mine, and I'm reminded of a future voyeur room experience with her. I can't wait to have a more intimate setting with her. *And to be naughty in the dark, so taboo and forbidden.*

With all the dancing and a rush of nerves going to my cock, I'm fucking parched. I offer to leave to get us drinks, and Niks agrees.

It takes a bit to make it there due to the crowd, but I push past the sweaty half-dressed bodies, eventually making it to the bar. Not sure why tonight is so busy since it's not a holiday, but oh fucking well. I already have my voyeur room plans with my girl.

As I wait, I can picture it already. *Niks and I are in the back of the room, watching a couple beyond the one-way glass. She's in my lap, leaning against me as I tease her with neck kisses and body caresses. I tease her by whispering dirty things in her ear as I tug on earlobe. Of course, there would be others in front of us, watching and doing whatever, as Niks and I have our own fun in the dark.*

Just before I imagine running my fingers towards her wet cunt, the bartender asks what I'd like to drink, interrupting my little reverie. I take a deep steadying breath, ordering something stronger for myself and a margarita for Nikki.

People are so close to me which makes me worry about Nikki as I know how she gets with crowds and overstimulation. Strumming my fingers impatiently, the drinks are slid across the counter, and I put $40 cash down before pushing my way through the crowd to get back to my woman.

The main room is packed, and I end up draining my drink dry due to impatience with all these damn people pushing against me. Searching for Nikki takes far longer than I'd like. Where the hell were we before on the dance floor?

When I don't find her on the dance floor, I frown. Worry coils in my stomach as I frantically look over people and try to spot her.

Think, Rory, think. Where else would she go?

The bathroom is my next guess. So, I start to make my way through people, but then someone familiar catches my eye off to the side. I run into an old fuck buddy, and she makes eye contact with me, indicating her head toward me with a mischievous smile that can be anything but good.

Shit. Fuck.

I drain the drink I intended for Niks, knowing I'll need it for this conversation. I thought about ignoring Rachel's ass, but I don't run—*not from anyone.*

Rachel and I had a sexual relationship off and on for scening and fucking at the club. It didn't go past that, even if she wanted it to. To get her off my back, I told her I work a lot.

Then, I ghosted her.

Sometimes women don't take a hint. Not that men are any better, but for fuck's sake.

"Rory, it's so good to see you," she says as I go up to her, wondering what the fuck she wants. She may be pretty with her long brunette hair and porn-star, dick-sucking-lips, but the ship has sailed. I haven't thought about Rachel in a while, even before Nikki. Rachel was a decent lay, but that was it for me. Rachel certainly didn't add more color into my life, not like my Niks does.

Rachel runs her hands up my chest as if putting on a fucking show and to proclaim some fucking territory. *This bitch is playing fucking games, and I'm already irritated.*

I growl low in warning, my face serious. "What do you want, Rachel?"

"I've missed you, and you haven't called." She purses her lips as if she thinks being a pouty little bitch will help her case or get me to sympathize with whatever the fuck she's after—*not happening.* "Then, I see you here with *her.* What the hell? You deserve better than her. *Me.*"

I'm getting more and more impatient, and her comment doesn't help matters any. I don't think when I aggressively push her back against the wall. Placing my arm next to her head, my brows furrow.

"What did you do? Where is she?" I say between clenched teeth.

"I did nothing! I just talked to her." The tone of her voice let me know about her little show. Something between the lines of *oh, poor innocent me,* but also, *fuck your new woman, pick me.*

I grip her chin, showcasing my anger. No telling what

the hell she told Nikki. No wonder I can't fucking find her, which only frustrates and worries me further. *Goddammit.*

"There's that angry Dom I adore," she breathes out, the lust dancing in her brown eyes.

"Knock your shit off, Rachel. Leave my girlfriend alone," I order, pushing away in disgust. I set the empty drink glasses on a nearby table where others have done the same. I quickly push through the crowd again to find my girlfriend. This time I'm frantically searching, looking back at the dance floor, the bathroom, then the bar.

Nearly ready to lose my ever-living shit, I find her on the dance floor with some fucking masked guy.

Why the fuck is she dancing with him?

Goddammit, Rachel. I know she said some bullshit to her.

Ignoring logic and reason, I tighten my fists, moving toward them as he does a dance move where he drops down and runs his hands up her body from the bottom up.

Hell no.

It pisses me the fuck off, and I go up to them ready for battle. To my fucking luck, Rachel appears at my side out of thin air, saying stupid shit that I'm not fucking hearing.

I see how irritated and hurt Nikki is when both Rachel and I approach her and the masked guy. It confirms my earlier suspicions about Rachel talking shit. After this situation, I want nothing to do with Rachel either. *Not that I really did before.*

The situation serves to remind me why I never brought women back home or did relationships before Niks. Women think they have a right to me.

Nikki storms off, and I turn to tell Rachel it's over and to fucking leave me alone. I glare at the guy, pointing at him in warning while I leave the dancing crowd. If I say anything to him, I'll start a fight and get banned from the club, which I don't want, so sometimes the best thing to do is walk off. I'm not staying to fuck around and find out this time. It was stupid of me to even go up to Rachel in the first place.

I check the same locations of the bathroom, bar, then outside area in the back for smokers to go. Nikki is nowhere to be found.

"Goddammit!" I kick at the wall outside, reminding myself to calm the hell down.

Running my hand through my hair in frustration, I meander back inside and down the long hallway. Near the bar area, I lean on one of the walls, not ready to dive back into the crowd. Trying to fucking think and grab some brain cell of sanity, I sigh, staring up at the red ceiling.

Moaning can be heard through the walls, and part of me wonders if the person is faking it. It sounded staged. Somehow with that thought, my light bulb brain burns bright. *Check the voyeur room.*

If she'll even talk to me, I decide to try my luck there as I highly doubt she left the club.

Quickly and quietly, I enter the voyeur room two doors down.

There is low lighting, and the large room divides in half.

While it's the 'voyeur' room, it's really for both exhibitionists and voyeurs alike. On the one side, people can watch others in various acts to whoever is behind the one-way glass. Whoever is on the other side can't see out, but the voyeurs can see everything. On the play space side, there's a setup of a bed, a medical table, BDSM pillory, and a long rack on the back wall of various toys and objects for pleasure. Sometimes, the room gets switched out depending on events and scenes for voyeurs to watch and experience.

Currently, there's a couple experimenting with the medical table.

There's a rule for this room if a certain couple wants anyone to join or not. At the far-side back wall of the room, there's an entryway with a small hallway to switch sides of the room. There is a green light if people can join in. If not, then it's red. A simple way of consent that doesn't involve speaking, especially if there's anyone in the middle of a scene.

Paying no mind to the scene quite yet, I'm half surprised there's already a decent amount of people in the room, but it's not nearly as crowded as it is elsewhere. *Thank fuck.*

I mentally cross my fingers, making my back to the back row of seats for voyeur viewing. There's a moment that I think I'll turn up empty-handed, until my heart stalls when I see my blondie in red.

Thankfully, she's sitting by herself. A rush of relief empties out my lungs of breath as I slide next to her. I don't miss the unhappy side-glare she shoots me either.

I hear softcore porn music start up that I'm not sure was playing before but I was too in-the-zone to notice. The music isn't too loud, but it's enough to echo around the room and muffle anyone's making out and low moans. Despite the nearly dark lighting on the voyeur side, I can still see my girl perfectly unhappy with me. Giving her, and myself, a moment to process, I decide to glance towards the one way glass, seeing how one of the play partners is tying the other one to the table which is more than likely the submissive for the scene.

Without making eye contact with Nikki, I lean to the side, asking her, "Why'd you run away?"

It doesn't surprise me that she huffs and puffs.

"I was overstimulated. *Again.*" My eye twitches. *Fucking Rachel.*

Ready to clear the air at once, I tell her honestly, "I told Rachel to back off and leave me alone." Hoping she believes the truth, I finish with, "I ghosted her long before I followed you around."

Her eyes meet mine with a blank look that I can't decipher her mood, but I gather she's still pissy. "I didn't appreciate her confrontation."

I cup her cheek, offering comfort. "I have ex fuck-buddies, and I can't control what they do. I'm sorry she felt she needed to do that when she had no right to, but *I* can control how I respond to them. I'll respond as I did today, by telling them to fuck all the way off. I have a sinfully hot girlfriend, and I'm not looking at anyone but her." My hand drops to her shoulders, rubbing gently. "Are you okay, Niks? What'd she say?"

Nikki doesn't answer right away which makes me all the more anxious. She exhales deeply, looking lazily toward the scene and then back at me. "I'm...*okay.* She said to back off, obviously—you are hers. Blah blah *this* and blah blah *that.* I told her to fuck off."

My girl melts my fucking heart with the shit that comes out of her mouth. Nikki is so fierce and lets no one walk all over her, and her honesty means everything right now in this moment. I untense my shoulders, relaxing slightly.

I can't help but feel proud to call her *mine.*

A smile stretches across my face. "Good girl."

My hand moves to grip her chin, turning her to face me. My eyes narrow as I remember that fucking guy's hands on her. "Why was that masked guy all over you? Or did you do that on purpose? Do I need to add him to my kill list?"

Confusing me, Nikki's expression changes, narrowing her eyes. It makes me tilt my head.

"Why were your hands on her?" she counters back in a sassy little tone.

Ah, *jealousy. Or envy perhaps?*

I shake my head. "It wasn't like that."

Her brow raises as if to call bullshit.

"I mean it," I add. "She was touching me first, saying stupid shit to piss me off. I didn't see you, so I assumed she got to you. I didn't *touch* her. I was trying to get a point across before I lost my shit. I was more worried about *you.*"

My hand drifts to her thigh, and I hear her heavy sigh despite the music echoing around the room.

"Looks can be deceiving, I guess." She tries to look away, but I use my other hand to force her gently to look at me. She continues, "I saw the interaction and got pissy again. I grabbed two shots from the bar and ran into a masked guy... You're right, I got impulsive in my anger, and I did it to make you jealous..."

I roll my neck, joining her in her sighs. "Well, you accomplished your goal."

"He's actually really cool. It was friendly until I *knew* you were watching. Remove him from your kill list, he didn't actually do anything nonconsensual."

"Not helping your case here, Niks." I growl low, tightening my grip on her thigh.

She shrugs, her eyes drifting away, and my other hand falls behind her back.

"I'm sorry about Rachel and for letting you think that my eyes and hands want to be anywhere other than on your delectable body."

My gaze travels to her perky tits, the red dress shaping them perfectly.

A familiar lust-filled look meets my own. Music and moans echo beyond the glass to the scene on the medical table. As great as this room can be, the only one I need is right in front of me.

"And where do you want your hands and eyes?" Her voice is low, but not so low that I can't hear the timbre of her desire.

"Can I show you?" My tone is huskier than I intended but *fuck it*.

She tilts her head up as I lean closer. My face hovers centimeters from hers, waiting for her permission. When she inches closer, I claim those lips.

I'm torn on whether I want to lick her pussy and worship her here or have her climb in my lap. *How discreet do I want to be?*

Deciding to prove a point, I pull her into my lap, my earlier fantasy coming to the forefront of my mind.

She's facing the scening couple. The other audience members are either watching the couple on the other side of the glass, masturbating, or making out heavily.

I pull her dress up, exposing her thighs. My nose presses into the crook of her neck, breathing in that sugary scent that I adore.

"Want me to fuck you right here while we watch?" I tug on her earlobe.

My hands travel up her thighs in slow tantalizing strokes. She leans into me more, a soft sound leaving her kissable lips. Without asking, she opens her legs further.

"Yes or no, Sugar." I pause, waiting for her response, even though I'm more than eager to be buried deep.

"Yes, please."

I place a gentle kiss on her neck, letting my hand wander under the dress and to her pussy.

"My little slut is already wet," I murmur in her ear while running fingers up and down her slit a couple of times before sinking two fingers inside.

"Fuck," she utters, nearly bucking off me.

"Don't disturb the audience," I warn before nibbling on that little ear of hers.

I pull my fingers out and tell her to open her mouth. "Taste what I do to you," I whisper.

She sucks on my fingers, and I nudge my hips against her where my dick is already hard.

"Is my cum slut ready for this cock?" I practically purr in her ear, ready to consume her.

She nods eagerly while I work to free myself, lifting her up to slide in.

"Watch the scene and feel exactly where I want to be. My hands are where they belong. No one else but you." While I speak, I run my hands up her thighs before caressing one of her breasts outside the dress's fabric.

Nikki grinds her hips, her eyes on the scene before us. I sneak a glimpse of what she's seeing. The non-tied up member is giving oral while the tied-up one is moaning and squirming against their bindings.

So far, no one has seen us except for when I first came into the room. Not that I care, either way, but *this moment is just for us*.

"You take me so well. I always want to come back to *this*," I say, before beginning to give her a hickey on her shoulder. Marking my woman has to be one of my favorite things, aside from tasting our cum.

My hands grip her waist as we work together gyrating our hips. Slow and steady wins the race. I do it purposely, so she feels each agonizing pump. How I fuck her and how she's made for me in every which way. Fuck what

Rachel says, it makes the animal in me come out, ready to play and claim the only woman who makes sense in my fucked up life—at least before Niks and I changed the game.

A toe-curling moan escapes her, and I quickly turn her toward me so I can taste it. A thought crosses my mind, and I can't wait to do it. *I want her to taste us once I come inside her.*

I kiss her desperately as my hands guide her hips.

For a few moments there are cries echoing around the room from others, until I slide my hand to her pussy, circling her clit while the other teases her nipple.

I taste her moans and soft sounds, moving my hips slightly faster. The sweet torturous agony of waiting until she comes for me first. Nikki is fucking dripping and I'm ready to devour.

Her pussy begins to swell, and I know she's close. "Come all over me, baby."

Those voyeur room eyes lock onto mine, and I feel my own orgasm rising with our foreheads pressing together.

"That's my pretty girl. Remember, you are mine, and I am yours. Don't let anyone take that away from us," I assure her firmly.

I still shortly after, filling her up with my cum, and she clenches down on me. Our soft sighs leave our mouths, and I kiss her before sticking two fingers in her. Feeling our release intertwining on my fingers does unspeakable things for me, and I make sure she can share in the taste of us too.

"Open that lovely mouth and taste what is only ours."

Those fuck-me eyes are glazed over, opening her lips slowly to my command.

"I want to taste too; spit in my mouth," I tell her as she hums on my fingers in her mouth.

I stick a single finger inside her again before repeating the process.

Holding her beautiful, perfect face, she exchanges our taste with me.

Moaning into her mouth, I'm ready to fuck her again, despite my cock being sensitive.

"I'll be licking that up at home later," I promise.

She huffs a laugh as the couple on the medical table finishes their scene. They leave the glass room, and someone else replaces them.

"Ready to continue this at home?" I ask, leaning into her back to catch my breath and hold her.

"Yes. I'm done with this place for a while," she admits.

I run my fingers through her hair.

"I second that."

I stuff my sensitive cock back in my pants and help Nikki straighten up her clothes. After such an evening, I want to do nothing else other than lick her pussy.

XoXo
LOVE

Chapter Twenty Seven

Nikki

Staring in the mirror while holding up two different dresses makes me indecisive. Rory is waiting just outside.

I'm torn between the dark blue and purple one.

"I can't make a decision."

"Get both," he says, opening the curtain and joining me.

I meet his green-blue eyes in the reflection and frown.

"You're not helpful."

He wraps his arms around me, resting his chin on my shoulder. "Not that it's legal or approved for a work event, but I prefer your outfits to be *gone*."

I huff out a breath. "You're ridiculous."

He nuzzles the side of my face, and I can't help but let a small giggle slip.

"Maybe, but I know what I enjoy."

"I suppose I'll get both," I say, giving in.

"Good. I'm going to be taking them off you regardless." He kisses my neck, and I shiver under his hold.

I can't believe I'm actually falling for this guy.

Not that I have the words to voice it yet. I'm sure it will

come in time. I'm still not ready for the words to be true, and I know I'm fighting it.

Emotions are hard.

"Alright, let's go find you something." I wiggle in his hold.

"Yes, ma'am."

Turning around in his hold, we share a brief kiss, and I can tell he's dragging his ass, wanting to remain there in the dressing room.

"Come on, Romeo."

He grabs the dresses from my hands and goes to checkout. I follow after him and it doesn't slip my notice that the lady at the register is eyeing him. She frowns at me as I appear beside him.

Rolling my eyes, we get out of there and continue through the mall to the men's store.

Rory doesn't let me hold the dresses even when I offer.

I take the initiative once we're in the men's store and a suit makes eyes at me. It matches perfectly to either dress. It's simple and elegant, being all black, which I know suits his tastes, yet on the jacket, there's a blue and purple outline at the edges. It doesn't look cheesy as it fades into each other as if they're perfectly paired colors.

"This one. That way it won't matter what dress I wear."

I turn to find him standing beside me with a smile. "That works for me, Sugar."

He plucks his size off the hanger and asks for a dressing room.

The guy working nods politely before smiling at me.

I snatch my dresses from Rory and let him try the suit on while I wait outside.

Worker-guy turns to me once Rory's in the changing room. "Are you two together?"

"Yes," I say already annoyed

The guy sighs. "That's a shame. You'd look better on my arm."

Ignoring him, he walks away, and I roll my eyes again.

What is it with people today?

I can't tell, but I *think* I hear a grumble from the dressing room.

Did Rory hear the guy?

After a couple of minutes, he emerges from the room, and all I can do is stare at him. The suit is perfectly made. A little color to his black wardrobe, and I'm already fucking drooling.

"Yes?" He does a full turn for me that I appreciate.

I nod my head, taking him in. The black suit hugs his body perfectly and I want to lick him. His ass looks fucking *great.*

"You look edible," I compliment him.

His husky low laugh tickles my ears as I blush.

"Just what I was hoping for. So, this is the one?"

"Do *you* like it?" I interrupt as he nods. "Then yes, this is the one," I confirm honestly.

He gives me a panty-dropping smile. *As if I wear underwear half the time.*

Disappearing into the room once more, I leave the area to look for matching ties. I can feel the worker-guy's eyes follow me around the store which is unnerving to me. I hate attention like this unless it's from Rory.

I find three ties I can't decide between. A blue, a purple, and a black one—*just in case.*

Arms go around me, and I startle, thinking the worker-guy got brave.

"It's just me," Rory whispers.

"Sorry, I thought it was the worker guy. He was flirty earlier."

I turn around, holding up the ties for him to see.

Rory is frowning. "So, I heard. Want me to kill him?"

I flick his arm hard and shake my head. "Let's just check out and grab food. I'm hungry."

He leans in to kiss my forehead, and I close my eyes briefly, enjoying the forehead kisses which are some of my favorite things to receive. It expresses sweet tenderness in my eyes, and it reminds me that relationships aren't always about sex and kinky shit. Little moments like this matter too.

"Me too."

Once at the counter, I begin to shift uncomfortably due to the tension and grumpy looks from the two men.

What is it with the unnecessary dick-measuring contest?

Rory pays, and I tug on his hand to get us out of the store.

"Put your dick away," I mumble, and he chuckles.

"I'm starving. Chinese food in the food court?" I add, my stomach growling so loudly that I'm surprised the whole mall doesn't hear it.

"Sounds good. I won't steal your food this time, or you might eat *me* like some Hannibal Lecter," he teases, poking me in the stomach.

I shoot him a look and shake my head over his silliness.

I'm grateful when we arrive at the Chinese takeout spot with no line.

Fidgeting until we're next, I order crab rangoon, an egg roll, and sweet and sour chicken.

He orders something similar but gets ribs. *And I'm the Hannibal Lecter?*

We pay and take our trays of food and find a cozy spot away from people in the middle of the room next to half-wall of fake plants.

I do one of those happy-to-be-eating wiggles when I catch Rory's eyes sparkling in amusement.

"Do you want to go out on Halloween or stay in?" he asks.

I think about it for a moment and shrug. "What do you have in mind?"

"Well... I was hoping we could go out," he starts to suggest.

Intrigued, I can't help but laugh. "Did I domesticate a killer?"

Rory chuckles in amusement. "Yes, actually." He looks around, making sure no one heard what I said. *Whoops.*

"Well, I'm flattered. Sure, let's do it," I say quickly.

He grins, seeming at ease and content to eat there with me in the noisy food court. Shaking my head, yet finding him adorable, we finish eating and leave the mall.

Malls and crowds, I don't care for, so I'm grateful to finally leave. The work event is just a couple of weeks away, and at least I don't need to stress over what to wear anymore. Sure, my medication takes the edges off the anxiety, but I still fret over small things like *what the fuck to wear*. A normal thing to stress about, I suppose.

The work event arrives in a blink, or so it feels.

I got my hair done the day before to refresh my blonde color and got some layers added in. To my surprise, Rory got his hair cut too. Not that he wasn't handsome before, but I find how much I enjoy him with shorter hair since it grew out over our months together.

Still can't believe I domesticated a killer. Life's fucking weird—the future title of my memoir.

Rory takes a full mirror photo of us, and I'm happy with my choice of the purple dress.

"We look good," he says, kissing my cheek.

"Indeed," I agree before we head out the door.

My purple dress goes to my knees and accentuates my curves, and dare I say, I look good on Rory's arm tonight.

Rory drives us through the city until we arrive at one of the tall buildings and he pays for valet parking. He takes my arm, and we walk inside, heading up to the twentieth floor.

"Do you know many people here tonight?" he asks quietly as we ride the elevator.

I shake my head. "I'll probably introduce you to my boss, and my work-friend, Tanya. We're only here because I'm required to show my face."

Rory hugs me to his side. "Fair enough, Sugar."

Once the elevator dings, we exit, and there's already too many people to my liking. The room is large, and there's piano music playing from somewhere.

"I'll be surprised if I last an hour," I grumble under my breath.

Rory grabs my hand, squeezing it in comfort. "I'm here; don't you worry your pretty little head."

Somehow, his words are soothing enough to relax my shoulders. "Alright, let's do this," I say more to myself than to him.

He keeps his hand in mine, and we make our way through the crowded room. Anxiety floods my nervous system, and I desperately need a damn drink to help calm my nerves to get through however long I have to be here. *I hate work events and masking.* Who wants to play pretend at these things anyway?

The room chatter is almost too overstimulating the further we walk in.

I can't deny the relief I feel when I see the bar. Dragging Rory with me, I order wine for myself as Rory grabs whiskey. I'm not even a sip in when my boss walks over with her husband. *For fuck's sake.*

"I'm so glad you could come, Nicole," my boss says in greeting as she smiles and introduces her husband while I introduce Rory.

She hands me an envelope and grins. "This is for the excellent work from last quarter."

Finally, a nice bonus check. I never would've gotten this with the old bitchy boss I used to have.

I thank her politely, and she mentions that Tanya is nearby with her husband. My newer boss knows me well enough to notice that I talk to Tanya frequently. Tanya is at least a decade older than me with kids of her own, and we work together in the same department.

My boss tells me dinner is in an hour, and to sit with her and her husband. I nod and smile, feeling uncomfortable right before she walks away to mingle more.

I sigh out in relief once she's gone from earshot. "I suppose we can stay for the food at least."

"What did she hand you? A bonus?" he asks as I start sipping my wine to gather what liquid courage I can.

I nod toward Rory, and we meander away from the bar. I debate on looking for Tanya, but she finds me first. The woman herself is smiling big when she sees me. She's all dolled up with a blonde fancy updo, and friendly, smiling blue eyes. She even wears a matching blue dress that brings out her eyes.

"There she is! There are so many people, I almost didn't find you!" She hugs me tight, and my anxiety peaks at the reminder.

"And who's this fine specimen on your arm?" She nudges me, and now I'm focused on something else. So, I introduce Rory.

The man himself seems smug when I introduce him as my boyfriend. I resist the urge to roll my eyes, but I also can't help but melt internally over his reaction.

"Nice to meet you, Rory. You two look lovely together. Right, Joe?" Her husband suddenly appears next to her, nodding his head. He has more gray hair than she does, but they still look like a happily married couple.

I began to wonder if I'd ever have that type of marriage, or if I was even made for it. In a sense, it hasn't been a thing that I've wanted in life. Not with this brain of mine.

Ignoring my turn of thoughts, Tanya guides us to a standing table feet away to chat more. She knows I don't care for crowds, and I'm so grateful she knows me well enough to take the initiative.

Joe is mostly quiet while Tanya and I chat, until she asks Rory basic questions about his job and such. He answers politely, keeping the conversation light for a social outing. I know Tanya wants to grill him further since she's never seen me with a man, or friend, period. *How sad is that?*

When she asks about what Rory does for fun, I stiffen. *Do not open your mouth, Nikki—don't do it.*

Rory notices and wraps his arm around me. "Mostly, keeping up with this one."

Relaxing with relief, he rubs my upper back. "No lies detected," I confirm, grateful for his response, so that my poor brain didn't fuck anything up in public by muttering *killing*.

Tanya and Joe chuckle, and I direct the conversation away from Rory and me to ask how her kids are doing. She proudly talks about them, and soon I realize my wine glass is empty.

Politely, I wait for a break in conversation to excuse myself. "Tanya, will you and Joe keep Rory company while I grab some more drinks?"

Thankfully, Rory's is empty too, and he gives me a look that almost reads, *"Are you sure you're okay?"*

I offer him a smile before telling them I'd be back shortly. I can feel Rory's eyes follow me until I disappear into the crowd towards the bar. While one drink eased my social anxiety slightly, I know one isn't enough for me. I criticize myself and my brain internally before taking a deep breath.

You're autistic, not inept. So, what, places are noisy. Fucking relax.

To my continued discomfort, the bar is crowded. I fidget with my fingers slightly, waiting until it's my turn. I practice counting my breaths. Time passes slowly as I shift from one hip to the other.

Once I'm closer to being next, I notice someone is standing next to me, closer than I'd like. My senses all heighten, becoming more alert. A strange feeling of unease washes over me, and I dare to peek to see who's standing so close to me.

My heart drops to the floor, and a dark smile crosses the other male's face. A face I never expected to see again.

I'm standing next to my high school rapist.

XOXO
LOVE

Chapter Twenty Eight

Rory

Part of me is glad that Nikki has a friend in her life, and the other part of me is ready to leave this work event of hers.

The longer Nikki is gone at the bar, the more worried I become. I remember her mentioning she had issues with social anxiety and crowds. She seemed more at ease with chatting with her work friend, Tanya, but I know it's not a complete fix.

Anxiety floods me with anticipation. I nervously glance around, the crowd feels as if it's closing in. I decided to wait another five minutes, and as soon as I decided against it, Tanya places her hand on mine.

"She'll be fine, don't worry." She offers me the reassurance I didn't know I needed.

Removing her hand from mine, I take a deep breath. "I just worry about her, you know?" I admit quietly. A calm energy emanates from her as if she's used to this sort of thing. I find myself being honest to this stranger. "I'm still learning more about ASD and the woman herself. I want her to feel safe and secure in this big and chaotic world."

Tanya's smile is genuine, offering me comfort with her

next words. "I know. Even though she has her sensitivities, she's capable of a lot. Her heart is big, even if she doesn't always show it or express it properly as society says she should. I'm glad she has you in her corner, Rory." I'm not sure why, but her words relax me. "Her isolation was worrying me for a while," she goes on to say, and I see her take a deep breath. "I know her meds help level her out, but as her friend, I'm glad she has someone looking out for her and worrying too."

I give her a secret smile of my own. "I'm glad she's not alone and has you."

Joe nods his head in agreement as if to say silently that Tanya and he are a team. Something I aspire to be in the future with my woman. Seeing Tanya and Joe, although different than Niks and I, it gives me a hint of things to look forward to in the future.

"We invite her to dine with us on holidays, so she isn't alone," Tanya says with a thoughtful look.

I'm liking the couple the more I speak with them even if her husband is the silent support type.

Relaxing a little more, I look around and I find Nikki coming back towards us.

Something is off about her with the tense look on her face, even though she's holding two drinks. I can't put my finger on it. It's *almost* a blank face, but there's a slight twist of discomfort, if I'm reading it properly. That's when I see a male following her. He has plain brown hair and dark eyes. I'm getting predator energy from him.

It takes one to know one, even if we come in all flavors.

The alarm bells are ringing in my own head, and the energy near us is tanked.

Nikki is soon in front of me, handing me whiskey. It

doesn't slip past me that her hand is shaking. I can *feel* her tension even without her words to voice it.

The guy sizes me up, and I put my hand on her shoulder. *Oh, she's definitely tense.*

Thank goodness I'm learning to pick up better on her nonverbal cues and putting two and two together. "Who's your friend, Nikki?"

The exchange is unsettling as I meet the guy's narrowing dark eyes. Tanya's unsettled look reflects in my periphery. *Okay, I'm not crazy here.*

Nicole doesn't answer, and I rub her shoulder to offer some form of comfort; the stress is rolling off her in waves, making my hands itch to correct any wrongdoings on her behalf.

"I'm Gary. We went to high school together. I work for one of the companies that's a part of the charity tonight. I never thought I'd run into Nikki in the big city miles away from our hometown." A dark smile crosses his face, and it doesn't fucking sit right.

Gary turns his smile towards my Nikki, and I feel her stiffness under my fingertips.

It takes me all of him speaking for two seconds to realize *who he is.*

Murderous energy fills me to the brim until it begins to overflow.

Her wine glass is already empty.

There are too many fucking people to even think about killing him. Before I can consider causing a scene, we're saved by the dinner bell.

Nikki jumps at the sound, and I take control of the situation.

"Enjoy your evening, *Gary.*" I shoot him a death glare.

It's a promise not a threat, because I'll fucking kill him. *Without witnesses, of course.*

I get behind her, so the guy doesn't get any ideas. Tanya and Joe flank to either side of Nikki, after Tanya indicates her toward her husband. All of us form a protective barrier and walk into the large dining hall with round tables.

I ensure Gary isn't anywhere near her when we're seated at the same table as Nikki's boss and colleagues.

Thankfully, more wine is brought to the table.

Tanya and her husband sit on the other side of Nikki while I sit at her right.

I lean in and whisper in her ear, concerned for her well-being. "Are you okay, baby?"

She shakes her head subtlety.

I can feel her anxiety as if it were fully my own. I bring my ear closer to her mouth for her to whisper for me only, "I want to leave after dinner, *please.*"

The urgency and worry are clear as day. I rub her upper back, and I feel eyes upon us. I don't want to alert anyone else at the table that something is wrong, and in case Gary is nearby, I'm not going to let him think anything by it. Fuck him for thinking he can back me or Nikki into any goddamn corner.

Resolve fills me to the brim.

I'm going to kill Gary.

He's going to be number eleven, and I don't fucking care about the consequences. I decide with finality right there at the dinner table.

The food can't arrive fast enough, but when it does, there's some speakers yapping up at the podium in the front of the room about how much money was raised for homelessness for the city. Apparently, there are plans to make a homeless shelter to help get people off the street and get the help and assistance they need.

We'll see if they mean it. Businesses can claim philanthropy all day, but they're empty words without actions to follow them.

The longer it drags out, the worse it begins to feel on our side of the table. Tanya and I exchange a look at some point, and we seem to be of one mind as she indicates her head to Nikki. I'm not sure how much she knows about her ex in high school, or if at all, but she can tell that guy isn't good news either way. As a mom, she must know all about the protective energy which alleviates my rage momentarily to focus on getting Nikki the fuck out of here.

When I feel there's a break, they announce dessert coming. I stand and go over to Nikki's boss, leaning down to whisper how she's not feeling well, so we're excusing ourselves to head out.

A look of concern crosses her boss's face. "Tell her I hope she feels better. We have Monday and Tuesday off while we work on the shelter in the city."

I'm pleasantly surprised, inclining my head.

At least I'll have more time with Nikki without work to worry about. *I'll call out of work, too.*

I go back to Nikki and tell Tanya and Joe that it's nice to meet them. They return the sentiment, and I grab Nikki's hand and usher her out the room, but not before finding that prick's gaze in the crowd. I give him a threatening glare, and the asshole seems so satisfied with himself.

A familiar but different urge nudges its way inside me. Killing because I have to, not just for bloodsport.

We venture down the elevator, and I hold her to my chest the entire way. I wonder what's going through her mind this entire time. Nikki says nothing and lets me hold her in my arms.

I can't relate to her experience, and while I'm not morally sound, I don't fucking rape women.

This anger is hot as flowing lava from the earth.

Valet brings the car around, and I keep her hand intertwined with mine as we stand close. I tip the valet person, buckling Nikki in before hopping in my seat and taking off through the city.

Nikki is extremely quiet, so much that it worries me, since she's rarely quiet around me. I can tell when something is wrong by the empty expression on her gorgeous face.

Once we're home, she immediately goes to the medicine cabinet for a Xanax.

"Are you sure drinking with that is the best idea?" I frown, moving to stop her, but she put up her hand, shaking her head.

I freeze nearly inches from her as she swallows it down without water.

"It's a low dose. It'll help. I just want to sleep. If I don't do that right now, it'll be bad, Rory."

My heart cracks over her words.

"What can I do then? Do you need to talk about it more later or just sleep it off?" I offer, wondering how to best help her at this moment.

This is a new emotion. *Helplessness.*

"I don't know, Rory." She begins to walk away from me, and I catch her hand, locking my fingers with hers. "I don't want to have a meltdown tonight. I'll process it more after some sleep."

My thumb rubs the back of her hand. "Can I hold you for a while at least?"

"Sure."

I reluctantly unlink our fingers, feeling defeated as I loosen my purple tie.

She moves slowly, getting her pajamas from her dresser.

After a deep breath or two, maybe three, I make my way towards her, taking off my suit jacket.

"Sit, let me take care of you," I say, taking the clothes from her as she mindlessly makes her way to sit on the edge of the bed.

I see how unfocused her eyes are as I kneel in front of her. She's spacing the fuck out and it's scaring me.

Gently, I take off her shoes and tell her to put her arms up.

My fingers wrap around the bottom hem of her dress, pulling it up and off. I toss it aside and unbutton her bra, kissing her arm softly.

A tear fills one eye and sits in the corner at seeing her this way.

I lay my head on her lap.

"As a token of my love, I want you to know I'm going to kill him. Lucky number eleven."

Her hand rests on my head, moving a finger slightly. "What happened to quitting your bad habits?" Her tone isn't as snarky as I'm used to, but the fact that she's speaking causes my tears to blink away.

"This is for the good of mankind," I counter back, picking my head up before reaching for her pajama top. She pulls her arms through the t-shirt and simply stares at me. I can't read her gaze because it's another first for me. The fact that I'm ready to kill for her, shows how deep she's wedged into my once blackened heart.

I help with pulling up her orange pajama bottoms.

Nikki stands to pull the rest up before crawling onto her corner spot of the bed.

My throat constricts as I undress quickly, not bothering to put anything away. I leave my boxer briefs on and cuddle closer.

We lay there for a few minutes in silence as she sighs, turning to face me.

Staring into those watery green eyes, I touch my forehead to hers, rubbing her arm.

"I'm so in love with you, Niks. I hope you know that. I'd do *anything* for you."

I roll on my back, tucking my arm under her neck so she'll scoot closer. I'm so grateful when she does. I rub her back in slow, soothing circles.

Nikki drapes her arm over my chest, nestled nicely into my side—*and my heart.*

"You're just saying that because you love my pussy," she says, and this time there's a little more heart in her sassy tone than before even though it's not a normal-day version of it.

My laugh is short. "Well, I won't deny that I love your pussy, but I'm talking about you in your entirety. Your pussy is an added bonus feature."

I kiss the top of her head, and Nikki squeezes me slightly with her arm.

"You should be proud of me for not causing a public scene. I'm learning to read your nonverbal cues better."

"Good job, Rore."

I lean my head against hers, cherishing the woman in my arms. "Get some sleep, Sugar. You're safe with me. He won't hurt you again. *That's a fucking promise.*"

"Strangely, I believe you." She exhales before yawning. "I just need to sleep it off. I'll be fine... Thank you."

I feel her relax as I continue to rub her back, breathing in her sweet sugary scent. Her one arm is tucked into her chest as if guarding her heart from me still while her other is wrapped over mine.

I stare at the ceiling until her breathing deepens and her hand slides. Moving her hand back to its designated spot on my heart, only she can hold my heart like this.

"I'll make him pay, so you and no one else have to worry about such scum again," I promise quietly as I begin to go through in my mind just how to do it while she rests in the safety of my arms.

One last killing promise that I intend to follow through.

XOXO
LOVE

Chapter Twenty Nine

Nikki

I succumb to numbness when I finally awaken a day later.

My brain is weird. After going through my initial trauma therapy and finishing it, my coping and processing isn't the same. If I happen to run into serious meltdown moments, sometimes the best thing for me to do is to tell my nervous system to chill out and take some meds as needed. Instead of reacting and melting down, it's better for me to sleep first. Somehow, after I wake up, processing is easier. I can't explain my body and brain, but coping works differently for allistics and autistics, like me. *Thank fuck for my doctor taking over medication management after I completed therapy.*

My eyes open slowly, ready to process shit. I groan and stretch my stiff limbs from sleeping for so many hours.

I startle when I hear Rory's voice carry from the kitchen. "You worried me when you slept over twenty-four hours."

There's concern in his voice which makes me sigh, realizing that he cares enough to worry about little ole' me. "Sometimes I need to sleep it off before I can process. I know how to deal with my anxiety and some of my melt-downs in a way that works best for me. I don't expect you or anyone to understand," I explain quietly, sitting up in bed.

I meet his eyes from across the room. He's wearing black sweatpants with no shirt, cooking breakfast. We hold our gazes. I smell the air and my stomach growls at the notice that it's bacon.

"I was hoping I could lure you out of your sleeping coma with breakfast," he says to me, and I gather more motivation at the sight of him cooking for me with his tattoos on display, concern on his face.

"You know me so well," I comment quietly, getting out of bed. It takes me a moment to stretch my limbs again before making my way towards him to wrap my arms around him.

The smell of bacon and citrus is welcoming me back into the waking world, the comfort making everything easier for me.

"How are you feeling?" he asks, returning the hug. "I meant what I said before. Number eleven."

"Can we listen to The Getaway Playlist and add songs to it?" I suggest, wiping the leftover sleep from my eyes.

"Of course. I'll even add some songs of my own," he offers, giving me a sweet forehead kiss, and I melt a little more.

"Then I suppose I can justify one more. Can I at least kick him in the face?" I'm definitely motivated for the small act of deserved violence in my favor.

"I'd be honored if you did."

I tighten my hold, feeling better already.

Normally, I wouldn't condone violence, but I have strong opinions on rapists, especially after my own fucking trauma from it. The fact that I wasn't the only one, and how often he got away with being terrible under the guise of *good guy* makes me fucking sick to think about. Rory, despite all his lack of morals and faults, is a better person than Gary.

Fuck that guy right into hell.

Also, no one tell my old therapist.

"When do you want to do it?"

"As soon as possible, so I don't have to think about him ever again," I say nonchalantly while Rory puts the rest of the bacon on a plate.

He cracks some eggs into the pan as toast pops up from the toaster. "Alright, consider it done. What's his last name, so I can have an easier time finding him."

I whisper his last name while cringing as a small fear that he'll appear again crawls its way back into my brain.

"Thanks for the info, baby. Grab yourself some fresh coffee I made, and I'll bring the food to you at the table. Relax for me."

Placing a soft kiss on his right pec, I slowly make my way to grab a cup of steaming black coffee before going to sit at the table.

He sets all the food on top, bringing all that we need to eat.

"I'll make the plate for you, tell me what you want."

"One of everything," I say while sipping the hot coffee, a sense of relief for the bean juice giving me life and energy again.

I find Rory's gesture of cooking breakfast to be sweet. I can feel the effort and care that went into it. The words almost slipped from my lips.

I love you, Rory.

Instead, he hands me the plate of food he made, and I give him my sweetest smile. *You're a coward, Nikki.* I make note that while the feelings are there for love, my mouth isn't cooperating with my brain.

"Your smile makes my day, Sugar. Enjoy." He winks and piles food on his plate too, which is also some of everything.

I eat happily, wiggling in my seat and making pleasurable noises.

"What do you want to do today?" he asks, taking a bite of toast.

"Work on our playlist. Oh! Should we get a mask for me too?" Looks like no processing needs to be done. Revenge first, apparently.

He leans in his chair, smirking.

"If you'd like. I can arrange that. Can I paint yours if it's black?"

I grin in return. "Deal."

"I'll scour the internet to find him and order the mask and supplies. Do you want the same type of mask or something different?"

I consider him, thinking his proposal over.

"I like your signature look. I don't want to steal it. I'll leave it for you to decide."

"I'm so turned on right now." He closes his eyes briefly, sighing and adjusting himself.

I giggle, continuing to eat the rest of my bacon. There's no denying the small excitement of anticipation over what he'll choose for me.

Since finding motivation inspired by music, I eagerly finish eating.

"Computer is all yours while I clean up."

Instead of answering, I make my way to the shared computer and continue to edit The Getaway Playlist.

To cheer myself up more as a distraction from old feelings, I play some songs that remind me of Rory.

I hum to myself and let the music take me away.

"You are cheesy," I hear from somewhere behind me.

Turning to look, I find him on the couch scrolling through his phone.

'Wanted Dead Or Alive' is currently playing.

"Then add your own songs later. Don't hate!"

He chuckles as I turn back around and continue.

I purposely put on a cover song for *'Somebody's Watching Me.'*

When I check on him again, he's smirking.

"Mask is similar, but it's ordered. I also found an address. I'm going to take over the playlist while I plot and plan. Also, there's a box over there for you."

I get up and look around. He points to a box I didn't recognize before, and he switches spots.

"In two weeks, we'll plan for Sunday?" he asks from the desk while I grab the box.

It's not a large box, but it has some weight to it. I wonder what it is while I grab the tape from the side and rip it without scissors.

"Based on what I found at your old apartment, I wanted you to start anew. I hope this helps."

I open the box, half-listening to his words. Inside is a couple of adult-related coloring books with the coloring markers and pens. Some paints and colored pencils are also in there with a few small canvases; there's fancy charcoal pencils with some packs of drawing paper differing in thickness.

My eyes water, and I start to get choked up. I can't even describe what such a gift means to me. I didn't ask or say anything about wanting to pick up art stuff again. Rory just...*did it.*

Glancing up from the floor I'm sitting on, I find him watching me; my eyes drop and then meet his stare.

"Why?"

His image blurs until my tears trickle down my cheeks.

"Why not?" He pauses. "I can't tell if you're happy or not."

Rory stands and kneels next to me as I look between the art stuff on the table to Rory.

"I think I'm getting my period," I half-deflect. "I'm feeling emotional."

He cups my cheek, and I lean more into it.

"Period or not, it's okay. Do you like it at least? I tried not to get cheap stuff that wouldn't last long. At least from the reviews I read anyway."

The effort he put into thoughtfulness, causes me sweet anguish. I nod, hiccupping before he pulls me to his chest to hold me.

"Aw, Niks. What's the matter, Sugar?"

"You didn't have to be so thoughtful," I managed to finally say the words.

He eases his hold, moving my face to gaze upon me. His thumbs wipe away the wet tears. "I love you. Why wouldn't I want to do nice things for you?"

"I don't know. I'm not used to it, and it confuses me. Logically, I know people can be thoughtful, but I never experienced it firsthand until you. My domesticated killer is *sweet* to me."

"Only you, baby." He kisses me deeply, leaning his forehead against mine. "I care about you, more than words can do me justice for. I know I don't deserve you, Niks, but damn me if I don't at least try and be worthy of your love. Love that I hope to earn despite how we got to this point."

I release a deep breath, closing my eyes. *Be brave, Nikki. Just for today, take a step.*

"I never thought I'd say this, but...you're my sanctuary, Rore. I feel safe here with you. I feel protected and cared for. I also care about you in return, despite how we got to this point."

I open my eyes, seeing a sense of peace cross his face.

"I'll take it. I'll have you any way I can. That means a lot to me, Niks. *Thank you.*"

A genuine smile crosses my face, and I give him a soft kiss of appreciation.

"This means a lot to me," I indicate my head beside us towards the art supplies.

"You're welcome, baby. Come lay with me? I'll continue the playlist later."

Music drifts from the computer, and I agree. I move to the couch, laying on my side to face him while he joins me. There's much comfort in the way his arms feel like a protective cocoon of him and I in our own little world.

Although I haven't voiced it quite yet, I'm falling for him and he's making it the easiest thing I've ever done.

Chapter Thirty

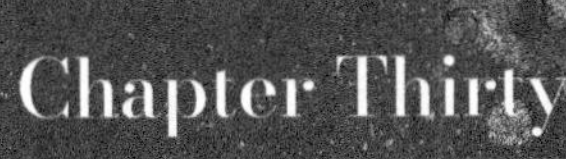

Rory

I find where that fucker *Gary* lives. His car is fancier than his small house in a nicer part of the city. *I bet his parents bought it for him.*

I spend the next week following him around to learn his schedule. I had some PTO to burn, so *fuck it*. It's for a worthy cause.

Capitalism can eat my dick.

Gary wakes up at 5 am every day to go to the gym, then he showers there and goes to work just outside the city. *Interesting*, in the opposite sense of the word.

I'm bored.

After Gary gets off work, he sometimes grabs a beer at the tavern near his house. A couple of times he'll bring a woman home. The women leave his house looking *displeased* for lack of a better word. On the nights he doesn't do this, he just goes home and stays there to repeat his cycle again.

It makes me realize while I'm stalking and scoping out his miserable dailies, how we're all so fucking boring in our mundane lives.

Stalking Gary aside, I work on Nikki's mask, which just covers her eyes and has a skull-like shape too. I try to match the gray tones like she did with mine, but I want hers to be more metallic. Somehow, I knew it would suit her better. She's certainly a gunmetal gray metallic color to me. Despite her darkness, she shines and radiates.

When I get home a week out from our plan of attack, I mostly have all the arrangements in place. I scheduled to pick up the clunker car from a guy I know to throw Gary in when the upcoming weekend arrives. There's a location with an abandoned house outside his *nice* neighborhood. Of course, I renewed my *kill-bag,* and it's lighter than I've had before. *Since this is my last planned kill, for the greater good.*

I'm going to give him a trial by fire. An old wooden house is easy to disguise. *Faulty wiring.*

Smirking to myself as I tally up my check-list mentally, I grab whiskey and find Nikki on the couch, watching true crime with a grin on her face.

I nearly spit out my drink, laughing. "Motivation?" I humor myself, and she scoots closer.

"Maybe. How boring is the stalking?"

"Boring," I sigh, downing my drink.

"Not surprised. Fuck that guy."

I turn to look at her. "How about we *fuck* that guy up?"

Her green eyes meet mine, nodding only just slightly. "I just want to kick him in the face a couple of times. This isn't my profession, you know. I'll leave it to the expert." She winks, and I'm tickled by her words.

Leaning my head back, a deep bellied laugh of excitement comes from deep within me. She stares at me in disbelief before joining in my laughter.

"I love you. You say the damnedest things, Niks."

Her smile is bright and unashamed as she takes my compliment.

I love her more and more each day. When she said she cared for me in return and that *I* was her sanctuary, I died and resurrected like Jesus. She's come a long way in our months together. While I long to hear those words from her divine lips, love isn't a simple, fickle thing to wave around randomly. It takes time and dedication. I can tell that when, and if, Nikki loves something, then it's truly worthy. Which is what I want to be for her. She deserves to be loved by every cell in my body. Every atom and molecule is hers.

I never knew what love was until she opened her mouth and threw insults at me. My insanity matches her energy. Like calls to like, I suppose. Nikki wasn't insane, she just views the world differently than most. A tune on her own wavelength. Her own light on the spectrum. Somehow, her light flows into my wavelength, shaping and molding it into something new.

I wish I was creative enough to paint her something or write sweet lyrics to her like the lovely songs she listens to.

It's just not me. She's already changed me, my life. How could I ever express such gratitude and my changing outlook?

Every day, that's how.

I can do little acts of thoughtfulness and be her sanctuary—that's enough for me. And be loved by her, if and when that day comes.

I hope it does.

XOXO
LOVE

Chapter Thirty One

Nikki

Rory and I tail Gary. We're in a junk car watching his house. I roll my eyes as soon as the random hookup woman leaves late Saturday evening.

"How involved do you want to be, Sugar?"

I mull over his words.

"Everything, minus the killing."

He cups my cheek fondly before moving his hand and placing a kiss there.

"Let's go kidnap the guy."

"Alright, balls to the wall it is," I say without thinking, grabbing the bat as he grabs the stuff to chloroform Gary.

With a snicker from him, we pull up our dark hoods and masks, exiting the car.

"This drunk asshole leaves his backdoor unlocked... *He's asking for it.*" Rory shakes his head.

My mouth is agape while I follow him in through the back. An interesting comment that resonates with me as most women, like myself, are fucking told that *we're asking for it.*

I melt a little more as Rory signals quietness while we gently make our way up the steps.

The house is dark and silent so it's taking a little to adjust, but there's enough natural outside lighting from the moon to guide our way. I'm holding the bat in my hands nervously.

What if Gary suddenly decided to get a drink of water?

My anxiousness is met with the sounds of snoring. I puff out a breath. *Okay, relax.*

We creep into his bedroom, and when there's a creak in the floor, I nearly piss myself. Rory pauses, waiting to make sure Gary doesn't stir on the bed.

He doesn't. *Thank fucking goodness.* This kidnapping business isn't my preferred job.

After a quick hand signal from Rory, we go to either side of Gary on his bed.

The original plan is for Rory to chloroform his ass, and we dip out. Yet, I feel like using the bat *now*. Familiar anger from years ago floods me like a tidal wave, and I make silent hand gestures to Rory, so he understands what I'm about to do.

Rory shrugs, shaking his head and holding back his laughter with thinned out lips.

Half-wondering if I've gone insane, I pull from my arsenal of inner anger and swing the fuck out of that bat, right on his chest.

Gary jolts awake. In the same instance, I jump on him and straddle him while Rory works the towel and chloroform over his mouth and nose.

"Heya, Gary-Berry, time to go night-night," I say as he struggles slightly before going limp.

Moving from the scumbag, I'm standing next to Rory, and he whispers, "You sure are something else."

Deciding not to ask, I move as he slings limp-dick Gary over his shoulder.

We make our way carefully to the car, and Rore tosses him into the trunk, tying his feet and hands together quickly. I watch in amazement, and it doesn't even cross my mind to check if we're being watched or followed. Granted, it is late at night and we're quiet in our masks and careful until now. Also, if Rory is unbothered, why should I be worried? *He's the expert here.*

We shut the trunk and get in the car, driving off to whatever place Rory found to do the crime in.

"Playlist?" I suggest, and he nods while driving us off.

I put on *Famous Last Words*, and hum along.

Without issue or delay, we arrive at an abandoned looking place after *Face Down* finishes playing.

The dilapidated building is standing solo away from nearby houses. While it's not secluded, it serves its purpose. Plus, it's wooden.

I grab the bat and the small kill-bag while Rory grabs Gary.

To keep myself focused, I wonder what song to play next.

As I ponder in my mind, having memorized all the songs on our getaway playlist, Rory leads the way.

When we're inside, I look around noticing how unsteady the place is. It creaks more than anything I've ever heard.

Please don't let this place crash down and kill us in the process.

I say nothing as Rory expertly ties Gary to a chair.

"I didn't give him enough of a dose to have him knocked out for too long... So, while we wait, play it."

Grinning happily, I put on *You've Seen the Butcher*.

Rory comes closer and his mask looks *so fucking good.*

Ignoring why we're there, my brain goes another direction with things. Seeing him in the mask *I* made him turns me on. *Mask kink aside.*

"Your mask does things to me," I whisper once he puts his hands on my waist.

"Funny, I'm over here thinking the same thing about yours."

"We make quite the pair, don't we?"

He lifts his hood and mask to kiss me. I can't help but clutch him to me and moan.

His hot tongue slides into my mouth, where I taste whiskey, hickory, and salt. Rory's hand slides down my ass, cupping and squeezing. I can feel his strength under my fingertips, those muscles are about to be used for killing.

While we make out, I hear a groan from nearby, then what I think sounds like a, *"what the fuck."*

"You two are fucking sick. Let me go!"

Rory curses under his breath. "Forgot to gag him."

"Let me go!"

"You're so fucking noisy, glad to know that hasn't fucking changed." I step out from behind Rory's tall shadow.

The moon reflects my face, and I take off the mask so he can gaze on the one responsible for him being here. Had he not decided to rape me and other women, we wouldn't be here.

Women may move on and heal, but we don't fucking forget. *Ever.*

"Nicole? What the fuck!"

The bat slides in my hand. *Thanks, Rore.*

"Shut up. You don't get to speak. *It's my turn.*"

His face is half in the light from the cracks in the walls,

painting him as a dark villain. People like him are the real villains.

Rory's not up for discussion on it.

"Why are you doing this?" he asks, and I turn back to Rory with a laugh of disbelief. He simply shakes his head.

"Why am *I* doing this? Did I not say the same thing to you fifteen years ago?"

His face contorts in confusion, those wheels in his head, burning fumes.

"You wanted it, Nicole, don't fucking lie."

Anger rises, hot like a burning star. "I told you no, *three* fucking times."

All he does is sigh. "Don't be a bitch about it. It was years ago. Get over yourself."

Rory steps closer, a low growl in his throat of warning. I ignore the rising heat between my thighs over the sound. A strange fucking place to be with all the unfurling emotions. Horny from Rory, and murderous over Gary's dumbass.

I take the moment to kick Gary in the jaw and happen to hear a snap.

He cries out in pain as I straddle him as blood pours out of his mouth.

"What's that Gary? *Sorry, I didn't hear you over the sound of me saying no for the third time.*"

Pretty sure I broke his jaw. *Sorry—not sorry.*

His dark eyes are blazing in anger that I've taken his right to speak away.

"You know, Gary, most women don't get the opportunity to kick their rapist in the face. Because that's what you are. A rapist. You get off on taking advantage of women who say no. You know consent wasn't always a thing, but you know right from wrong, don't you, Gary-Berry?"

He gives me a glare, trying to get the word 'bitch' out.

I laugh, debating on kicking his face in again before walking away.

"You're the scum of the earth. I feel better after breaking your jaw because you broke my mind. Fuck you all the way to hell, *Gary-Berry*. Your turn." I indicate my head toward Rory, turning and walking toward him, patting him on the chest as I walk by.

"I'll meet you in the car, baby," Rory says with a strange purr of approval in his throat.

Not sticking around for long, I take off the top layer of my clothes and toss it toward him. I had a black dress tucked into my hoodie and black pants.

Turning off the music that had been playing this whole time, I go to the car with my phone. Only when I climb and lay the seat all the way back do I take deep breaths to calm myself down.

How dare he. Even after all these years, he hasn't changed—*they never do.*

Chapter Thirty Two

Rory

Nikki looks so fucking sexy in her mask I painted just for her. If we weren't about to commit crimes, I'd take a photo of us in our black outfits and masks like two hot vigilantes. She was right before; *sometimes you need a little statement piece*. I've seen her at her best and worst. Nothing compares to how she looks in a black hoodie and jeans to match the mask. Her green eyes are bright and angry, getting the justice she deserves, along with so many others.

As she speaks to him after nearly kicking his jaw off his face, I wait for her to finish. She *could* kill him, but I know her well enough that she would carry it with her until it eats her up. Meanwhile, I'm mostly dead inside, minus the room I made just for her in my heart.

Nikki walks past me, patting me on the chest for my go-ahead.

I wait for her to leave, seeing her mask on the broken wooden floor. Sad over the work of art gone to waste, I make note to create another one for Halloween. Grinning beneath my mask, I hear the guy whimper as I waste no time and swing the bat clean against his head, knocking him out.

"That's for Niks, too. Bastard. This is the only kill I'm seriously happy about."

I jump from one foot to another, almost wiggling out my pent up emotion over this fucker.

He gets another hit for good measure before I open the kill bag, pour gasoline over the guy, and strip out of my first layer of clothes. I debate whether to keep the mask as a token of my affection.

It takes little time to decide I don't have the heart to burn it. I need to remember this moment, because this is a turning point. Forever.

Standing in my black shorts and t-shirt, I keep the mask on my head and shove our clothes under the guy.

Gary *naps*, and I light the lighter under the ass of his chair, stepping away carefully due to the unstable floor. I realize I have less than a minute to get out of there before the whole place ignites. Since I prepare ahead, the whole place is primed and loaded.

Making my way to the car, the mask is firmly over my face as the place lights up like a goddamn Christmas tree. Did I mention that I love Christmas? I'm only *slightly* sentimental.

Nikki and I stand there for a moment, her green eyes reflecting those burning flames. I can see her processing, yet she looks more at ease like a weight had been lifted.

"You make a great partner in crime," I step into her side as she turns those precious eyes to me.

The side of her mouth curls up. "Thank you, Rore."

Lifting the mask up, I take her face between my hands and kiss her until she needs to breathe again.

Not sure what it is about us, but post-kill kissing next to flames is fucking romantic to me.

Tugging her closer, I bask in the taste of mint from her toothpaste and how justified the last kill was. I want to take this moment in and kiss her so that it's forever engrained in my memory as one of the best ones, aside from when I didn't kill her.

By the time we pull away, we're breathless and the house is collapsing in on itself. The heat is radiating towards us more, and I want to make sure my woman is safe.

"We should probably go, Sugar." I bring her hand to my lips and plant a gentle kiss on top.

"True," she agrees, squeezing my hand before releasing it and jumping into the car quickly.

After I'm in the car, I start the engine, and we watch it burn for a long minute.

"I wish I had a picture to frame of you standing in front of the burning building after killing someone who deserved it."

I place the mask in her lap, reversing the car.

"That's some sexy shit," she utters quietly.

My laugh is husky as I release it. I haven't felt this good in a long time.

"How should we celebrate?" I ask, pulling away from the crime scene.

"I can think of a few things, Rore," she answers suggestively.

With the sexy look she gives me, I can't help but kiss her.

"I want to celebrate all the ways you're thinking. But first, we need to ditch the car. Luckily, I arranged it with a guy I know that takes scraps for parts. I told him I was working late, so he's already waiting."

I notice the sky lighten in the distance and make my way towards the destination. It is conveniently located by our place, so the walk back won't be terrible.

The Getaway Playlist plays from one of our phones, and I tap my fingers on the steering wheel to one of the drumming parts. Nikki rolls her window down and extends her hand out of it to feel the cool wind.

My smile sparks up at the look of ease on her face, a look of fucking peace. It's absolutely breathtaking to see this from her.

The city lights remind me of the home I've built here as I drive us towards the gated spot. I pull in and my guy opens the gate once I arrive. Nikki keeps the mask in her hand as we park inside the gate and exit the car.

"How was work? Late shifts are the worst, am I right?"

I nod, clapping him on the shoulder. "It really is."

Nikki gets out of the car, and I see her do something with the mask under her dress.

Before I can think about it, I turn to the guy, indicating the junk car. "Anyway, she's all yours."

He hands me an envelope of cash. "Thanks, man. I'm building something that requires another engine and parts, so this works perfect."

Not having a clue about what he's working on, I salute him.

"You need a ride?" he asks, and I shake my head.

"I live close, so we're good, thanks." I turn and wave toward him while Nikki falls in step with me.

My guy closes the gate behind us, and her fingers lace with mine.

"Let's go home, baby," I say with an exhaled sigh of relief, ready to be at home and in bed.

"Yes, let's," she says as we walk the sidewalks.

Although thirty minutes ago was romantic by the burning house, I find walking with her like this is, too. A new normal for me, and I find that it sits well within me.

"Where did you put the mask?" I ask minutes later as the sun rises higher.

"I attached it to my underwear, so it just looks like I have a bigger ass."

Moving my head to check and see, now that it's getting much lighter outside, I release a chuckle. *It does look bigger.*

"I can't wait to smell it later," I wiggle my eyebrows at her.

"Weirdo," she says, shaking her head over my antics and nudging her elbow against me.

"Only for you, Sugar."

Her smile is sweet, and we finally arrive for the sun to peak over the horizon.

"Can we watch more of the sunrise on the roof?" she asks, her green eyes full of life and love.

"Really?" I can't deny my shock that she wants to as she's never asked before.

She nods.

"Let's go." I lead her up the two sets of stairs near the elevator.

The city air hits us once we're on the rooftop. Clouds dance in the distance, the sunrise painting the sky in a cacophony of colors. Purples and reds with orange and pink sneaking in.

Nikki leans her arms on the brick of the building, gazing out at the city and sky. She looks beautiful shrouded in shadows, but most especially in the light.

My heart is full of her as I stand gazing at her.

"I love you."

She meets my stare, and I see her eyes water.

"I love you, Rory."

The world stops moving, and my heart skips a beat. I've waited on such words for months now, and I feel whole hearing them finally. We just committed a crime, my mask is on her ass, and I'm deeply in love with her. All is right in the world, indeed.

I wrap my arm around her, drawing her into me.

"I'll need to hear that at least a thousand more times until I'm satisfied."

The giggle she lets out makes me feel light on my feet.

"Is it too early to propose marriage?" I propose the question back to her.

She swats my chest. "You have zero chill. At least let me sleep before you go wild on me."

My hand moves of its own accord to rub her head. "I'm already wild, but I guess sleep is important."

"I'll be beside you, idiot." She pops her hip against me.

"Hey, I just killed a man for you."

"You *volunteered.*"

Well, she's got me there. A laugh leaves us both over that fact when I don't respond to her sass.

"Fineeee," I draw out, pursing my lip in a pout that makes her roll her eyes. "Murder, sunsets, sleep, and marriage."

"All in that order?" she asks me, turning to wrap her arms around my waist, looking up at me. A spark of joy is there as if she doesn't mind being tied to my ass for the rest of her life.

I kiss the top of her head, rubbing my hand on her back.

"All in that order," I confirm with every fiber of my being.

XOXO
LOVE

Chapter Thirty Three

Nikki

When I say those words finally, there's a sense of inner peace. Like I've been holding on to a baggage of emotion, and it's being set free into the wind.

Leave it to Rory to continue to be intense.

I love you means marriage to him. He does tend to move fast, and I'm expected to go along with his whims.

He's lucky I do love him, though. We're stuck like glue whether we like it or not at this point. Neither of us care about marriage stuff other than the legal piece of paper. Err, so I thought anyway.

Nicole Starling has a ring to it. *Rory Starling.*

I found mail by accident and saw his name; *how adorable.*

Yet, I'm finding myself wondering if I'm ready for that yet.

I just said I love you for the first time.

Halloween is coming up and Rory has something up his sleeve.

I don't ask when he orders new masks and paints them. It makes him happy, and I've been painting and coloring for fun with the paints he gave me. They've mostly been painted sunset and sunrise scenes because I'm feeling sentimental about it. If Rory caught on, he didn't mention anything. It's nice to finally feel like I'm coming back to myself with art.

The day arrives and I call out of work since it's during the week. I stare at the tall ceiling and grumble when he turns over in bed.

"Are you ready for tonight?" he asks sleepily, and I frown.

"How the hell am I supposed to be ready for something I don't know about?"

He rolls forward toward me until he sits up partially, leaning over me and rubbing my thigh under the covers.

"I've been painting masks... Did it not register for you?"

I give him my blank face purposely.

"Not even a little?" he pursues further.

"Rory, darling, light of my life... When I focus on a task, I'm focused; I'm not paying attention to you."

He has the audacity to fake pout. "We're going to be masked serial killers for Halloween."

My mouth falls open in shock, but then I start laughing and can't stop.

What a dumb, idiotic, but cute thing to do.

Nobody would know except us. A weird fucked-up secret between me and Rore.

"What's so funny?" he asks, hiding his smile and leaning down.

I shake my head, still laughing my ass off before burying my face into the pillow, rolling away from him.

He pinches my ass, and I squeal.

"Hey!"

"What's wrong with the Halloween idea?"

I turn to face him, thinning out my lips. "I think you could've been more creative, but that's just me. Also, it defeats the purpose of *laying low,* doesn't it?"

He sighs. "It's fine, Niks. I'm trying to appease your mask kink while doing kinky shit. Don't you want to fuck on the bed for all to see?"

I warm all over, a slow rising prickly sensation from my feet to my scalp.

"Well... *why didn't you say so the first time?*"

He chuckles while leaning in to kiss me. "I got us various things to choose from. Let's eat breakfast before deciding."

"Alright, coffee before talkie."

He stands up, revealing a lovely ass. I move quickly to smack it, relishing in the pleasant sound.

Smack!

"I'm adding to the tally of how many you'll be receiving later. Keep on." He's turned to the side, giving me a look that kinda means business, but not entirely. Not that I care either way.

I stick my tongue out, getting out of bed to follow him into the kitchen.

We make a quick breakfast and I down two cups of iced coffee with the fun cold foam from the store for some razzle dazzle. Since it's spooky season, it's pumpkin spice galore. *I live for it.*

The only time I come out of my black coffee habit is to enjoy all the pumpkin spice while it's in season. The nice thing is it's extending into the holidays with pumpkin eggnog. My fucking favorite time of year to feel alive.

"You are something else," he says, leaning on the counter.

"Where have I heard that before..." I finish cleaning up before telling him to show me outfit choices.

He indicates his head for me to follow him. Trailing behind him, I pause once he grabs a large box from in front of the bed.

"So," he begins, setting the box on the bed and opening it, "I had some different ideas, but I wanted to include you in them, of course. Remember what we talked about before with the collars?"

I tilt my head, giving him my blank thinking face as he pulls out two leather collars with a metal hoop in the front.

Soon, it clicks.

"Oh! When we said we'd both wear one to show our devotion to each other?"

He inclines his head, setting it to the side along with a double-sided leash. I can't deny the way I find the gesture endearing and heartfelt. Rory still continues to surprise me. My domesticated killer.

Next, he lays out some weird shaped garments.

"These are binding and restrictive clothing *and* crotchless."

He holds up one for himself that looks like a small chastity cage that would cover his cock.

"Mine has a snap that lets me loose," he says once he notices my look of confusion when he holds his up.

The one for me has a chest harness with open breasts and it connects to a corset looking thing that connects down to my hips and thighs. It leaves room in the neckline to add our collars.

"Okay, what else have you got in there?" I move next to him to touch the material, enjoying the leather feel.

The next one is a cute pleather dress that spans out at the bottom, so it isn't tight nor restricting near my ass. Even though I enjoy leather, I don't mind the pleather. The next one is a full body harness that's pretty and crisscrosses all over.

How am I supposed to make a decision like this?

"Why do I have to choose?" I pout, and he chuckles.

"Well, you don't if you don't want to. Either way, you'll be wearing all of these at some point. You get to decide what you want me to fuck you in tonight. *With an audience.*"

As if summoned by a magic spell, my pussy seems like all the ideas. *You're no help either.*

I take a deep breath. "You pick, Rore," I confirm, not having the bandwidth of energy to decide. *Not when all I can picture is our collars connected and being bent over and fucked on all fours.*

"If you're sure." He cups my cheek.

"We'll be wearing masks, so that can protect us a little bit. I know I'm not the only male in there with tattoos."

"You kept your OG mask I painted, didn't you?" It's not quite a question, but more of a statement of confirmation.

Now that I think of it, I only saw him vaguely working on *mine,* but I could be wrong.

He turns toward me, scratching the back of his head. *Caught him.*

"Would you hate me if I said yes?"

I shake my head *no.*

"While it's probably not the smartest of choices, I appreciate the sentiment." I reach for his face and cup his cheek.

Rory leans into it, cupping my hand before kissing the inside of it.

"I love you. I didn't have the heart to destroy it. I wanted to practice more on yours... I wanted us to match this time."

I find myself pulling him closer and melting into him.

"I love you, Rory," I say back, smooching him sweetly.

A moan leaves his lips. "I *love* hearing those words, each and every time."

Smiling up at him, he reaches inside the box and grabs a smaller box.

"What's this?" I ask as he gets down on one knee.

Oh, no.

"It may be too soon for this, but I don't care. I'm putting a ring on that finger. There's no way in hell I want to live the rest of my life without you. We don't have to make it official until you're ready, but please do me the honor."

He slips the black ring on my finger, a simple but elegant design that I find suitable for someone who never pictured getting married.

"I love you, Nicole. Say yes?"

My eyes water. This guy is dead serious right now.

"I suppose," I tease, and he jumps up and hugs me tight.

"I'm going to fuck you so good for saying yes tonight. *Claiming you officially in front of everyone's eyes.*"

A thoughtful smile crosses my face before I kiss him. "I look forward to it."

Chapter Thirty Four

Rory

She said yes.

There's more pep in my step as we get ready for our Halloween outing.

Nicole Starling. *Such a perfect ring to it.*

I choose to go with the leather binding-restrictive choice for her and put fun tassels on her nipples. For myself, I went with a fun chest harness and the restrictive bottom piece.

In the bathroom mirror, I watch her finish her makeup. Although I'm going to fuck that red lipstick off, I can't help but admire my future wife and bask in our progress with each other. A point I never thought we'd reach with each other.

I catch her green eyes in the mirror as I slip the collar on her, and my cock is restrained even though he begs to come out and play just from looking at her. The collar symbolizes so much, not just D/S dynamics, but who we are to each other.

Her breath hitches before playing with the metal hoop on the front. We are tied together—*bound* because we choose to be.

"Beautiful," I murmur, kissing the crook of her neck.

I braid her hair, stealing glances in the mirror. Tonight is important for us both. Public play and giving up control for the other. There are some nervousness and excitement, because it's new for me. Seems I have all these new experiences with Nicole. No wonder she'll be made wifey soon.

The woman herself smiles in the mirror as I finish braiding her hair, kissing her shoulder. Nikki reaches for my collar on the counter.

"No one's ever done this to me," I confess as she begins to put it on.

A sweet look crosses over her as she meets my eyes. "I'm honored. Just as I'm honored to be wearing *yours*. Hell, *I am yours*, Rore."

My neck prickles over her sweet words as I exhale, watching her closely as she fastens and secures the collar. For once in my life this feels right. I've known that since I met her. This woman changed something inside me, giving me a reason to care and not continue as I was.

"I can't wait to fuck you," she says with a growing smirk, almost taking the words right from my mouth.

"You have no idea, Sugar," I say, kissing her cheek.

To make our lives easier, we put on our long black trench coats and make our way to the car with our masks in her lap.

I waste no time starting the engine, listening to the purr of her. I rub the steering wheel fondly before pulling away from our building. Nikki grabs my hand, holding it as I drive.

"Once we park, we'll put them on," I say, referring to the masks in her lap while driving through the city.

She squeezes my hand. "Okie dokie."

"The bed is reserved and cleaned for us tonight, I made

sure of that," I add on, making sure the mental checklist is said aloud for her.

I pull into the private parking lot then. After I pay and park, I kill the engine.

"You're sweet for making sure everything is taken care of. Strangely, it didn't even cross my mind if that bed was cleaned between uses... Priorities, I guess."

I chuckle. "It depends on the person. People have their fluid kinks too," I tell her, unbuckling myself as she does the same.

We mask up and step out of the car.

"Ready for the best night ever?" I grin at her even though she can't quite see my full face, and she pokes at my side.

"When are nights with you not entertaining?" I hear her teasing tone and lacing our fingers together.

"True. Before we get started, let's grab a drink and relax, and see what others are up to. I know you like watching to get warmed up," I offer as a suggestion as we walk inside and pay for the night.

She squeezes my hand, pressing into my side. "Yes, Sir."

"That's my perfect girl."

Once we get our orange bracelets for *switches*. They take our coats, and I feel her tense up slightly. She hasn't been this exposed at the club before with her gorgeous body on display for all to see. *I'm salivating over her.*

"Eyes are on me," she says as I take her hand and gently tug her to the quieter bar area.

I'm not surprised the club is in full swing tonight. Halloween is one of their busiest nights due to fun costumes and even kinkier outfits. All the fun freaks come out to play and explore. There's an energy in the air; the energy of sexual freedom to be who you truly are.

"They're looking at you because of your outfit, Sugar. You are *lickable*."

I order us something strong to drink, and we move away from the busy bar, receiving more looks. I'm sure there's an aura of mystery with our painted skull masks. Yet, we aren't the only ones in masks. There are a few *Scream* masks from the horror movies, and others that vary from other familiar ones like *Halloween* and *Terrifier*. Some have painted skulls on their faces that I find artful and well done. It looks different than mine and Nikki's though, but I appreciate the efforts people put in regardless.

"There are amazing looks tonight," she says as if we're of one mind. We stand off to the side and people watch.

"Agreed," I say and see she's finishing her drink rather quickly, replacing her mask afterwards.

"One more?" I ask, catching her nonverbal cues by how she shifts her stance which shows her nervousness. A low chuckle leaves me when she nods. "Be right back, baby." I say while downing mine and walking away quickly.

Part of me is curious to see who dares to go up to her, but the other part of me doesn't want to stress over it. Tonight is too important for us both.

Thankfully, the bartender doesn't take long and I'm back before I can find out.

"I'm glad to find you here and not kidnapped," I joke, handing her the last drink.

She pokes me hard in the ribs, making me burst out into laughter which is partially over the gesture and the other half being that it *tickles*.

"You're lucky I love you. *Or I'd have to kill you for that.*"

I stick my tongue out as I lift the mask to drink and see her give me a cheesy grin.

"Cheers to us, Granite and Sugar," I say with all the love and adoration in my heart.

"Are those our killer names?"

I grin and she shakes her head with a smile, clinking.

"To us, Granite and Sugar."

God, I could kiss the lipstick off her.

Finishing up quickly, we meander around the place. There are all sorts of shenanigans happening everywhere we look.

The dance floor is packed, and so are the others who are in scenes.

In the corner, I'm pleased to find the bed enclosed by a plastic plexiglass type of wall, meaning *no one will be able to join us.* I want people to see our dominance over each other while both of us are in full exhibitionist mode.

I specifically requested it and paid extra for the fun set up. The place was nice enough to give us two hours.

"Ready?" I ask, leading her over to the setup.

"Why is it enclosed?" she says, sounding confused.

"So, no one can even *think* about joining us."

"A sadist through and through," she teases.

I merely shrug as we walk around through the small opening in the back.

"Are you comfortable with keeping our masks on?"

She nods in confirmation.

"Good. Remember your colors, Sugar. Get on the bed for me."

"Yes, Sir."

I proudly watch her stalk to the bed before looking out towards the people out in the dungeon.

"Keep your eyes focused on me," I instruct, seeing how she freezes.

To my delight, she listens as I stalk around the bed, watching her eyes follow me. Nikki sits on her knees; I indicate my hand towards the floggers already laid out at the front edge of the mattress. I wiggle my toes excitedly, seeing how the club put restraints at the top of the four-poster bed as I requested.

Pointing up over her head, she slowly looks up seeing the cuffs and restraints.

"Stand up for me, Sugar."

I watch as she does, and I crawl on all fours toward her.

Once I'm in front of her and sniffing her cunt, she runs her fingers through my hair in a way that makes me melt, submitting to her just as much as she's submitting to me.

"I love you," I whisper for her ears only as music begins to play in our space. I made sure to put various songs together to fit tonight's mood.

"I love you," she says as I move to cuff her feet in place, then I rise.

"Tonight's about you and me. Nothing and no one else. A symbol of our future and how we're tied to each other."

I tug on the leash that's dangling down her body and bring her lips to mine.

She keeps her eyes on me as I cuff her arms, so that she's spread out in the famous x-shape.

"How's that feel?" she asks, meaning the cock cage I'm wearing.

"I'm good... Now, to play with *you*," I say while getting off the bed, smirking beneath the mask.

I grab the floggers and go behind her, giving her the light sensory play experience.

"How's this feel, Sugar?" I ask her sweetly.

"Neon green."

I smile to myself before increasing the pressure enough to hear her make audible noises.

They aren't loud noises, but ones I'm familiar with when she's enjoying herself. A cue I learned to pick up on anytime we do a scene of some sort.

Her ass is absolutely *bitable,* and I ease up with the floggers just so I can have a nibble.

A cute little squeal leaves those tasteful red lips that I know are under that mask, and I move to the front side of her as her head rolls to the side.

I give her more sensory flogging that isn't hard on the front side of her. Then, I switch to a harder hit across her thighs.

"Don't go subby on me yet," I demand, placing the floggers down, coming to her side and smacking her ass.

An "O-oh," sound leaves her, and I crawl on the bed behind her.

"How wet are you, I wonder?" I kiss her lovely ass and use a finger to swipe up her cunt. "Mmm." I taste for myself. "Just as I expected."

I hear her soft sighs as I tease her, already feeling her swell.

"Not yet," I warn, teasing her with my finger before lifting up her mask so her lips are showing. "Have a taste," I tell her, and she opens her mouth willingly to taste herself.

It's so fucking hot that I growl low. "I'm going to let you come, and then you'll suck on what I have waiting for you."

"Yes, please," she says so sweetly that I want to rip off my cock harness and fuck her.

I lower the restraints that's holding her up until she's on her knees, and I want the crowd to witness her sit on my face. I check in with her and make sure she still gives me the green go-ahead.

When she does, I crawl in front of her once more. After lifting the mask, I kiss her sweetly before moving around. Her cunt is towards the watching crowd. I clip the other end of her leash to my collar as I position my face directly under her perfect pussy.

"Sit."

As she does, I begin to devour the divine. Curling my tongue on her sweet spot, her sounds struggle to remain quiet as her mouth falls open.

She tastes so fucking good, and I'm a hungry soul waiting to eat and consume. My hands wrap around those delectable thighs as they tighten around me until it's only her and those flowing juices.

With my raging cock, I find how eager I am to get her off. I tug on the now leash-collar with one hand and get her eyes to look down at me between the valley of her breasts. *Fuck. This is the best view.*

My eyes are watchful and focused; she bites her lip and releases noises that I longed to hear.

Releasing the leash that begins to drape around my head, I swirl and tease her clit in the same rhythm I know gets her off as long as I don't ease up.

"Oh, God," she cries out before squeezing my skull with her luscious thighs and comes all over my tongue.

I don't know what it is about tonight, but she's irresistible, more so than normal, and I'm so eager to feel her mouth around me right before I slip back inside where I belong. She shakes above me, and part of me wonders if I slipped into my own kind of space. The space where I can keep continuing like this. Just her and I.

With her heaving breaths above me, I give her ass a playful squeeze before I undo the bindings and restraints. I have her then lay on the side of the bed on her back.

"Show our audience how you suck a cock that is for you only," I say in a low, needy tone as I undo the snap and my cock springs free towards her waiting lips.

Her mouth opens as I gaze down at her, watching her take me slowly, stretching her throat. Seeing my cock in her throat drives me fucking wild.

"Tap my leg if it's too much, Sugar," I say to her as a Deftones song begins.

She says nothing since her mouth is full of me, and I continue to slowly fuck her mouth, seeing her lipstick come right off. Just as I originally intended.

I smirk and begin to play with her breasts. "That's it, Sugar. Take me—*all of me*," I say as she deep throats me.

Releasing a groan of pure bliss, my head tilts back as I increase my pace slightly faster.

I'm uncertain if I hear gagging or humming around my cock, but since she hasn't once tapped my leg, I keep going knowing I'm going to edge myself because I want to come inside her instead.

Losing myself in the sensation, I nearly do.

I jerk myself away, taking all sets of reserves to calm my dick down from coming.

Panting heavily, I lean toward her and smear the lipstick across her face.

"There, much better," I say sweetly, adjusting our masks back in place since our playing around moved them slightly.

Once she catches her breath, I tell her to strap my arms and feet and do whatever she wants to me. It's a huge risk of trust I'm putting into her, but I can't deny how much *I do* trust her. With my life.

She tells me to lay on my back while she secures my wrists and ankles to the bed restraints; another lovely addition that I didn't have to ask for. I watch her through the mask, noticing how cute she looks attached to our leash that's tugging on us both.

I let her have some fun with the floggers. It doesn't take me but five seconds to be hard as fuck from seeing her focus on me as a flogger caresses my skin.

I haven't been in subspace in a long time, if ever, now that I recall. So, I'm feeling *wonderful.* Subspace works differently but similarly for everyone. Sometimes, it's not about hard impact and can be for others to enjoy the sensory experience. There's no right or wrong to it, other than making sure partners are taken care of. Can't forget the aftercare.

A smack to my face causes me to regain my sanity as the floggers are dropped at the side of the bed.

Nikki straddles me, lifting my mask to claim my lips urgently, a sense of sexy desperation there before her tongue slides in to mingle with mine.

"Now, it's my turn to fuck you, darling boy."

I shiver at the words as she sinks down on my cock, her nails scraping down my chest.

Fu-ck.

I gasp with her and bask in how we both top from the bottom and vice versa. A fun dynamic that I'm learning to enjoy from this scene. Not that our relationship was ever conventional by any means.

Nikki and I play by our own rules.

She rides me, and I politely ask if she'll release me because I want to touch her too.

Pausing, but not before rolling her hips, she bends back and releases my one foot before moving and doing the other.

"Sit on my face while you do my arms," I whisper as she sighs and does what she's told.

I taste us as she sits and leans to undo my arms. Her moans give me life as I lick her.

Once my one arm is free, I hold her down against my tongue.

"How am I supposed to let you free when you're teasing me?" She gives me a pouty moan that makes me smile and squeeze her ass.

"Hurry up then," I murmur against her pussy.

Thankfully she does get my other arm free, and in one instance, I playfully roll us around until she's in my lap giggling.

"There, now I can look you in the eyes and hold you."

"So sweet," she says, kissing me before allowing me to glide back into her warmth.

I adjust the leash, so it's untangled while she rides me.

"I'm going to pump you so full. Then, I'm going to make you come on my tongue again while I taste us."

"You insatiable man," she huffs out, making lively noises that I want to hear more of.

"I can't wait for you to be my wife," I express honestly, and her eyes open and fall onto mine. I can see those glittery green gems even beneath the mask.

Her lips open for me to claim as we hold each other tight, and I know deep within that it won't be long until that awaited day comes, but for now, I'll love and cherish her in this moment in front of all these people watching us claim each other. *It's so freeing,* exhilarating even.

My cock swells, and I tuck my head into her neck to release my finishing moans for her. I love the way she clutches me to her while I fill her up. She releases a small gasp of her own, and I tell her to roll on her back.

She does and I waste no time tasting my cum in her,

lapping up our fucking divine taste, the finest cuisine on this goddamn planet.

When she releases for me and I taste us both, I swear I'm soaring beyond the stars with how good we taste together.

No wonder I'm so obsessed with my wife.

XOXO
LOVE

Chapter Thirty Five

Nikki

Rory has me spread on all fours, fucking me rough and hard after I come on his tongue two more times. He loves tasting us after he comes inside me. I don't mind it and find it flattering how much he worships it.

We're still in the club on Halloween Night, finishing our *showcase performance*. Our public display of our love and devotion to each other.

After he told me to focus on him, I did. The rest of the world drifted away and all there was, it was me and him enclosed in our own space.

A tug on the leash distracts me as I arch my back and deepen my stretch towards the bed, so my ass is exposed as he pounds into me.

I can't help the ungodly sounds that leave me as his hands grip my hair. I'm so in love with him, *with this*, that I begin to float on his cloud of marriage too.

This every day?

Obviously, sign me up.

I lose all thoughts and reasoning when it comes to him. I guess that's what love truly is.

When we come for the final time in our exhibitionist session, I collapse into the bed and so does Rory.

"We have ten minutes to remain here and cuddle for a few."

As we do, we practice breathing techniques to bring us out of our sexy space we created together. His warmth, our smell of sex, and how slick we are of sweat. We still have our things on, and suddenly I'm ready to take everything off because of how hot I am. Yet, I can't bring myself to move just yet while embracing him.

"I love you," I whisper to him as he kisses me, repeating it back.

The minutes fly by, and I'm vaguely aware of him cleaning us up. He uses a wipe for my smeared makeup on him and I.

Someone comes in after us to clean up, and we make our way to a quiet room that's around the corner where the bed setup is. Apparently, it's for reservation only.

There's a large couch with a blanket and pillow to go with it. Rory sets the mood lighting to a glow of red and puts on more music that sounds like it's from The Getaway Playlist.

I smile to myself as we strip nude and snuggle on the couch under the blanket.

"You did amazing," he says, wrapping his arm around me from behind.

"So did you," I compliment right back.

I focus on the comfort of the moment and aftercare, and I'm not sure when it happens but I fall asleep, only to be woken up by a loud knock on the door.

"Ah, our time is up. Here's some dark chocolate and some water, baby," he says, sitting up with me.

Rory takes some chocolate for himself and drinks half the bottle of water before handing it to me.

"Thank you," I say, yawning.

He gets dressed in his sexy clothes from before, and I eat the chocolate and finish the water off.

It helps me feel slightly more awake as I try to find the energy to put anything back on.

Rory assists and puts my nipple tassels back on as we leave the room. Our masks are secured back in place, and once the door opens, the masked guy from months ago that I made Rory jealous with, gives us a thumbs up before going into the room.

I can't help but giggle as Rory leads me to get our coats.

"I'm ready for bed, how about you, Sugar?"

"Yep, I'm not done snuggling," I say sleepily and he kisses my cheek.

It takes me a minute to realize he's wearing the leash on his collar this time around, letting it dangle.

I can't deny that it's quite the look on him.

Once our coats are given to us, we put them on and head home.

"Let's shower before bed, Sugar?" Rory offers once we get inside the door back at home.

"Yeah, we probably should."

Once we're naked and free of clothing, we shower together. During it, he showers me with his own sweet, consuming kisses and caresses. I let him bathe me and wash my hair, finding it to be the best thing to ever receive. It makes me feel pampered and spoiled without it being a selfish thing, more of a *I love you, let me care for you;* an unspoken worship.

I return the favor and see how this tough, tattooed man

melts under my touch. I don't think I've seen him so relaxed before.

When we finish, I kiss him soft and slow before turning off the water.

"I'm tired but I could go for another round before bed," he says, pulling me closer.

"Can we at least get *in* bed?"

He showers cute kisses all over my face in response.

"Of course."

Smiling, we dry off and do exactly that.

Chapter Thirty Six

Nikki

Ring, ring!

Since when do I leave my cell phone ringer on?

I get up from the couch and see, since no one ever calls me, well, minus Rory, but Rory's in the kitchen cooking.

"Hello?" I ask whoever is on the other line.

"About time you answered your damn phone." Ah, the voice of my mother. *Lovely.*

Also, when did she call?

My mind vaguely runs through all the times in the past couple of months I've rejected the call. In my defense, she's been pressuring me to let her come visit, but I simply didn't feel like it.

"I've been busy with work. What's up?" *A natural, non-argumentative thing to say of me.*

I hear her sigh and grumble into the line which makes me frown.

"The holidays are coming up. Are you going to host this year or what? You haven't been back in years, so I decided to come to you. I'm not taking no for an answer."

My frown deepens, and I find myself getting riled up.

"At least let me ask first. I don't live alone anymore, *mother.*"

She doesn't like my tone. I hold the phone away from my ear the minute I hear her go off. *"Alone? Who are you living with? Is it a man? Why didn't you tell me you're dating?"*

"One second," is all I say into the phone before I mute her.

I turn around to find Rory with his arms crossed, leaning on the counter with a playful look on his face.

"My mother is demanding—"

"Demanding? Nicole!" I can hear her shouting, and I realize the mute button wasn't pushed, so I correct it.

"My mother is demanding to see me for the holidays which means my brother will arrive with her. Are you okay with having them? I'll see if they can stay elsewhere, but they want to visit."

I sigh heavily, unsatisfied.

"Is that what you want?" he asks, moving toward me and squatting down to look at me closely over the couch.

"Not really, but I've avoided a visit for a couple of years now."

He takes a few strands of hair and plays with it around his fingers.

"So, we'll host. No worries. I'll make sure to hide any evidence."

He winks before standing up as I scowl.

I unmute the phone and tell my mom that we don't have the space to have them stay with us, but we'll host the holiday dinner.

"Don't think you're off the hook. Who are you living with? Is he a boyfriend?"

"I'll tell you all about it when you get here. I have something to do. I'll talk to you at Christmas and send the address before then. Bye!"

I quickly hang up and silence my phone in the event she calls back.

Tossing the phone on a nearby chair, I flop back on the couch.

"Problems in paradise?" I hear Rory say before peeking over the couch at me.

I grumble.

"My mother is very... nosy and demanding. She still treats me like I'm five. My brother isn't much of a talker and loves playing on all his technology gadgets."

"How old are you again?" he says before I throw a pillow at him.

"You're an elder millennial, I don't want to hear it!"

His laughter follows behind him as he goes back to making food.

I play with the ring on my finger to calm me down. Once I get it together, I sit back up and watch Rory in the kitchen. The smell of something spicy permeates the air, and my stomach growls in calling.

"When do you want to get married?" I ask randomly as soon as the question pops in my brain.

I hear him drop something on the ground and he quickly picks whatever it was up and tosses it into the sink.

Rory faces me now.

"When do *you* want to?"

I think on it.

"I've never gotten married, so how should I know how it works?"

I pause again. "I know I don't want what other people want. Like reception and everything where the money adds up quickly and ends up being about other people rather than the couple, all on the words of *tradition*. It's dumb, if you ask me. I don't like my family that much, and I only like Tanya and Joe. And, well, *you*."

Rory grins. "I'm estranged with my family, so I'm in agreement. People like traditions, Niks."

I frown, for what feels like the millionth time today.

"*I'm* not people. I'm a person, me—Nicole—a single person. I don't like doing what society expects of me, nor my family. I speak and see them out of obligation. What I do is my business. And if we're going to do this, I'm not doing what people expect."

"Yes, ma'am; we aren't regular people, so traditions don't apply to us."

"Well, what do you want out of marriage, or the day, rather?" I counter back, since he's not being very helpful right now.

"Like you, I never thought about marriage until you. I think I'm in agreement, though. I want to keep it up with the unconventional." He gives me one of his panty-dropping smiles, and I could kiss him for it. Today, I actually put on underwear.

"Go on." I indicate with my hand as he turns around to flip what's in the pan before turning off the stove.

"What are you making anyway?" I ask and he says over his shoulder, "Spicy chicken tacos."

Yum.

He sets out the plates and ingredients on the table with glasses of water.

"Come eat and I'll tell you."

I get up and sit at the high table with him, making my plate.

"This smells amazing, Rore," I praise him, and he beams like a little lighthouse beacon at me.

"Why, thank you. It's one of my favorites to make, and I realize I hadn't made it for you yet."

I do a happy food wiggle and take my first few bites and make my *happy food sounds* to go with it.

Rory begins eating and sighs in approval.

"So, there's a special event going on in the city next week, and they do it every once in a while. At the court-house, they do marriage day, where costs are cut to go get legally married. It's a quick thing that involves signing your life away and getting that little piece of paper. You can bring two witnesses with you and make it all official in their little chapel altar. I've looked at pictures and obsessed over it for weeks, and I think it'd be perfect for us."

My eyes move up, focusing on him, and water. "You've thought a lot about this, haven't you?"

He nods, eating more of his tacos.

I'm getting choked up over it and start crying into my food. "That sounds fine," I manage to say, and I immedi-ately hear him get up.

"When you cry at the table, I think my food's bad, Niks," he says sweetly before wrapping his arms around me.

"You're being sweet, and it still makes me emotional sometimes."

"That's okay, Sugar. You're allowed to. You are also the only one I do this stuff for, like ever, so if that says anything."

I wipe my face, and gaze into his blue-green eyes that I love getting lost in.

"It means everything."

XOXO
LOVE

Chapter Thirty Seven

Nikki

That Wednesday morning arrives before I know it. We take the rest of the week off and settle on something easy, a beach resort with privacy for a quick getaway honeymoon after our piece-of-paper binding.

Days beforehand, there's a follow up news report of a case being dropped after a body was found burned to a crispy potato chip.

Serves that asshole right.

Rory simply grins from beside me, overjoyed.

I can't help but join in on his joy.

Looks like we're both fucked in the head.

No wonder we're getting married soon.

Speaking of... Rory is already up with the biggest of smiles on his handsome face, laying beside me in bed.

"Are you ready, Sugar?"

I decide to tease him as I roll on my side to face him.

"Not sure. Never thought I'd ever be at this point with anyone. Or that I'd have a choice in the matter."

He pokes at my side.

"You could've said no."

"You're persistent, what can I say? I'm a captive to your love."

He sits up, leaning down over me.

"Oh, is that so?" I can hear the sassiness in his tone along with seeing his smug look, and I'm living for it.

"Mmhmm," I echo at the back of my throat.

Without warning, Rory hits me with, "I'm a psychopath, remember? I'm *delulu in relulu*."

My mouth falls open in disbelief, and he gets out of bed, laughing as he does.

When was the last time I said those words aloud?

"Oh my god, Roryyyy," I drag out the 'y' in his name, pulling the covers over my head to cackle at his antics.

"Is funeral black alright with you, Sugar?"

I throw off the covers and sit up, blowing the hair out of my face. He's already holding up black pants and a suit jacket for me to see.

"Sure. Pick out my funeral attire too. I need coffee."

He laughs silently to himself and indicates his head.

"Go on, morning gremlin. I'll find something for you."

Getting up, I grab my sanity-juice, and lean against the counter, inhaling the scent of caramel coffee beans in liquid form.

"This is already an unconventional marriage, you know that, right?"

"Is anything about us normal, Niks?"

"True," I say, sipping my coffee in utter bliss. My eyes drift down to my simple but pretty ring.

"I like that the ring you chose will match anything I'll wear."

"I agree. I told you black is the best color, Sugar."

I roll my eyes. "What am I going to do with you?" I say it in a joking way and don't realize how he's walking over to me.

Nearly startling, I make sure my cup of joe is okay before the handsome man in a suit is upon me in all black. *Jesus, he cleans up nice.*

"Love me, of course." He leans down for a kiss, taking my last breath away.

No wonder I'm referring to this day as our funeral day. *He's going to be the death of me.*

Then, the fucker has the audacity to take a sip of my coffee.

He shakes his head at the taste, making gross noises and turning away.

"Ugh, I forgot you drink it black. So gross."

I can't even be mad because all I can think of is how the domesticated killer is complaining about how I drink *my coffee.* I shake my head over the thought, laughing quietly.

"What's so funny?" he asks, leaving the bathroom.

My mug I'm drinking from has a skeleton hand giving the middle finger. "You are."

"Hm?"

"A domesticated killer is giving me lectures about how I take my coffee," I say without thinking.

He comes toward me to make his own cup and rolls his eyes, "Can we take that off my resume already?"

"I'll think about it," I say over the brim of the mug to finish it off.

He makes both of us another cup, and I quickly apply light makeup and go to the bed where he lay out a high-neck, black dress with double leg slits.

My smile grows as does the warm fuzzies inside my rib cage.

"Nice choice, Rore," I say with praise, pulling it on and making sure I have enough deodorant on for all the sweating I'll be doing for this new activity of *getting hitched.*

"Let's get married, come on!" He's rushing me, and that's not helping.

I reprimand him with a look as I spray my favorite sweet-smelling perfume that's vanilla and bergamot which kind of reminds me of a creamsicle.

"What is your problem today?"

"I want to get married. Am I not allowed to be excited and happy about it?"

I consider him as he impatiently taps his foot. "It's weird. I can't match your energy, bud. Well, maybe my meds will do the trick since I've only had coffee."

"Coming right up."

This guy is ridiculous.

I take my meds and pin up my hair so that it's half in an up-do before mister ants-in-his-pants continues to rush me. After my hair, I call it a day.

Let him be happy about you, Nikki. He's a fool in love.

A domesticated killer in love.

I put on my black platform shoes and put my black skull clip in my hair to add to the mood where my hair is already pulled back. Then, I add some small dangly skull earrings.

"There. How's this?" I turn around to find him with a skull on his collar, in place of where a bow tie would be.

"Well, damn," he says, letting his eyes rove over me from head to toe and then again as if once wasn't enough.

"I clean up well sometimes," I say with a cocky grin, adding, "You look perfect too. Let's go get hitched?"

His smile is absolutely dazzling. "I thought you'd never ask." He holds his arm out for me, and I join in on his antics.

He leads me all excitedly on the way to the car.

Putting on The Getaway Playlist, we sing along to *Blood Sport* plus another song until we arrive.

The old courthouse building comes into view as he parks the car across the street in a lot. It looks like any other gothic Victorian architecture piece in most downtown cities, well at least this one is. Grabbing my small bag, he leads the way in with my hand squeezed tight in his. *He's as nervous as I am.*

Due to my anxiety and weird excitement, despite other people thinking the same thing about getting married that day, the process is shorter than I imagined it to be. We hand over our IDs and documents Rory already submitted, *to no one's surprise.* Afterwards, we're ushered into a room where something like *"I do's"* are exchanged in front of someone, then we leave with our marriage license certificate thing.

It's that easy.

During the short ceremony, Rory slides me his ring and I put it on him, which is a simple black band.

As we leave, I can't help but notice how Rory has the most heartfelt smile I've ever seen on him as we walk down the steps to be greeted by a scream of excitement.

I turn my head and see Tanya running toward me as her husband Joe shakes his head. I'm engulfed by her hug before I know it, and she's as happy as Rory is.

"I have an extra hour for lunch today, so let's go celebrate missy!"

I smile before tossing Rory a look. "Did you plan this?"

He shrugs with an innocent smile, and I huff and puff.

"Thank you for coming," I say to her as we leave the area and go eat nearby.

The place we walk into is all floral and pretty inside.

Once we're seated, Tanya and Joe are across from us when we order our food.

"So, Nikki, how's it feel being married for all of five minutes?"

I think about what response I want to give, but my mouth runs for me instead.

"I'm already irritated."

"Welcome to my world," Joe pipes up, and Rory and I both look at him.

Tanya nudges his side. "Love you too," she mumbles under breath before I glance at Rory and we both start to laugh.

His happiness is exuding its own presence, radiating like his own burning star. I'm flattered beyond belief to know what it's like to be truly cherished by someone, to know he chose me with all of my specialness. My brain can't process it. My senses can't process it, but my heart? She feels it.

I was lying when I said I was irritated, I've never actually been happier.

We chat about the upcoming weekend honeymoon at the beach and Tanya is excited while Joe remains mostly quiet. Rory keeps his smile and we spend those two hours chatting away. It's really nice, dare I say, and I never imagined such a day as this one. Who knew it would be in the cards for me?

Once they pay and leave, Rory and I stay for dessert.

"I want you to know this is the happiest day of my life, Nicole."

Woah, not the government name.

I offer him a smile, unsure how to react. Sweet words make me uncomfortable, and I've never been able to figure out why.

"I'm shocked anyone would want to be tied to a nut like

me, but somehow, I'm not surprised it's *you*. I love you, Rory. Thank you for choosing me."

It's not my best choice of words, but it's the best I have.

He turns my face and kisses me in thanks.

"Thank you for insulting me, and telling me how ridiculous I am," he says with a cute, secretive smile that has me melting into the seat like goo.

"Anytime." I wink playfully.

We hold hands under the table until our dessert arrives. We're smiling like idiots looking at our rings as we eat the sweet and savory treats.

Who is Nikki, and where has she gone?

Rory's energy is rubbing off on me, and I can't help but fall into his mushiness.

"This food is yum," I say between bites.

"You're yum."

I stare at him while he does the same, a smirk growing.

"No, you," I counter back playfully, finishing up the tasty dessert.

Rory finishes at the same time and asks what I want to do next.

"Are you ready to go to the beach, or did you want to do anything else in the city?"

He pays with his card, and we finally leave.

"Hell no, take me to the beach, *please*," I say honestly.

Grinning, he pulls me into a loving embrace outside the place, kissing me there for all the world to see.

"Let's kick off this marriage with sex on the beach," he says suggestively, taking my hand into his.

Leading us back to the car, I question him. "You mean the drink, right?" *I know it's probably* not, *but I can never be too sure.*

"We can, but I'm talking about fucking you."

I sigh. "Sex is a given, Rore."

"Good, because I can't wait to have you naked under me as I claim you as *my wife*."

I shiver, swallowing hard.

Is it hot out here or is it just him?

"Yes, Sir."

"That's my Sugar."

Chapter Thirty Eight

Rory

The night is dark, and the beach is private. Now, at least I don't have to worry about getting arrested for fucking my wife on our wedding night out in the open.

She's wearing a thin white robe, and I catch her perfect face observing me as I spread out a large blanket. The natural lighting makes her blonde hair appear paler in an angelic sort of way. She certainly swooped into my life like one. I've been baptized by her and made anew.

My obsession. My religion.

My goddess to worship.

It's her and I.

Taking off my robe, I move onto the blanket and sit, watching her slowly remove hers.

"How would you like me?" Her voice dips low, straight to my cock.

"Any way. *All the ways.* Bring that ass over here." She's nude now, and I reach for her hand, tugging her toward me.

My wife straddles me, claiming my lips while I hold her snug in my arms where she belongs.

We make love to each other slowly, savoring the time

amidst the crashing waves. Nikki rides me in a sensuous way that urges me to join her in our union. Leaning back to steady herself, she rolls her hips in a gentle rhythm. My mind is vacant yet full of her. All I see is the beautiful woman bathing in the moonlight, my divine lover in this life. She says I chose her, but she's chosen me just as much.

I hold her hips and mimic her movements. I feel the rising sensations giving in as she swells and starts to pulse with me. We are of one heartbeat. When I come, she comes, too.

I can't remember the last time I came to gentle lovemaking, if ever. I'm finding that it doesn't matter as long as it's with her.

I pull her up with me and hold her with me still inside.

The wind and my voice carry the words of how much I love her. I'm in awe of this woman every day, who has overcome so much, even when I came in as a trainwreck. I'm caught up in her design, beautifully so. The hollows of my heart, or lack thereof, let her in just enough that she sprouted and bloomed. Yet, I know where I'm meant to be.

The cool waves crash at my feet. The sun is setting, and everything feels absolutely perfect. I have *my wife,* a boring mundane job, and a home that actually *is* one. For once in my life, I'm fucking satisfied and happy. I spent my entire life wondering what happiness is, at least until a blonde woman came into my life, or I came into hers. Now, neither of us can tell where we begin and end.

Our connection is unlike anything else. Her molecules are molded to mine. Two colliding atoms that split and forced themselves back together by invisible forces of the universe.

My soul belongs to her alone, to do with as she wills.

Every time she says she loves me, I become one with the earth even more. Her green eyes are the only eyes I want to see for the rest of my life.

"This is a great honeymoon." Nikki's sweet voice lures me out of my lovely thoughts about her.

"The best," I add on, squeezing her hand briefly.

"I love you. Thank you for all of this. I know I'm awkward with romance and sweet words, but they do matter. I cherish them. *And you.*"

I pull her into my arms. Her warmth, and the sound and feel of the waves cool on my feet, are soothing to me just as I know how they are for her.

"I know you do, Sugar. I love you, and I'm happy to be sweet for the rest of our lives. You deserve a happy, safe life, Nikki. One with me. I still feel like I have a lot to make up for with how I brought you into my life by force."

She nuzzles her face into my chest, and suddenly I wish my t-shirt were gone so I could feel her skin to skin.

"Thank you for choosing me, too." She meets my eyes, amusement swimming there. "Oh, woe is me, I've been forced into a relationship by a guy who takes care of me and loves me better than I've ever been loved in my life."

I breathe out in relief.

Part of me is glad she's forgiven me for all I put her through in the beginning, and the other parts of me are reminded about where I've been and don't want to be. It's a huge stress relief that she doesn't look at me as if I'm the bane of her existence, or the fear. I changed for her, *because* of her. She's reshaped my entire world, and I love her all the more for it.

"I'll happily keep you ungagged for the rest of your life," I tease back, licking the tip of her nose to hear that precious giggle.

"It seems we've both changed in our time together, haven't we?"

Touching her face, I breathe in her light and fresh vanilla-ocean scent. Her scent changes when she's on the beach versus non-beach times. Not that I mind it one bit. She's mine to breathe in for the rest of my life.

"Happily, I might add. I'm enjoying marital bliss on this beach with you. No matter what our journey brings next, I'm with you, Sugar."

Nikki tilts her head back, seemingly content.

"I'm also with you, Rore."

XOXO
LOVE

Chapter Thirty Nine

Nikki

Christmas is here and Rory and I are busy in the kitchen when a knock arrives.

I try to ignore the uneasy feelings about my mother visiting.

"Check the ham while I get that?" I say to him, wiping my hands on my cooking apron as I get the door.

My mother stands in front of me a few inches taller with dark hair and eyes that I inherited; my brother is also standing beside her thin and six feet tall with short buzzed brown hair.

"Something smells good; go inside and hug your sister, Nathan."

He does as he's told, and I sigh, patting his back.

"Couch is over there, buddy." I indicate to the side.

"Okay," he says, going to do exactly that and play on one of his handheld consoles.

I awkwardly hug my mom as she stands near the door, watching Rory.

"Alright, you kept me waiting long enough, Nicole." She looks expectant of me, and I sigh heavily.

"Mom, this is Rory. Rory, meet Mom."

He washes his hands and comes over to shake her hand. She takes him in, no doubt ogling how good he looks in his all black business casual dinner attire.

Mom raises her brow at me as he walks away to put one of the casseroles in the oven.

"Where did you find him?"

Are you sure you want to know that, Mom?

"Rory, do you have a brother that likes older women?"

"Mom!" Okay, so she's going to settle on embarrassing me. *Great, love that for me.*

I hear Rory's laughter echo and run my hand through my hair. Remembering that I should put it up, I go to do so, but not before my mother snatches my hand, tugging me to her.

"Nicole, what is this on your finger?"

Fuck! I forgot to take the ring off. Shit, fuck—damn!

"I, uh..."

"Nicole," she says more sternly, and I feel like cowering in on myself.

Rory sidles up next to me, showing his ring. "We've been dating for a while, and I asked if she would marry me. There was a special event going on at the courthouse, so we took the opportunity to do so to save money. It wasn't our intention to keep it from anyone."

Thank you, you gorgeous man.

My mother takes in our rings and sighs in defeat. "I would've come was all, but I get it, it's your business. Your marriage." I can't deny my inner shock that this wasn't an argument.

Rory gives her a sweet, adoring smile that I know is melting my mother's temperament down. He kisses my cheek before getting back in the kitchen.

She looks up at me with tears in her eyes. "Don't you think something important like this deserves to be told to your mother? Did you not want me there?"

Well...now that you mention it...

"Come on, it's not like that," I say as calmly as I can. "I don't like when things are made a big deal. We did it in the middle of the week anyways, and it's not like you could've just taken off work when we decided a week before to do it. We just wanted it to be about us, no one else. That's what marriage these days should be about, right?"

She sighs again and pulls me into a hug, weeping. I keep feeling more awkward, which I know is my processing and autism, but it is what it is.

"I'm sorry," I say to her, rubbing her back for comfort as she sniffles.

"Did you at least take any pictures? I would've liked to have been there, but I respect your decision, I guess."

Rory comes over with tissues and hands them to her. She mumbles, *"thank you,"* before blowing her nose and wiping her eyes.

"We took a few selfies. Let me make the deviled eggs and then I'll show you on my phone, okay?" I try to compromise as she nods.

"Do you two need any help?" she offers shortly afterward.

"We're good," Rory says from the kitchen, and now it's my turn to sigh. I keep fidgeting from one leg to another.

"Well, alright, I'll go sit with Nathan. Do you want some background music on the TV?" Mom says, going to do so, and I show her how to work the remote.

"Christmas tunes are fine," I tell her before stepping beside Rory to make the deviled eggs.

"I don't know if you know this, but Christmas time is

my favorite time of year," he whispers to me as music cues up.

I turn my head to the side, feeling like I don't know my husband at all.

"Who are you and what have you done with the *real* Rory?"

He sticks his tongue out before nudging me with his ass.

I vaguely hear my mother talking to my brother about the game he's playing, and then Rory takes notice and says to me, "They seem nice, Nikki."

I puff out a breath. "Sometimes, I guess. I'm just a grouchy ass."

After I finish speaking, he pinches my ass cheek. "*My* grouchy ass."

I decide to bite him on his upper arm to exert my dominance, and he bursts into laughter.

"What's so funny?" I hear Nathan's voice call from the couch.

"Nikki just bit me," Rory says in amusement as I mix up the stuff for the eggs.

"Really, Nicole?" my mother says, the same tone of voice reminding me of all the times I got into trouble after I did something when I was younger.

"You might need a rabies shot," my brother adds, and I pull in my lips to hold my smile.

"All of you hush," I tell them, and finish the process of deviled eggs, adding the paprika on top.

"Baked mac and cheese is in the oven. Now, we wait," Rory says as I clean up the dishes to make room for preparing the other sides.

"Sounds good! Mac and cheese is my favorite!" Nathan really can't help but not have a filter. *Guess it runs in the family.*

"Wife, scoot over, and I'll help you."

I make a noise of complaint as he nudges me over, and all my ears catch on is the way he's addressing me, *wife*.

"Thanks, *husband*."

He gives me the cheesiest grin, and I lean into him before focusing on the tasks in front of me.

We finish the dips and various salad dishes, such as fruit salad and potato salad, plus the green stuff Nathan doesn't like. I remember a time when I hated veggies growing up, too.

Before I know it, the various timers are going off for the food, and I get overwhelmed. I excuse myself to the bathroom once we take things out.

"So many things, all at once. Too much going on," I mutter to myself and take off the apron. I fix my hair again, making a tight bun on my head, and get myself together. I can't go all flappy hands over Christmas dinner, not when the visit is going better than I thought it'd go.

I splash cold water on my face and wash my hands. After wiping both dry, I take deeper breaths, feeling slightly better. Thank fuck, Rory turned the music down to a softer noise level.

"Want to watch a Christmas movie after dinner?" Nathan asks no one in particular.

"Sure," I agree as I set the table, and smile at the fact Rory bought two extra chairs just for this visit.

"What movie?" my mom asks him as she plays on her phone.

"Something funny!"

"How about The Grinch?" Rory offers as a suggestion.

"I like that one," I say, appreciating him for joining the conversation.

"Me too," Nathan confirms.

"So, we'll watch that one then," my mother says, not really caring, although the sparkle in her eyes is there from having her kids together.

"Well, load up your plates, dinner's ready," I say after I hand everyone their empty plates.

"Oh wow, you guys made a lot of food!" my mom says with an impressed look.

"And you both will be taking plates home tonight too," I tell her, knowing she'll leave all the food with me if I don't say anything.

I hear her sigh from behind me as I move out of the way to make sure everyone gets their plates first. Feeling worn out by cooking and preparing everything, I put the pies in the oven to bake while we eat.

"You two have a cozy place here," my mom says, finally looking around and taking her plate.

The string lights are on above us, dangling from the ceiling, creating an ambiance that's fitting for a family dinner. For shits and giggles, I convinced Rory to have a tiny desk tree with colorful lights on it.

"Thanks," Rory says as he lets them get first dibs before handing me a plate.

"You first, baby," he whispers in my ear.

"Nathan, save some mac and cheese for everyone else, not the whole damn plate!" my mom chastises him.

"Fine, Mom!"

I chuckle, remembering how I said similar things as a teenager.

"Sit anywhere at the table," I tell them both as they grab what they want and sit down.

"These chairs are almost too tall for me," my mother says once she's up in the seat.

"That's cause you're shorter than me, Mom," Nathan says casually, digging into the mac and cheese.

Rory and I both catch the look she gives him, and we load up our plates with all the fixings too. Ham, mashed potatoes, green bean casserole, mac and cheese, and salad.

"The water on the table is good for everyone, right?" I ask them.

They answer with their mouths full that it is. I shake my head, remembering when I used to get yelled at for answering with my mouth full.

Once we're all seated, my mother dives right into the questions for Rory.

What do you do for work?

Where are you from?

How'd you meet? Which is the best question, in my opinion.

"Well," Rory begins as the oven beeps, and that's my cue to escape the conversation.

My ears are on high alert as I listen in as my brother decides he's done and goes back to the couch to continue on his console.

"We bumped into each other on the street."

That's one way to put it, Rore. Obviously, we couldn't tell my mom the full truth. Well, *I* could.

I decide to be funny and confess, "Actually, he kidnapped me on the street, nearly killed me, decided he liked me enough, and then we got hitched so I wouldn't spill his secrets."

My mother shakes her head at me. "Nicole, enough with your ridiculous antics. Let the man talk," she scolds.

Rory's face relaxes as I gave him a pointed look.

"What happened after you bumped into each other on the street?" She asks him directly, ignoring my stupid grin.

Of course, the truth is fucking wild, no wonder she doesn't believe me. It's too hilarious either way.

Rory sighs heavily, not finding it as funny as I do. "Well, the bumping led to a tumble, and she landed on top of me."

I can't help but snicker, setting the pies on the stove and turning off the oven.

"Nicole is clumsy, so I'm not surprised," my mother comments, and while she's right, that's not what happened. Well, in that order anyway.

"I felt bad, so I treated her to coffee next time I saw her, and the rest is history."

Again, not in that order, but sure.

"How fascinating. Nicole is a coffee-over-people person. She probably got that from me," my mother admits.

Damn right.

Murder is wrong, but coffee isn't.

"Alright, *alright.* I'm right here, you know," I complain and move to turn on the movie, done with all the talking. "Let's eat pie and watch this movie," I say after I find it on the TV.

Rory takes it upon himself to bring out the pies to us as we settle in.

I sit next to Rory on one end of the couch while my mom is next to me and then Nathan on her other side.

"This is a great Christmas," Nathan comments, and my mom agrees.

With a mouthful of pie and a side glance at Rory, my lips curl up. Domesticating a killer isn't so bad, after all.

XOXO
LOVE

Epilogue

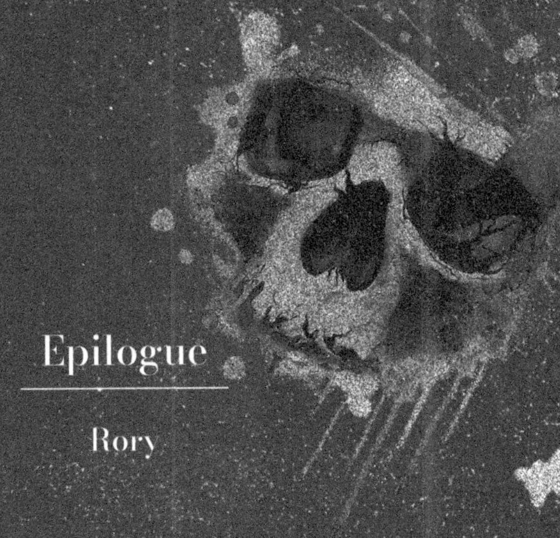

Rory

I'm grinning as I stare at the computer screen upon finishing my *Domesticated K!113R* playlist.

I have a casserole in the oven as Nikki comes fresh out from the shower.

After hooking up the Bluetooth speaker, I place it on the counter while I set the table and watch her steal a t-shirt of mine to wear. A sight that still has blood rushing right to my cock.

"That smells good," she says, walking over to me and kissing my cheek.

I'll Follow You by Shinedown plays in the background as the oven timer beeps.

Nikki steps to the side and grabs us wine and water, placing it on the table while I cut the casserole and serve it with dinner rolls. Remembering the lactose pills, I place them on the table for Nikki as she sits down and smiles sweetly.

"Thank you, Rore. My stomach also thanks you in advance." She winks and does a cute little salute.

I chuckle, settling into the chair and digging in.

"I've heard this song before, I think?" she comments after finishing her food. "Is this a different playlist?"

Hold Me Now by Red plays as I wipe my mouth. "It's a new playlist."

Her brow shoots up with curiosity.

"Guess the title," I say, smirking while I sip white wine, my own brow quirks up.

"Title of what? I'm full and don't want to use up brain energy to think."

I wait until my glass is empty to answer her to leave her in suspense.

"Domesticated Killer."

Her eyes light up in amusement. "You're so grossly sweet, I can't stand it."

"You married me," I say, standing up and moving to her side of the table.

I confirm that her smile is all I need for the rest of my life.

"I should be saying that to you," she says as I lean in for a kiss.

After a few precious moments, I lean my head back to catch her eyes staring right through me.

"You're right, though, I did marry you. Let's not divorce like everyone else does over an argument, alright?"

Leaning my forehead against hers, I sigh. "I'll kill you first, you millennial."

"Likewise, you elder millennial ass," she says, poking me in the side before offering to clean up.

"I'll find a crime show to watch?" I offer, but not before I see her roll her eyes.

I swiftly smack her ass as she stands.

"Yee-ow!" Her brows scrunch with a frown before

giving me her sass. "Obviously that's what I want to do with my domesticated *killer*."

"Good," I say, returning the kiss to her cheek.

After cleanup, we settle into domesticated bliss, happy with the calm of crime TV.

The End

Drag Me Under

Teaser

Haddonfield, NJ

Danny

Present Day

Halloween night is my night.

It's also the anniversary of my family's death, just like another famous killer from some slasher movies I enjoy. There's something about it I can relate to, and it gives me inspiration to prowl the streets each year to find my next victims.

I don't just choose anyone though. Men or women, it doesn't matter to me. I call myself a martyr, killing for the sacred act of cleaning up the streets of bad people. My own call to justice. Only on Halloween as it's revered for me. The rest of the year, I spend plotting and waiting.

I'm always on the lookout.

Always making my list and checking it twice, like Santa Claus. Like that fat fucker, I'm the one in red doing poetic justice. I wear dark red so that when blood rains down and splatters, it blends in nicely with the leather. Something a woman with tastes like me can appreciate

To be continued.
Coming in 2026.

Acknowledgments

Hello Preylings.

I hope you enjoyed the chaotic journey of Nikki and Rory. If not, that's also valid as their chaos isn't for everyone.

Mental health is important, and while Nikki's diagnoses don't fit everyone's bill, it's unique to her experience.

Any who, onto the acknowledgements!

I first want to thank Amy for alpha/beta reading and believing in the chaos of this book. Thank you for cheering them on and their weird sense of humor. You've been supportive since we found each other, and I can't wait to see what else we accomplish together. Love you!

To my dearest beta readers, thank you so much for helping me make this book come more to life. To name a few: Lily, Chloe, Kristen, Anuschka, Kayla, and Amy.

Lily, you've been with me since day one of Parasite, always supporting and encouraging this weird brain of mine even if some tropes weren't your favorite, but you still kept with me for these past few years. I can't imagine anyone else I'd want on this journey with me and the support and incredible insight you bring. Chloe, my book author bestie, I'm so glad we found each other when we did. I can't wait to continue to see each of our growth with future books and journeys I love you! Kristen, you're newer to the beta reading family, but I enjoy your reactions, and your insight and help is fantastic! I hope you'll stick around for future projects and this crazy, chaotic journey that is books and reading. Anuschka and Kayla, you've been with me for a while, and I continue to cherish having you on the team and on the hype squad! Thank you for all that you do!

ARC readers, I'm speechless when it comes to you. You also stick around whether you like certain tropes/aspects or not. I'm happy and grateful for each and every one of you who volunteered and dedicated time out of your day to read. You make this all possible and are a great part of the hype squad too!

To you, the reader, no matter how you came here, thank you for giving this neurodivergent author a chance.

Until we meet again.

Author Note

While your mental health is important, remember that authors are people who bleed and cry onto the pages to create stories. Whether you like the books, writing, scenes, or not, that is perfectly okay, but please be aware of how harmful your words can be to others. Not just for me specifically as a person, but other authors and readers too.

The world needs more kindness and empathy, not hate and assumptions.

If you ever need to address a situation or something you consider hurtful, please address it directly. I am a person just like you who is learning and growing and doesn't always get it right.

Please note that this author doesn't support the following: homophobia, transphobia, anti-LGBTQIA+, misogyny, racism, abuse, genocide, anti-mental health, and violence.

I'm sure there's more, but those are the important ones.

Mental health is real, and so are varying diagnoses.

Don't be the reason someone gives up on their dreams because you want to be a prick, or yuck someone else's yum!

That's all folks!

With love, R.N.

Other Books

The Para-Series
Parasite
Para-Psych
Para (book 3 standalone)—coming soon

Triad Bite Series
Into the Black
Into the Red
Into the Blue
Into the Fire

Standalones
Poa
Lee
The Misfortunes of Tommelise

The Horns Trilogy
Horns & Heat
Horns & Flames

About the Author

R.N. Arcadia is a neurodivergent, day-dreaming Pisces. They live in New Jersey with her family.

When R.N. isn't writing or working, they enjoy traveling, going to the beach, binge-watching/binge-reading whatever series they finds themselves engrossed in, and listening to all sorts of music to stay sane.

https://linktr.ee/r.n.arcadia